THE TEAR OF TYBALETH

A FELLOWSHIP OF THE FLAME NOVEL, BOOK 1

A. R. SILVERBERRY

TREE TUNNEL PRESS

Cover Design © selfpubbookcovers.com/LaLimaDesign

Print Edition ISBN - 13: 978-1-7375173-0-6

Published by Tree Tunnel Press, P.O. Box 733, Capitola, CA 95010

❀ Created with Vellum

PRAISE FOR A. R. SILVERBERRY

Praise for Wyndano's Cloak

"**Constant suspense . . . impossible to put down**. You're going to be very tired in the morning!" Feathered Quill Review

"**I was entranced** . . . Silverberry is a master at characterization. Few are his equal . . ." Readers Favorite

"**I loved it!** If you like a tight, well-written, exciting, moving, and, ultimately, satisfying book, then this is for you, regardless of your age and gender." The Book Sage, Review by Lloyd Russell

"**A tale of intense imagination and wonder**. An adventure we may only find in the deepest corners of our imagination. A. R. Silverberry's story was one that I will likely be re-reading very soon." Allbooksreviews, Review by Kirsten Bussière

"**A grand adventure . . . a coming-of-age soon to be classic.** Silverberry's creativity and imagination are second to none." Review by William R. Potter for Reader's Choice Book Reviews

"**An extraordinary heroine** . . . captures the courage and sense of adventure that lies in the heart of all young girls." Sandra Martz, editor, *When I Am an Old Woman I Shall Wear Purple*

"**Mystery, treachery, intrigue** ... and a magical cloak that may prove just as dangerous to use as not to use. Delicious!" Eric A. Kimmel, author of *Hershel and the Hanukkah Goblins*

"**A magical tale** ... chock full of everything a great fantasy novel needs; dashing young men, adventures galore, treachery, love and intrigue ... I highly recommend this book." Thesupermom.com, Review by Karlynn Johnston

"**Hard to put down!!!** Breathtaking and Captivating tale of a brave and daring young girl!" Marcia Freespirit, CEO, JimSam Publishing

Praise for **The Stream**

"**Wend's story is heart-breaking,** joyous, desperate and exciting ... Masterful storytelling and a thought-provoking read." Five Stars! Readers' Favorite Review

"**This book is nothing less than a treasure!**" Janetti Marotta, PhD, author of 50 Mindful Steps to Self-Esteem: Everyday Practices for Cultivating Self-Acceptance & Self-Compassion

For my father, who first taught me story magic

CONTENTS

PREFACE

When I wrote *Wyndano's Cloak*, I intended it to be a single novel. All was wrapped up, so what more was there to say? But an idea started percolating in the back of my mind: what was happening in Purpura before events in the above book? I had some things to go on.

1. There was a pretty bad actor in the queen of Purpura. In fact, they don't come any worse. She was spiteful, vengeful, relentless, and if that's not bad enough, she commanded a hefty arsenal of sorcery.
2. There was a resistance striving against her.
3. There were some determined characters opposing her. I began to wonder what they had been up to before Jenren took up Wyndano's Cloak.

And so the *Fellowship of the Flame* series was born, tales of brave fighters striving against a dangerous adversary. While the stories are interconnected, with overlapping characters, they may be read as standalones. Still, I recommend reading them in order, if only for maximum enjoyment.

In the series prequel novella, *The Fellowship of the Flame*, we find the ten-year-old Little Captain colliding headlong with the queen in his attempt to join the resistance, and in the process, getting a deadly human bloodhound on his trail. While the main character is a child, and children will enjoy the adventure, the story was written for readers of all ages that love fantasies. The novella takes place five years before the events of *Wyndano's Cloak*.

Book 1 of the series, *The Tear of Tybaleth*, is also a fantasy adventure, but with a strong romantic element. For that reason, it's geared toward adults and teens. The story begins twenty-six years before the start of *Wyndano's Cloak*.

Book 2 of the series, *The Treasure of Trenalon*, carries on the tale of Briar, *Tear's* heroine. It's due out summer, 2024.

And so, without further ado, meet Briar in the pages ahead …

PART ONE

CHAPTER ONE

*B*riar's first memory of her father was as a towering wall of granite. That he rejected her from birth was clear from the stories she'd heard, not just from her wet nurse, but from half a dozen servants who were more than happy to throw it in her face. As the story goes, it was a dawn in the dead of winter. Snow struck the shuttered windows like sand, and the wind snarled and hissed like a catamount outside the manse. Her father, the baron, paced the wooden floors of the anteroom adjoining the birth room, indifferent to the screams from the chamber beyond. When at last the door was opened and the midwife came out with Briar, washed, rubbed with salt, and swaddled in bands of fleece, a small flame lit the baron's eyes.

"Well?" he asked.

The midwife was too shrewd to answer, but merely pulled aside the bands to show him the baby's sex. The baron's gaze never looked to that part of her anatomy but remained fixed on the wild jungle of black, scrawled atop her crown, as if it were a sign of the plague.

The spark in his eyes snuffed out. "Throw it in the well."

He pointed to the strands, shining like oil.

From her bed, exhausted and beaded with sweat, Briar's mother had been looking up at the baron's face, framed in the doorway. From the quickening when she first felt Briar stir in her belly, she'd clung to a ray of hope that in this one small way she could please her husband. Now his glacial expression left her chilled and lifeless. Too desolate and downcast to cry, she turned to the wall.

As though she'd understood her father's words and her mother's sorrow, Briar unleashed a torrent of angry wails that sent the baron to the farthest corner of the manse, his private study where he kept his stock of fine pipe weed and apricot brandy. But Briar's cries refused to be denied. They pierced the walls like the shrieks of an avenging eagle, sending the baron cursing and pacing and belching out torrents of smoke until a cloud hung over the room. Unable to bear further torment, he retreated from the house and out into the storm, preferring the slap-cold wind and snow to the wails of the creature he'd spawned. Even there, the bawling followed him, borne on gusts and flurries like the cries of an accusing ghost.

So the story went, and from her earliest memories, Briar could believe it, for the baron's manner toward her never wavered. He never turned the warmth of a smile upon her and always walked away when he encountered her. She was forced to eat on a hard wooden chair in the kitchen. Infractions were swiftly punished—she was denied dinner or locked in the cellar, and he was not averse to sending her to the housekeeper for a strong dose of hickory. He never played with her, never walked with her, never watched her take her first steps, say her first words, or take her first courageous canter on a pony. Her room was situated on the opposite corner of the manse from the baron's, and she was certain that, if he could, he would have moved her into the servants' hovels, but for the poor impression that would have left on visiting nobles.

Indifference would have been tolerable, but he was determined to bend Briar to his will, for there was one thing he desired from her: to grow into a lady—quiet, meek, and refined.

Briar had her own ideas, and it wasn't holding teacups with her pinky extended or sitting in the parlor jabbing her fingers with a needle. If she was put into anything lacy or frilly she soon wriggled out of it. She chased butterflies in the fields and tramped far into the countryside, her rainsoaked breeches dressed in mud. She rode her pony like a man, whooping and charging down mountain trails with reckless abandon. But the offense that most piqued the baron was her fascination with swords. One hung with a dagger in the great entrance hall, and Briar was often found before them, pretending to hold one in her tiny fist, swinging with the fierceness of a gladiator. She progressed to stick battles with the servants' children, her black hair whipping wildly in the wind. After a few bruised arms and legs, they refused to fight her. Briar was not deterred. She took her skirmishes into the woods, where she fought the worthier foes of her imagination, stabbing and slashing the stout trunk of an old oak tree to her heart's content.

When she was six, she returned from one of her woodland journeys with an abandoned baby weasel she'd found, and a few weeks later, a fox puppy. She was forbidden to bring them into the manse, but she sneaked out when the house was quiet, and the next morning the pets were found snuggled beneath her blankets. The result, in a few months, was the devastation of the chicken house. Soon after, her pets disappeared. The baron told her sternly that wild creatures couldn't be tamed; eventually they run off. Briar knew the truth. He'd destroyed her furry friends to spite her.

She rarely went to her mother for anything, but now she did, tramping up the seemingly endless flights of stairs, down a long lonely hardwood corridor, the dark paintings of her ancestors glaring down on her. At last she tapped on her mother's door and entered at the murmur from within. With the curtains pulled closed, and in the dim light, her mother was almost lost, sunken in her chair.

Briar understood little about her mother. There was nothing here to amuse. No watercolors, no needlepoint, no books. Her mother's gaze was always cast to the floor, but she raised it now and blessed her daughter with a faint smile.

"Briar," she said, as if awakening from a dream and seeing an old acquaintance. A bit of color crept into her pallid face.

Briar leaped to the point. "Why does he hate me?"

Her mother's gaze traveled over Briar's tresses, as black and glossy as ink. "Best not cross your father. You know how it vexes him." She reached for a small silver casket she kept on an end table and opened it. Inside, a ring with an enormous ruby gleamed and sparkled, even in the dull light. "One day, this will be yours."

This was the extent of motherly love and protection Briar received. As for her question, it remained unanswered.

She got little more from the servants. They turned away at her queries with a mysterious gleam in their eyes and mockery on their lips. Nor did she find love among them. They greeted her with deference or indifference, and more than a few seemed to take quiet glee in her troubles. Not one of them took her under their wing, consoled her, or soothed away her tears. Some looked upon her with simmering hostility and suspicion, as if she were a trespasser or had stolen a loved possession. She often came upon groups of them grumbling, but she could never get close enough to hear the origin of their complaint, and when she drew near they parted and moved on.

The one corner where Briar found an absence of ill will was in the hut of the old blind woman, Racca. How long Racca had lived on the estate, Briar never learned. It seemed she was related to no one. The other servants left her alone, and quite a few appeared frightened of her. Briar had no illusions that she would receive more information from Racca than she had from her own mother, but Racca, blind as she was, seemed fully aware of who Briar was. Once, when Briar stood too close, the old woman grabbed her arm, pulled her near, and with the other hand ran gnarled, questing fingers roughly through Briar's hair. When she was done, she shoved Briar away. What this signified, Briar never understood. Her questions were answered with silence.

Racca seemed to care little whether Briar stayed or left, and when she spoke in that cracked and croaking way of hers, it often seemed that she spoke for her own amusement rather than because Briar had entered the hut, with its bunches of herbs and bulbs of garlic hanging from the low ceiling. Briar sat on a stool and waited, while Racca stooped over a large kettle, stirring milk for cheese with a broad stick. The old woman appeared to be gazing at something beyond the walls of the hut, and her unseeing eyes twitched back and forth and shone brightly in the lantern light. At these times Briar's patience was rewarded, for Racca told stories of the forest and mountain beyond the estate, stories that left Briar's eyes wide with wonder.

"You've got pine needles on your boot," Racca said one day, sniffing the air. "You've been swimming in Abunary Pond. Then you lay among the wildflowers in the meadow beyond the eldara trees."

Briar had done just that. How Racca knew was a mystery, for Briar could detect no telltale scent. Sometimes she thought Racca must look into her steaming pot and find visions there.

"Stay clear of the pond and the woods beyond," Racca continued.

"Why?"

Racca's black stick scraped the bottom of the pot rhythmically. "Spirits dwell there."

Briar had been all around the pond and the woods beyond and had never seen anything but the glorious arms of the trees and the sun dancing on the dew. She would have thought Racca was teasing her, but the old woman's expression was stone serious.

"What kind of spirits?" Briar asked.

"The kind you don't meddle with," Racca replied sharply. "You think because you haven't seen them that they aren't there. They stay invisible if they want to."

Briar crept closer and peeked into the swirling mists of the pot to see if the spirits were revealed there. "Are they good or bad?"

"Ah, that's a question."

Briar waited for the answer. When none came she asked, "Where do they come from?"

Racca stopped stirring. In the light of the lantern she looked like a great gray toad. "The night."

Briar pressed her face against the dim and grimy window and stared in wonder at the dark forest hugging Mount Einor, its peak wrapped in mystery beneath the clouds. To think that she'd tramped up there alone. Rather than filling her with dread, she longed to explore the pool and the woods all the more. Through autumn, she ventured deep into the trees, talking to them. Except for warblers flitting among the leaves and the occasional squirrel leaping from branch to branch, she saw nothing.

Then winter came and fierce storms kept her from exploring the countryside. Her battlefields snowed in, swordplay denied her, the manse cold and cheerless, and no friendly faces to greet her, she sought refuge in Racca's hut. The old woman's tales left her enraptured. The mountains were home to more than spirits. Face-changers walked the land, creatures capable of human shape or that of beast. Whether they were one, the other, or both, Racca couldn't say. But they were canny and wise, and a great snow tiger was foremost among them, and all other animals did its bidding.

During one violent storm, when the winds buffeted the hut and even the hearth fire quailed and shrank with fear, Racca set aside a shawl she was knitting and hobbled to the window, listening. Briar listened too, for she knew a tale was coming.

"Long ago, when the rivers and seas had a different shape and mountains dwarfed the ones we see today, a terrible army swept over villages and towns, driving all before it like a cold machine, enslaving the strong, casting aside the weak, leaving a path of destruction and starvation in its wake. One of the gods, looking down upon the suffering below, wept in sorrow. A single tear fell to earth. Some say it was hard and bright as a diamond, others that it was clear and shone like oil. Whatever it was, someone found it, and wherever it went, people were healed and hope flourished. Or so they say. What would I know about these things?"

Racca stumped over to a kettle simmering over the fire and ladled out two bowls of stew. She cut slices of cheese and hard black bread and arranged them on two plates. She dropped a spoon into each bowl and shoved the food toward Briar. Briar ate gratefully in the silence that followed. She couldn't remember a better meal, not one in her mother's lonely room, nor one in the kitchen, where she was served the same fare the servants ate.

After Briar washed the dishes and returned them to a small wooden cupboard, she and Racca sat through the afternoon and long into the evening, even though it had stopped snowing. It was full dark when she returned to the manse. No candles illuminated the foyer. She paused and listened to the house. Rather than sleeping it seemed to be holding its breath, and a strange foreboding set in. The urge to run back to Racca overtook her, but the old woman had no blankets to spare on a night such as this. She crept forward and almost collided with the wall of her father, who stood silently in the gloom.

"Where have you been?" he asked, his voice deep and edged with threat.

"Why do you care?" she flung back.

He raised his hand, like the head of a battle-axe in the darkness. She was ready to dodge it, but a voice—one she'd never heard before and that made her shiver more than the storm—came from one of the chairs lining the wall. "If you will, my lord, I'll handle this."

The form of a woman emerged from the shadows and stepped beside her father. She was stiff and imposing in a straight black dress that fell to the floor. Briar could make out little else in the gloom, save the woman's eyes, which peered down upon her like small pale moons through her narrow spectacles.

"Henceforth, you are this woman's charge," said her father. "You will obey her or suffer the consequences." He lit a taper. In the flickering light, his face appeared yellow and waxy. It may have been a trick of the candlelight, but it seemed that a glint, satisfied and cruel, came into his eyes. "Your tramping days are over."

She heard the words but understood little of what he said. The woman held her transfixed. A cry rose to Briar's lips like an animal caught in a snare. Before they could stop her, she spun around and darted out into the night.

CHAPTER TWO

*W*ind tossed snow in a confusion of flurries. Cold as it was, colder was the vision in Briar's mind of the woman shrouded in black, who seemed to reach with icy, ever lengthening arms to drag Briar back. Briar didn't dare look behind but charged on, certain that if she didn't get away, a terrible fate awaited her.

But where was she to go? Racca slept in her chair by the fire, leaving no warm spot to curl up in. Even if there were a place, Briar couldn't be certain she'd be welcome. She'd never imposed on the old woman.

She sped into the night. The squat servant hovels rose before her, no more inviting than brown lifeless hills. No kind face had greeted her there before; none would greet her now. No mug of steaming broth had been pressed into her hands before; none would warm her now. She turned at last to consider the manse, in time to see the door close. All was dark, save for one dim candle that glided from window to window, then up to the second floor, where it lingered at the baron's bedroom and then snuffed out.

She flung herself through the whirls and eddies of the

storm, filled with despair and longing and a good dose of hot rage at her father's indifference. Hadn't she seen the servants run with fright and then sweep up their small children with tenderness when one had fallen from a fence or skinned a knee? For the thousandth time Briar puzzled over why he hated her, why he hadn't thrown her in the well that day when he had the chance, when she was nothing more than a tiny bundle whose squalls would die as quickly as fading echoes.

The barn loomed in front of her and she slipped inside. Hollow and bleak, she cried herself to sleep in one of the stalls, vowing to never return to the manse, her father, or the fate he'd hatched for her, for even as troubled dreams overtook her, she seemed to see in them two cold pale moons, leveled on her from behind spectacles.

**

Morning found her shivering in the straw. Dullness clouded her mind. For the life of her, she couldn't recall why she wasn't in bed. Then memory of her flight descended on her like ice water. She listened for sounds of the groom or the blacksmith working his bellows. Nothing broke the stillness but the horses stirring in their stalls and the questioning *who* of an owl in the rafters. She rose, dusted off straw, and made a beeline to a barrel where apples were kept for the horses. She bit into one hungrily and stuffed another in her pocket.

The sky was graying when she stepped from the barn. Snow cloaked the fields and crusted the ancient oak on the southern lawn with icy lace. The slopes of Mount Einor appeared remote and bleak, while the manse with its imposing front columns stood cold and unmovable.

Where was she to go; where was she to live? Not in the manse, not with the stiff-backed woman in black.

No candles burned in the windows, though a few began to flare in the servants' huts. A plan hatched in her mind. She would never return. She would run to the forest. If squirrels could live on nuts, and birds could find seeds and berries, so could she. Before anyone saw her, she took off down the road, streaking across the white-blanketed fields and into the woods.

Her stubborn nature kept her there long past reason. She climbed into the boughs to keep dry, for the heat of her body quickly melted the snow on the ground. But these perches were uncomfortable, and the wind penetrated her coat. Out of season, no nuts, seeds, or berries could be discovered among the barren branches. All the nourishment she secured was snow, melted on her tongue.

The sinking sun found her trudging back to the manor, defeated. It was almost dark when she slid through the kitchen door and into her spot at the great cutting board that served as her table. A plate of mutton stew was laid out for her. She no sooner took up her spoon than the baron burst in. The woman he'd brought to bend Briar to his will trailed behind him, tall and imposing in her stern black garb. Her hair was tied in a bun so tight and exacting, no strands escaped. Her lips were thin, her eyebrows precise, and between them a deep disapproving line was chiseled.

The baron's indifferent gaze fell upon Briar. "You are forbidden to eat here," he said.

Briar rose, the stew cradled protectively in her arms. She eyed the back door, calculating her chance to dash out with her meal. If the kitchen was cut off from her, the barn would do. And the horses would be better company. Something in her father's tone made her pause. It wasn't kindness—his demeanor hadn't thawed a drop. Whatever it was, it invited curiosity.

"Where'll I eat?" she demanded.

"Come with me." He waved toward her meal. "Leave that slop."

Hunger clawed at her stomach, but she put the stew down reluctantly and followed him through the house to the dining room, the tall woman gliding behind.

"Henceforth," said the baron, "you will eat here."

Briar gazed about her in awe, more than half convinced this was a cruel joke to punish her for running away. She'd passed through here not more than a dozen times her whole life. The long white table trimmed in gold leaf, the cushioned chairs, the crystal chandelier, the blazing candelabras, the silver terrines of trout, roast beef, and honeyed baby carrots left her dizzy. She took a tentative step toward the feast, but the baron stopped her with a raised a hand.

"I require three things of you," he said. "You will arrive punctually for meals. You will do as Mistress Budge tells you." He indicated the woman with his hand. "Last and most important, you will become a young lady, *a young lady*, do you understand me?" His gaze traveled up and down her soiled clothes, lingering on her tangled mop and grimy face. What he said next surprised her. "Praise heaven, at least you're not ugly."

"Best not fill her head with vanity, my lord," the woman said with a righteous smile.

"Quite right. I leave her to you." He bowed and strode from the room.

The obstacle of her father removed, Briar was drawn to the feast like iron to a lodestone. A strong hand locked on her arm.

"Ladies dine here," Budge said, tightening her grip, "not little vagabonds. To the bath with you."

Briar was dragged unceremoniously to the bathroom where she was scrubbed raw. Afterward, she was put to bed without supper, so she could contemplate the worry she had caused her father. Briar doubted her father had given her one thought, but saw no point in saying so. Regarding Briar from the doorway of the darkened bedroom, Mistress Budge seemed a frightful specter. Under any other circumstances she would have crept to the dining hall and filled her stomach. And if the feast had been removed, she would have searched high and low for that bowl of stew. But long after the woman's footsteps faded down the hall, Briar remained fixed to her bed as readily as if she'd been tied there.

***

The next morning, one of the servants escorted Briar to a fitting room. Mistress Budge awaited her at a table where bolts of fabric were unrolled. She scrutinized Briar's hair, examined her hands and nails, squeezed her arms and knees, and peered at her teeth. At last, with a sigh that bespoke a heavy burden, she said, "Do as I say, and you'll eat in the dining room. Defy me, and you'll starve." She leaned in, her breath like foul cheese. "We'll get along fine." A smile that wasn't a smile accompanied her words.

Briar squelched the urge to take a step back. Her stomach growled at the aroma of bacon and freshly baked biscuits wafting from downstairs. It seemed like last week that she'd eaten those two apples. They *would* get along fine, she decided, for the feast she'd seen last night seemed fit for a queen, and a tiny spark flared in her breast that at last she might find love in the dining room.

But the morning passed little to her liking. She was trussed up in a dress that was too small, must have belonged to a long dead relative, and smelled of dust and mildew. She wasn't allowed into the dining room until her parents left. She would not partake with them—she was told—until she'd learned manners, etiquette, and deportment.

The hours ground by. Which fork to use, which direction to pass a plate, where to place the napkin, where to put the spoon, how to cover a cough, where to put bones and pits. Briar's head swam with rules. If she was graceful climbing trees or dueling with her stick, she was awkward and clumsy with a teacup. Jelly dropped onto the tablecloth; goblets of milk overturned; spoons, knives, and forks clattered to the floor. And the rules fled her head like startled birds.

When at last she was released for a break, she was dizzy and lightheaded, as much from lack of nourishment as from the drilling of lessons. *That* was a torture she wouldn't wish on an enemy. Feast or no, she was through, and dashed into the crisp outdoors. Up the road, through the meadow, into the woods she fled. Taking up a stick, she battled her old foe the tree trunk, telling him he was a little fool, a sorry child, a worthless baggage, the misery of his father, that he would never become a gentleman or hold a teacup correctly or lay a napkin in the right direction—in short, all the insults hurled upon Briar through the morning plus one of her own: the moon would fall from the sky before he was loved.

Dusk found her sliding into the barn. She squatted near the barrel and ate apples until her belly ached. Only then did she steal through the kitchen door. No one waited for her; no bowl of stew sat steaming on the cutting board. She hadn't expected any. Mistress Budge had made her terms clear. Briar crept to her bedroom, wriggled from the horrid dress, and slid beneath the covers. A few minutes later, footsteps approached her door. They paused there a moment, candlelight glowing faintly through the gap at the bottom of the door. A key turned the lock, and the footsteps receded.

She was far too tired to think more about it and soon fell asleep.

***

Morning brought hope. She would try harder. How difficult could it be? But her door remained locked. If Mistress Budge wanted to play tough, Briar could play tough too. She jumped into leggings and tunic, slipped out her second-story window, and scrambled down a tree.

She couldn't look at another apple for as long as she lived. She made a beeline for the garden. Surely she could dig up something. Roots could be roasted; squash could be boiled. But when she got to the neat rows of vegetables carefully tended and cleared of snow, the chief gardener, a man with leathery skin and squinting eyes, blocked her way past the gate.

"Sorry, Miss Briar," he said, looking more pleased than sorry. "Them in the house says the garden's off limits."

"Who in the house?" she demanded.

"The new lady. So sorry, miss—" Looking more pleased than ever. "You'll have to take it up with the baron."

Briar could think of no counter argument. What argument was there when the cold wall of her father shadowed everything? Yet a new idea came to her.

Racca!

But the gardener added, as she turned with excitement, "Don't be botherin' old Racca. The baron'll turn her out if she helps you."

With heavy steps, Briar returned to the manse. Mistress Budge awaited her in the foyer and escorted her to her bedroom. With dismay, Briar found the carpenter hammering bars over her window.

Victory gleamed in the woman's eyes. "Ready to resume your lessons?"

"I'm hungry," Briar said, her voice a feeble croak and almost unrecognizable.

"You should have thought of that before you ran off."

Briar was taken to the fitting room and given a crust of bread and a cup of milk. Soon, her head cleared. She didn't care about dining with the baron, and seeing her mother was like viewing a cloud, wispy and far away. But food was a great motivator and she applied herself to her lessons. She made few mistakes, though Mistress Budge watched her like a hawk, a thimble on the end of a forefinger. That thimble never saw needle or thread, but the hard end found a use on Briar's head if she slipped.

Satins and silks, velvets and brocades were draped over Briar, and a needlewoman took careful measurements. The first gown arrived a few days later. Briar would have been happy with just the shift and knee stockings, but then came petticoats and the inner dress. By the time the outer gown was pulled over her head, she felt as if she was wearing lead.

"Just for the dining room?" she asked hopefully.

"All day," Budge replied, "though you may change into formal attire for special guests."

If this wasn't formal, what was? Briar wondered. She held out the voluminous sleeves, which hung in long loops. She had a bad feeling about what would happen when they resumed her table lessons.

After her hair was brushed and gathered behind, she was turned toward a full-length mirror. The dress was astonishing, spreading from a tiny waist like a big tent. Briar gasped. The girl in the glass was unrecognizable—except the black eyes, staring back in wonder—like a princess, and Briar had the urge to curtsy as Budge had taught her.

"How does it fit?" Budge asked.

Fingers to her waist, Briar tried to loosen it. "It hurts."

"Suck in your stomach. You'll get used to it. Try walking."

Briar stepped across the room, the dress so long it splashed about her toes. Worse, it was cumbersome and her movements so restricted she felt like she was in shackles. No sword fighting in this thing, she thought, and saw red. "I don't *want* to get used to it. I don't want it at all." She began yanking at the ruffled collar, but the dress was buttoned in the back, and besides, it had taken a lady's maid to put her in it; it would take one to haul the dreadful thing off.

Budge folded her arms. "Wear it or starve."

"I can't do anything in this thing."

"You can and will."

But Budge's idea of what a lady does was at odds with Briar's. A lady sat with an erect back, hands folded like useless petals. Briar sat cross-legged on the chair, dress hiked to her knees. A lady steps so lightly she floats, she was told. Briar shook the hanging sleeves. "I'm a bird!" she cried, and ran about the room, flapping her arms.

She kept to the house for the next week, wandering the halls, looking for something to do when she wasn't receiving lessons in deportment. The gown rustled everywhere she went, to her annoyance, since it was always better to be out of the baron's notice. But he did notice, scrutinizing her as if she were a prize pony.

"Hello, Father," she would say, but he would only nod curtly and return to studying the estate books or simply gazing out a window.

She often lingered before the sword and dagger in the great entrance hall. The sword was too heavy for her, but the dagger—long and thin as a switch—suited her well. It was too high to reach, even standing on a chair on tippy-toes. But she shadow fenced before it—cutting, thrusting, and parrying as if she were defending the manse from a hundred attackers, and despite the terrible restraint of her gown, her movements were liquid and lethal.

Even the dagger couldn't hold her attention long. With nothing left to see in the house, and clouds fleeing before an unusually warm sun, she ventured outside. Despite the gown, she climbed trees, forged deep into the underbrush in search of rabbits, chased a wren through fields muddy with melting snow, and plunged into the waters of Abunary Pond in pursuit of a frog.

It was almost sundown when she started home. She was flying down a hillside when thundering hoofs and the scrape of wheels rose from the road below. As she reached the bottom, a carriage came charging around a bend. It was like nothing she'd ever seen, polished rosewood gilded with gold, alabaster, rubies, and emeralds. Harnesses shone like obsidian; apricot and blue ostrich feathers on the bridles waved like the wings of a giant bird. The coachman, all in black and brass buttons, yanked on the reins to avoid her. Briar dodged. The carriage veered to one side. Before it plunged on, a lady looked from the window. Her glance fell on Briar, standing on the side of the road, conscious now of her ripped and muddy gown, and her hair tossing wildly in the wind. The woman's eyes were ice—sending shivers down Briar's spine, frightening her more than Budge or the baron ever had. Then they dismissed her, brushing her aside like an insect.

Briar felt the slight, though she couldn't put it into words. That instant, she decided she hated the woman. But the carriage shot around the next bend and was gone.

When she arrived home, Briar was surprised to find the carriage parked in front of the manse. The slight still stung, and Briar determined to march through the great double doors of the entrance, muddy gown and all, to confront her enemy. Before she was halfway up the steps, two stout manservants latched onto each of her arms and carried her kicking to the kitchen.

Budge towered there, her face red with rage. "Where have you been?" she snapped. "The queen's here. Rule number one, what's rule number one?"

Briar scowled up at her tormentor. "I don't know, and I don't care."

Budge caught Briar's ear and began towing her upstairs. "You better care." But Budge's voice dropped with every step through the house. "One peep and I'll snip your ear off," she hissed.

They came to the bathroom, where two lady's maids waited with steaming water and a giant bar of tallow soap.

"Do it fast—there's no time to waste!" she told the maids.

Briar was scrubbed with haste. Afterward, she was yanked from the tub, and towel after towel were vigorously applied to her hair. As a new gown was dropped over her head, Briar overheard Budge talking to the baron, just outside the door.

"Is she ready?" he asked.

"Leave it to me," Budge replied.

"Her error is your error. Do I make myself clear?"

"Perfectly, my lord."

Briar's hair was brushed until it shone, and a necklace, bracelet, and ring she'd never seen before were added to her costume.

"Rule number one," Budge said, as she escorted Briar to the drawing room, "never, never, never keep important people waiting." She stopped. "Curtsy the way I showed you."

Briar bobbed a stately curtsy.

"That'll do. Now smile."

Briar smiled.

"Good. You're not completely hopeless."

When they neared the drawing room, Budge stopped

again and her face swooped within an inch of Briar's. "One mistake, and I'll lock you up for a month. Understand?"

Briar nodded and entered the drawing room. Dozens of candles on the walls and a crystal chandelier illuminated the room and gleamed on a silver tea service. Delicate sandwiches and pastries were arranged on a platter, reminding Briar she hadn't eaten since that morning. A ferocious fire crackled on the hearth, and the heat prickled beneath her shift, inner and outer dresses, and heavy cape sewn at the shoulders. Four upholstered chairs were arranged in a semicircle over a burgundy rug, laid before the fire.

Briar's mother was posed in her seat like a pale wax statue, her eyes empty glass. The baron sat beside her, dressed in a blue velvet suit, his moustache well waxed. He smiled at Briar—the kind one might see on a marionette—and waved her over. Briar glided to him as Budge had taught her, head poised, footsteps light; only the rustling of her gown marked her passing.

The queen studied her, and strangling fingers closed over Briar's throat. Would the queen recognize her after that brief encounter on the road? Briar couldn't read the frosty blue eyes inspecting her. The interval gave her a chance to make her own appraisal. The queen was in her twenties, and tall—as tall as the blacksmith—with powerful hips and shoulders. Her hair was a deep chestnut, her eyebrows thick. What was more remarkable is that she didn't wear a formal gown. In fact, she wore no gown at all, sporting loose pants, blouse, and vest instead. Briar's second impression was the same as her first: she hated this woman. But now an inkling of danger vibrated in her bones, and Briar's hand stiffened imperceptibly, as if she held that dagger hanging in the foyer.

"This is Queen Naryfel, Briar," the baron said with a grand sweep of his arm. "Queen of all Purpura."

Briar curtsied and forced a smiled.

The queen, who had dropped her head into her hand while examining Briar, roused at last. "Well done, Baron. She's dazzling, ravishing as a sapphire." To Briar, she said, "When you're older, I'll have you at court."

The Baron drew Briar onto his lap. The fingers of one hand burrowed through the folds of the gown, out of the queen's view, and pinched Briar's hip—not enough to make her yelp, but enough to convince her to do what she'd been taught in her long and tedious lessons with Budge.

"Thank you, Your Highness," Briar replied, inwardly shrinking at the idea of going anywhere near this woman. "I shall like that."

The queen took up one of the pastries and spread cream cheese and strawberry jam on it. "You can't imagine what I encountered on the way here. A filthy little grub almost collided with the carriage. I've never seen anything so wild or untamed. Like a little animal. Belongs to one of your servants, no doubt."

The baron paled. "Gypsies camp in the hills about here. Perhaps one strayed." He tightened his hold on the flesh of Briar's hip. It was all she could do not to cry out.

"All the more reason to help me against the Turlians," the queen replied.

"Nothing would please me more. There have been skirmishes across the border west of here, and they continue to file petitions of ownership on our estate. The servants grumble in their cups over it, believing they have a claim."

"Well then, Baron, we have a mutual interest."

"Indeed we do." He eased Briar off his lap. "Run along, dear. You may dine with Mistress Budge."

But Briar didn't dine with Budge. She was hauled back to her room.

"Father said I was to eat with you."

"Naughty girls who roam like strays dine on stale bread.

Think about that the next time you have the urge to tramp around like a little beggar." Budge left and locked the door behind her.

Shut in her room, Briar fumed for a week. Why try if they were only going to punish her? She hated Budge, she hated the baron, and she hated the queen most of all, for it was clear to Briar that this exalted lady was behind everything. Why else, when her father showed no interest before, would he want to show her off like a trinket to the queen?

Briar declared war, but picked her battles. When she could no longer stand her room and prisoner's fare, she cooperated with the lessons. But once a week she broke free, lured by the scent of spring. She stole breeches and tunic, belonging to a servant's child, from a clothesline. Then she carefully took off her gown, folded it, and hid it to keep it safe and dry. In her outside clothes, she romped to her heart's content, her only respite from the drudgery of lessons.

"Now that the queen has seen you," Budge said flatly, "there will be visitors, important visitors."

The lessons started in earnest.

"Arms off the table."

"Eat silently, girl. You chew like a starving wolf."

"White or dark meat, it matters not. Let others choose for you."

"Sit poised. You must be as delicate as a flower."

"Ladies should be ornaments, to enhance the general ambience of the room."

And so on.

From sunup to sundown, Briar was drilled. This was how you fluttered a fan; this was how you flipped it open. This was where you held it, not that high, not that low, small dainty motions, no, no, no, oh, you're hopeless!

It was all too confusing, like being told to go left when

you naturally go right. Budge's mood was a rising tide of annoyance, giving way to frustration and then all out anger. Throwing down her napkin, she fastened her nose to Briar's. "I won't be defeated, you little animal. I'll break you first."

But Briar was also at the end of her tether. "Girls grow up," she said, "but they don't forget. Their fathers die. *Then* where'll you be?"

Budge paled. "That will be a very long time from now. Presently, and for the foreseeable future, you have me."

If she made progress, if she pleased anyone, Briar couldn't tell. Her father didn't acknowledge her now any more than before. But Briar heard him demand, "Well, is she ready?"

"Soon, your grace," Budge replied.

"You're overdue already."

After that the lessons continued far into the night. A manservant hovered near if she tried to escape, and she was locked in her room at bedtime. She once tried to appeal to her mother for relief, but her mother's mind was as vaporous and far away as ever. It seemed certain that if she ever descended to earth and saw what was happening, she would shatter like fine china.

Then one day a ray of sunlight streamed in.

CHAPTER THREE

The baron's conversation with the queen stuck like a burr in Briar's mind. It took less than two seconds for her to work out they had a plan for her. Less than that to see they wanted to marry her off. Oh, not today —she was only eleven and wouldn't be of age for five more years—but at some point. All of the lessons in etiquette and deportment, all of the punishments had been with this end in mind. When, on a warm day with wildflowers springing up and scenting the hillsides, and birdsong, pine, and honey-suckle filling the air, and Briar itching to fly into all of it like a lark; when on this day of all days, a carriage—only slightly less elegant and imposing than the queen's—rolled up to the estate, and a family of four alighted in all their state, she knew she was in for it.

She stood on the front steps. Her mother floated like a cloud beside her, eyes lost in the blue. On Briar's left, her father attached his fingers to the flesh behind her shoulder, ready to twist. At a deferential distance, it seemed Budge's eyes drilled into Briar's back.

A footman climbed down and opened the carriage door,

gilded in silver with a crest of two crossing torches. A tall middle-aged man emerged first. Briar would have thought him handsome, with his waves of blond hair and bold nose, but he took in the grounds, the assembled servants, the manse, and Briar's parents with an expression that she took for disdain. When his gaze fell on Briar, he blew out a breath like a bellows.

The footman's announcement was like a trumpet: "Lord Durem D'Arté, Fourteenth Earl of Pendley."

The earl's wife descended next. Her face was wan, her eyes small, her body as narrow as a reed.

"Countess D'Arté," proclaimed the footman.

A younger version of the countess stepped down next, but her face was far more pinched, reminding Briar of a rat. She was in her early twenties. Her eyes glowed at the sight of the manse, and well they should—it had been scrubbed backwards and forwards, and the front gleamed with a new coat of paint.

"Miss Patrikka D'Arté."

Patrikka's lips pulled back, exposing teeth, as her gaze fell on Briar. It was all Briar could do to not glare, but her father's fingers warned on her shoulder.

"Viscount Vance D'Arté," the footman intoned.

From behind the wall of the earl, his wife, and daughter, came soft singing, half hummed as if to oneself. The tune was an old peasant song, something the baron would consider uncouth, but Briar had always liked.

The wall parted and out stepped the viscount, a boy not much older than Briar. The top of his shirt was unbuttoned, the collar flapping lightly in the wind. He'd taken off a green doublet and thrown it over one arm. In one hand he clasped a heavy book, in the other he held a cushion.

He handed the latter to the earl. "Your pillow, Father."

For a moment, the stone melted from the earl's face as he

smiled down on his son and took the cushion, but hardened again just as quickly. "Let's get on with it." And the earl blew out another breath, as much a growl as a sigh.

If the sister was cut from the same mold as her mother, the viscount was the image of his father. He had the same wavy hair, soft and fine as silk. And the same broad brow. But where the earl's was unyielding, the boy's was thoughtful. He had no interest in the manse or Briar's family, but was wholly absorbed with the assembled servants, who stood shifting in their worn-down sandals, their hats and bonnets clutched in calloused hands.

His sister took him by his shoulders and turned him toward Briar. He scowled and shrugged away from her hold.

"Say hello to Miss Briar, Vance," Patrikka said, reattaching her grip on his arms.

Briar jerked a curtsy. Vance swept into a slow bow, but came up frowning. Briar simmered. This wasn't what you wanted from a spark, even if she wasn't going to marry him.

The air thickened.

The baron waved his hand toward the cool shadows beyond the manse doorway. "You must be tired," he clucked. "Rest, freshen up, and a small repast will revive you."

"That would be—" began the countess.

"Kind of you," Patrikka finished.

Before anyone else moved, the earl stalked inside.

Over the next hour, Budge drilled Briar on the fine points of manners. It was moot. When the two families assembled in the dining room, Briar knew what to do. She had no interest in the D'Artés or her parents, nor was she frightened of punishment, but the baron had outdone himself, and the "small repast" was more lavish than any she'd seen. She'd had a growth spurt, and a diet of bread and water left her dizzy. Besides, if she was ever going to wield the sword hanging in the foyer, she required more than prison fare.

"I hope you had a pleasant ride," the baron said to the earl.

"Tolerable," was the crisp reply.

"You found the roads dry?"

"Dry enough."

So it went, the meal grinding on like a rusty wheel. Further attempts to draw out the earl fell on deaf ears. He glowered at the hearth, and the flames seemed to shrink from his glare. Briar's mother prattled now and then. The young viscount sat beside Briar, his eyes glued to the window, where a gentle breeze stirred the curtains and hinted at the garden beyond. His lack of interest suited Briar fine. She focused on devouring her meal with as much gusto as decorum would allow.

Patrikka's lips pulled back, exposing those teeth, and she nodded toward Briar and Vance. "They make a lovely couple, Baron."

The baron slopped a piece of roast beef around in his mashed potatoes and brought the bloody mess to his lips. "Indeed," he replied, without a glance at either Briar or Vance.

A flush burned clear to Briar's neck. Half seeing it, she reached for the nearest thing at hand, a sugar bowl, and passed it to Vance. He glanced helplessly at the sugar and then resumed his contemplation of the window.

Patrikka's comment made Briar steam. If she married at all—and she wasn't at all sure she wanted to—she'd choose her own husband.

"What about you, Miss Patrikka?" Briar asked sweetly. "Anyone sparking you? I bet you'd make a lovely couple."

Patrikka's eyes darkened. The baron went white, and Briar was relieved she wasn't sitting beside him, or she'd get a sharp pinch beneath the tablecloth.

But she knew what she was about—the lessons in deportment hadn't all been in vain. She plowed on. "If I had a brother," she continued, wrapping her words with an air of innocence, "you could marry him."

Patrikka laughed. "You have an accomplished offspring, Baron. And what a beauty."

The baron beamed and quickly turned the conversation. No one took further notice of Briar except Vance, who gazed at her thoughtfully and then resumed his contemplation of the window.

The meal lumbered on. Patrikka and the baron talked of unruly peasants, "the Turlian Claim," and the queen's campaign to secure the borders. Dessert was a long way off, coffee and cordials even longer. Briar was kicking restlessly under the table, dreaming of a good stick fight with an imaginary foe, when Vance reared from his seat.

"Father, the day's wasting," he said. "May Miss Briar and I go outside?"

The earl roused from his gloom and glanced to the open window, as if he wished to escape there himself. "You had better." He flashed a rare smile.

"By all means," said the baron. "Briar, give Master Vance a tour of the estate."

Aware of the watchful eye of her father, Briar offered her arm. Vance looped his around hers and they hurried into the sunshine. As soon they were down the front steps, she pulled away.

"There's the manse, there's the servants' quarters, there's the garden." Briar pointed out a road. "Walk that way. You'll see it all in an hour." She gave him a push to get him going.

Vance raised an eyebrow. "What about you?"

Briar hooked her thumb in the opposite direction. "Someplace else."

Amusement curled his lips. "You don't like us."

She folded her arms. "I like rats better."

"You don't even know us."

"I know all I need to."

"Like what?"

"You've been looking down your nose since you got here. Your father too. We're not fancy enough for you."

His smile broadened. "I like you."

"That's another thing. I wouldn't marry you if you were the last man in the world." Something had been fluttering inside of her since they'd stepped outside. It felt new and strange, and she wished she could take back her words as soon as she'd said them.

"We could be friends," he said.

"Never." She was like a runaway cart, hurtling down a hillside, and now she couldn't stop. He winced and turned away. Her heart sank.

But he stopped. "Father's in pain. And parties are hard for him—he doesn't hear well."

He started down the road. Briar watched him, feeling very foolish. Now that she thought about it, the earl's stiff walk might mask a limp. Vance paused when he came to a small rise and stood staring down at the servants' quarters. His face soured.

Curiosity got the better of her. When she'd caught up with him, he pointed. "That roof's sagging," he said. "It leaks when it rains. And that wall's as thin as cotton. Wind blows right through it."

"I didn't know that."

He turned on her. "Father says that an earl who doesn't take care of his people has no right being an earl. Better to give it all to them. That goes for barons too." Velvet brown eyes pierced her. He spun and continued down the road.

She hurried after him. "I can't tell the baron what to do."

"You could try."

"Like you do with your sister."

He winced, and she knew she'd hit home. They walked on

until they'd passed the garden and sat on a fence overlooking sheep and horses grazing in a pasture. This was one of Briar's favorite spots, but she hardly saw it. Her mind was spinning, first, over what he'd said about the estate, and second—more importantly—over this strange boy whose mind peered deep into things and shone like a bright flame. Hot shame burned her from the first. The second left her breathless.

He gazed with dreamy contentment at the hillsides, sloping gently upward and painted with poppies and daffodils. Neither had spoken since her jab about his sister. Grasping at straws to break the silence, she plucked out the first thing that came to her.

"Do you fight?" she asked.

"When I have to."

"No, I mean with a sword."

"Then I would really have to."

She elbowed him good-naturedly. "No-o-o, playing, silly."

He smiled. "Sometimes."

She scooted from the fence, found two sticks, and offered him one.

"I can't fight you," he said.

She slashed the air with her weapon. "Why not?"

"We're dressed up."

"I don't care about the dress." She brandished the stick. "Come on, let's see what you can do."

He took hold of her stick and pushed it aside. "We will. I promise."

That night, Briar marched into the baron's study. He was seated behind his desk, reviewing an account book with knitted brow.

"You know better than to come here," he growled, without looking up.

"You'll talk to me."

He put down his quill and raised stony eyes to meet hers. "Why's that?"

"The servants' quarters are falling apart."

He snorted. "When did you start caring about anything but your own single-minded needs?"

"Since now."

"The buildings have stood this long; they'll stand a little longer." He took up the quill and began scratching calculations on a piece of parchment. "Run along. It's not your concern."

"Right, it's yours."

His nostrils flared. "Don't think for a minute I won't throw you to Budge for a dose of hickory, guests or no guests."

"Go ahead. Poof!" Her fingers wiggled to imitate a cloud dissolving. "There goes your plan for me."

He tossed the quill aside and stared at her. "What the devil do the servants' quarters have to do with it?"

"Rats couldn't live in them. Vance will never propose as long as they're like that. And the earl won't give his blessing."

Something in the way of cracks spread across the baron's face. "Vance told you that?"

She smiled—one of those pretty smiles Budge had taught her—and left him looking in dismay at his account book.

At breakfast the next morning, Vance was as good as his word. After he'd bolted down his meal, he asked, "Father, can Miss Briar and I go exploring?"

The earl roused from his contemplation of the fireplace and looked with distaste at the adult company. "I think you'd better."

Vance took his napkin from his lap—shiny in a new velvet suit—and folded it over his plate. "Mother, can Miss Briar and I change? These'll get dirty."

"That would be—" his mother began.

"A splendid idea," Patrikka finished. "Don't you think, Baron?"

The baron didn't appear at all pleased. Perhaps he was considering whether Vance would unearth more expenses.

In clothes they could romp and tumble in, Briar and Vance made a beeline to the pasture. They took up their positions, armed with the sticks of yesterday. Briar darted in with an attack so swift and unexpected that it slipped past Vance's guard and caught him squarely on his heart.

He frowned. "Where did you learn that?"

Briar shrugged. "Nowhere. Stop talking and fight."

Before he could set himself, she struck again. Ferocious, raw, unschooled strokes rained down on him. He backed up, his feet shifting in subtle ways that baffled and moved him away from Briar's power. She kept up a perfect storm of slashing and stabbing, but the element of surprise was gone, and now he parried and countered, his motions spare and graceful. She knew she would tire. In a desperate surge, she retried that first gambit, which had landed before. The next thing she knew, her stick went flying and he scored.

She stalked to the fence, turning her back on him. Blood pounded in her veins. The field beyond blurred to hazy red. It seemed his eyes were on her. The back of her neck prickled; suddenly she wanted to be as far away as possible. In one fluid motion, she vaulted like a deer over the fence and tore up the hillside. She ran, heedless of where she went. His calm demeanor now seemed smug, and his sister's haughty expression was pasted over his. He thought he was better than her, that's all there was to it, and he was flinging it in her face.

You aren't so high and mighty, Vance D'Arté, with your fancy carriage. And you can forget marrying me. Exhausted, stinging with humiliation, she plunged into water. Only when she was well in it did she realize she'd come to Abunary Pond.

Eyes closed, she floated on her back. The coolness of the water, the fragrance of the pines, calmed her mind and allowed her to consider.

No promise had been made to her father. After the servants' quarters were fixed, he couldn't unfix them. More whirled through her mind about Vance's growling bear of a father and helpless mother and that goad of a sister, Patrikka. But curiosity began to intrude. She emerged, dripping, from the pond and lay on the grass. Allowing the sun to dry her, she began to wonder how Vance had beaten her. It was no longer the fact of losing. She had to know how to fight like that. Would he teach her? She would ask. If he refused, she would watch him like a hawk, memorize his motions, and then practice them until they were second nature. Even better, she would get that dagger hanging in the foyer, by hook or by crook, and drill with an intensity that would put Budge to shame.

Cold wind snapping through the branches roused her from her reverie. Shivering, she glanced at the sky. The sun dipped toward the horizon. She sprang to her feet and hurried home. Lunch was long past; dinner would be well on by the time she returned. The presence of guests made her absence a double offense.

Crimson and pink were spreading above when she came upon a curious sight in the yard just beyond the shacks. Half a dozen servants' children had formed a circle. The youngest, a boy no older than eight, stood in the center, clinging to a fur hat like it was his life. A strapping lad about Briar's age pushed the smaller boy into the dust and then latched onto the hat, trying to yank it away. Briar knew the ruffian well, a sullen lug named Jemmo.

What riveted her attention was Vance, striding toward the group, his eyes blazing. He wore the same play clothes from the morning, suggesting he hadn't returned for lunch or dinner either. What he did next sent a thrill through Briar. He shoved the other lads aside until he came to the chief culprit, who now dangled the hat before the nose of its former owner.

Briar was close enough now to overhear what was said.

"Give it back to him," Vance said.

"Who's gonna make me?" Jemmo sneered.

"I am. Return it, or I'll be forced to take action."

Jemmo's piggish eyes lit with malice. "Lookee here, boys, the lord o' the manor."

It was evident to Briar that Jemmo didn't have a clue who Vance was. He probably thought Vance was the son of a new servant or one of the tenant farmers from nearby who came to sell fruit and vegetables at the manse—not the visiting viscount. He sized Vance up. They were nearly the same size, but Vance was slim and not as broad in the shoulders. Jemmo must have liked what he saw. A nasty grin spread the pockmarks on his face.

"Last chance." Vance began rolling up his sleeves. "I will pay you the value of the hat. That's what you want, isn't it, a quick profit?"

Jemmo handed the hat to a compatriot and waded in, hands cocked. He threw a wide, arcing right. Vance sidestepped the blow and delivered a straight left, followed by a right. Jemmo blinked, momentarily stunned, then charged, bellowing like an enraged bull. Vance caught him coming in with a quick right-left-right combination. But Jemmo's head must have been as hard and as thick as a door. He bore in throwing punches, most of them wild. Vance demonstrated the same sneaky footwork that had baffled Briar earlier. Jemmo's blows fanned air, except one lucky roundhouse that grazed Vance's cheek. Otherwise, Vance was as slippery as an eel and countered with sharp and efficient blows. In a matter of moments, Jemmo was bleeding from his nose and mouth, and his left eye was swelling shut. A shot to his body buckled his knees. Then came a clean right to the jaw, and it was over. Jemmo fell face first into the dust.

"I'll take that hat now," Vance said. The cap was plucked up and pressed it into the grateful hands of its owner. Then Vance knelt over his opponent and turned him over. Jemmo stared up, dazed. A good dousing from a bucket soon restored him. He was led from the field of battle, not too worse for wear. The victor began heading out of the yard.

"Vance!" Briar was about to rush down to him but Budge seemed to come out of nowhere. She latched onto Briar and hauled her unceremoniously into the dining room. The baron was bringing a large slice of veal to his lips. He was leaning toward Patrikka, who spoke near his ear. A servant was pouring wine for the countess, who held out a goblet to him. The flushed and puffy condition of her face suggested she'd already quaffed several glasses. Briar's mother was white with agitation, and her eyes darted to and fro. It was not at all clear that Briar was the cause. The earl pushed his food about his plate with bored resignation.

"Where have you been?" the baron asked, chewing a wad of meat and leveling his fork at her. "We've been worried stiff." Briar almost laughed at the idea of her father worrying about her. He fretted more over his livestock. Of course, in that case he should be anxious about her—he was trading her like a farm animal.

He took in her clothing, wrinkled and muddy from Abunary Pond. "No, don't answer, I can see well enough." He turned to Patrikka. "You see what I'm up against? How is this sort of thing handled at Hartwell House?"

Patrikka exposed her teeth. "A strong dose of hickory."

Briar's mind raced for an excuse. She could see a tall shadow in the hall beyond the dining room and knew that

Budge was just behind the door, ready to carry out Patrikka's suggestion.

The baron looked rather pleased with the notion. He rang a bell beside him. Budge hurried in. A moment later, Vance entered through another door.

"It's my fault," he said. "I begged Miss Briar to take me into the hills. If anyone should be punished, it's me. She wanted to come home sooner. But I couldn't tear myself away from the trees and meadows. It was so beautiful."

The baron pointed to Vance's cheek, the color of raspberries, and his knuckles, like swollen grapes. "And how did that happen?"

Vance turned his hands before him and laughed. "This? A slip down a hillside. I should have listened to Miss Briar. She told me the rock was loose."

"I don't think so." The baron turned to Budge. "You know what to do."

The earl reared suddenly from his seat, red-faced. For the first time, he looked directly at the baron. "My son doesn't lie."

The baron paled. "No ... certainly ... Your Lordship."

"If he says he fell, he fell," the earl snapped. "If he says it's his fault, it's his fault."

"But surely both children—"

"If he says he should be punished, he should be punished."

The earl turned to his son with tenderness on his face. "Three days indoors. Is that sufficient?"

Vance was beaming. "That should do it, Father."

That night, Briar was ordered to her father's study.

He leveled his quill at her. "Don't think for one minute you're off the hook with me. When you're late, when you arrive like a muddy waif, when you're not dressed like a lady to dine with her class, you paint an ugly picture of yourself.

And you embarrass me." This last was spoken in a way that indicated it was the greatest of her crimes.

He waited as if to see the effect of his words. She glared at him with all the stubborn pride and indifference she could muster.

"If it were up to me, I'd throw you to Budge. But it seems I'm overruled." His gaze swept over her. "Well, the little viscount likes you, that's certain. Maybe this will work out after all."

He took up his pipe and lit it. When he'd blasted out a furious cloud, he added, "One more stunt like that and I'll take you in hand."

The whole day was a revelation to Briar. The earl called the shots, not the baron. Then there was Vance. Taking her punishment. Beating her neatly that morning. Then fighting for a defenseless boy. His stance, his poise, the subtle movement of his feet in both battles was like a light illuminating a secret previously unknown to her. In her room that night she tried to imitate his form, the angle of his feet, the bend of his knee, his advance, his retreat, his double retreat, his thrust—his slide, jump, and lunge. She practiced into the wee hours.

For the next three days she was free to roam. She hardly thought of the outdoors but sought out Vance first thing in the morning. The bruise on his cheek had deepened to purple, painful to behold.

She touched the spot with the gentleness of a butterfly. "Does it hurt?"

"Not now." He grinned. "You should go outside. It's what you like best in the world."

How did he know!

"Nonsense." She took his arm and they talked while she showed him the manse. They started on the third floor where she took him down the long corridor lined with dusty portraits. He pointed to one of a man posed before a mass of silvery eldara leaves, his black coils falling wildly to his shoulders, his eyes flaring and burning strangely.

"Who's that?" Vance asked.

"My Uncle Faelán."

"I would like to meet him.

"I would too."

He stopped and looked at her. "You haven't?"

"No. He may be dead. No one speaks about him."

They passed down a flight of stairs. The topic of her uncle troubled her. It seemed as taboo as why the baron hated her.

She quickly changed the subject. "You do fight."

His face grew serious. "I told you. When I have to."

"He was bigger than you."

"Size and strength don't matter."

Briar thought about that. She was strong and had outwrestled most of the boys she'd met. But she would never be as big or as strong as the earl, say, or Vance when he was fully grown. It irked her.

By this time they had reached the foyer where the sword and dagger were hanging.

She stopped and gripped both of his arms. "Can you show me? I want to fight like that."

"Pretend you're holding that knife on the wall. Fight the way you were yesterday."

She proceeded to battle across the flagstone. "Well?" she asked when she'd returned to him.

He hesitated, biting his lower lip.

"Let me have it. What am I doing wrong?" she asked.

"Everything."

It stung, but she resumed her stance. "Show me."

There beneath her father's weapons Vance tutored her, adjusting the placement of her feet, her posture, the angle of her body. Over the next hours she learned to thrust and parry, to guard and to turn a blade. A strange exhilaration overtook her. This was what she'd yearned for, to take all that energy bursting inside her and direct it.

Vance told her without discipline she would never be great—with discipline she was unstoppable.

"Even against you?" she asked.

"I don't have your fire for it. I dream about other things."

This intrigued her, but she wouldn't learn for some time what that might be.

It rained the day his punishment ended, spoiling her plans for a stick fight in the field.

They headed to the barn, but watching the stalls get cleaned offered little amusement, so they ducked into the tanner's shed next door. Vance was delighted and asked dozens of questions about how to skin, stretch, and scrape a hide clean. And how to soften it.

Briar had seen this before. Wanting no part of it, she tugged on Vance's sleeve. "Let's go."

But he insisted the tanner show him how he simmered the animal's brain and then worked the mush into the hide.

"It's disgusting," Briar said outside, as they skittered around puddles pocked with rain.

"You've seen all that?" Vance asked.

She nodded, gratified she'd known something Vance hadn't. "I can do lots of stuff."

They rushed up the front steps and into the foyer.

His face lit with curiosity. "Like what?"

"I can start a fire with sticks."

His eyes sparkled.

"It's not that hard. The groom's boy showed me." She twisted water from her hair.

"What else do you know?"

He pulled a deck of cards from his pocket. For the next few hours they played triumph, a card game he said was all the rage in salons and drawing rooms across Purpura. Briar seemed to have a knack for the game. After she learned the rules and lost a few hands, he rarely beat her. At last he threw down the cards in disgust, and suggested they do something else.

They were seated cross-legged beneath the foyer window. Rain pattered on the glass and ran down in streams, blurring the world beyond.

Briar cleaned away a little of the condensation and peeked out, but she couldn't see farther than the south lawn with its ancient oak, and both were vague behind the falling curtains of gray. "What's it like ... the rest of Purpura?"

He drew a map on the glass with his finger, showing Purpura's borders, main roads, rivers, and mountains. "Here's Einor," he said. "That's Turlia. Farfaeron's to the east. South of it is the little kingdom of Marendel."

"What's this?" She indicated an unnamed area to the west.

"The ocean."

Briar gazed at the glass in wonder.

Next morning dawned bright and clear. Briar and Vance flew back to the pasture with the fervor of geese returning home after winter. They took up their sticks and the lessons continued. Vance still beat her. At first. But very quickly the outcome of their battles seesawed, first one, then the other triumphing. She had been raw, red-hot metal; now she was tempered steel. Or would be, soon. She could feel it.

The visit came to an end far too soon, with both families assembled in front of the manse.

"Are you free next Sunday?" the baron asked the earl.

The earl cupped his ear. "Am I Phoenix Sunday? What the devil does he mean? He knows damn well that's not my name."

"Are you free? Free, papa!" Patrikka shouted in his ear. "They want us next Sunday."

"You don't have to shout. I heard him quite well. We'll see; we'll see."

The guests trundled into the carriage. Vance's feet seemed heavy and echoed the weight on Briar's heart. He was the last to go in. As the carriage rolled away, kicking up dust, his face was pressed to the window.

Later, Briar peppered the baron as to whether he'd heard from them.

"You'll be the first to know," he replied. "And stop that infernal pacing. You're like a wild animal—you'll wear out the carpet."

Fortunately, the D'Artés returned on Sunday and often afterward. Every day they were there, Briar was the first to stir. She was up rapping on the door of Dolly, her chambermaid, who came out bleary-eyed and hauled a heavy gown over Briar's head. Fully dressed, Briar was waiting in the breakfast room when everyone arrived. As soon as the meal was over, she and Vance changed and were off to the pasture where the cracking of their sticks filled the air.

In the beginning of each visit, he sent her sword flying.

"What's that?" she asked, the first time it happened. "You're holding out on me. I never saw that before."

"If I stop getting better you'll best me." He laughed. "Then you'll lose interest and won't want to see me."

"Never! Show me that move."

Then they were back at it until neither of them could say who was better.

More than sword fighting occupied them. She showed him another fox and weasel she'd rescued and hidden in the woods, out of sight of the baron. Briar showed how she fed them from her hand. He swore he never saw anyone do that, and though he tried, neither animal would allow him near.

She took him to Racca's. Instead of the hard black bread, Racca served warm biscuits; instead of peasant cheese, she served warm cream and strawberries. How those ingredients suddenly appeared, Racca wouldn't say, and Briar grew a little jealous over the old woman fawning over him. But Briar never stopped taking Vance there. Racca told him the tales about the forest spirits and face changers and the single tear that had fallen from the sky. The Tear of Tybaleth.

Vance was entranced and insisted Briar show him Abunary Pond and the mysterious woods that surrounded it.

"Racca's right," Vance said when he looked upon the trees and the water. "There's magic here. That eldara's a king, that one a queen."

"If they're magic why don't they move?" Briar asked.

"They move at night and then go back to where they were in the morning."

"We should find the Tear," Briar said, and then they were off on a new adventure, though of course, they didn't find it.

On the way home, Briar asked, "Have you ever seen the ocean?"

"Of course. Haven't you?"

She kicked up a cloud of dust. Never having been out of range of the manse or Einor, her face flamed with embarrassment.

Perhaps sensing her discomfort, he said, "I'll take you there. My father has a ship, The Golden Gull, moored at Misty Cove. The beach is as enchanted as Abunary Pond, with gold and emerald sands that sparkle in the moonlight."

"We'll play pirates right on your boat."

"We would have it all to ourselves. Few people know the way to the beach is through a cave hidden at the top of the cliffs."

Briar could almost hear the gulls and smell the sea, or at least how she imagined it. Soon after, she thought the time was right to offer her father some advice.

"We won't be needing Budge," she said, glancing meaningfully at his account book. "And I'll need a larger room— the one with the veranda and climbing vine—so I can keep my dresses in a wardrobe. Or moths will eat them."

Stroking his chin, he eyed her gown, a rich burgundy that set off her raven tresses. The next day, a sobbing Budge was sent packing.

"Cruel girl, wicked girl," she wailed. "After all I've done for you. Mark my words, you'll get yours tenfold and bring ruin on them all."

Without Budge hovering over her every move, Briar could suddenly breathe, and she didn't give the woman another thought. There were more important things to focus on. Like the butterflies fluttering in her heart when Vance was around. At dinner parties, she stole glances at him, burning to the roots of her hair when he caught her looking at him. Her breath quickened when his hand accidentally brushed hers. At night, she pressed the spot to her lips.

They took long walks as silent and profound as the night sky, but when he spoke she hung on every word.

He wrote long letters. She read and reread them, and kept them in a secret place in her room. Not having his way with words, she sought Dolly's advice.

"What do you write to a spark?" she asked.

"Does the girl love him or not?" Dolly asked archly.

"Never you mind, just tell me."

Dolly's suggestions must not have helped. Dozens of Briar's attempts were crumpled up and sent flying across the room.

On arriving at the manse, Vance rushed to her and took her hand. Then he dazzled her with tales of kings and queens and court life and a thousand other visions of the world beyond, for besides her own explorations into the hills, she had never ventured beyond the borders of the baron's lands.

Years passed, but one thing remained fixed: there was

sunshine when Vance entered a room, sunshine in his step, sunshine in his smile, and even the dim halls of the manse brightened when he passed through them.

Then, in almost the same spot where Briar had first seen it, the queen's carriage came flashing down the road, and a shadow fell.

CHAPTER FOUR

*S*ummer wasn't summer. The season should have been well on, but the days were overcast and chilly, as though winter were clinging to spring. That didn't stop Briar, now in her sixteenth year. She rode on Dondle, the baron's prize stallion. Point of fact, she was the only one he would carry, and he was universally acknowledged as her horse. She let him now extend his legs, gathering ground beneath his feet, and they flew through the pines. As they neared the road back to the manse he slowed to a walk. No one looking would have seen Briar signal the change of speed with her reins, nor would they have seen even a minute pressure from her knees or a whisper in Dondle's ear. The connection between rider and horse was so complete that the stallion understood what Briar wanted and answered accordingly.

He padded soundlessly on the forest loam. In the distance came a thunder of hoofs.

Vance! It must be! He'd been away longer than usual and was overdue for a visit.

Dondle responded. With a leap he was racing through the

pines toward the road. Caught in the wind, Briar's mane flew behind like the sable wings of a bird. As she broke through the trees, she found she was too late. The carriage was bouncing away in a cloud of dust toward the manse. But even from the back she knew the owner, and her heart sank. There couldn't be two such rigs of polished rosewood and glittering gems. It wasn't the D'Artés. It was the queen.

A cold finger traced down Briar's spine. Dondle looked backed questioningly, as if uncertain of this new emotion and what was expected of him.

Briar patted his neck reassuringly, but she was looking down the road with hard determination. A moment later, Dondle shook his mane and sent out a battle cry, and they were streaking again through the trees.

***

Briar secreted behind a large rhododendron. From this vantage point, she remained unseen to anyone passing by, and she could peek past the curtains of one of the drawing room windows. Riding home, she'd debated what to do. Her father might want to show her off to the queen, as he had done many years before. But he wouldn't expect Briar back. They'd come to an unspoken agreement. She roamed as she pleased but played the part of a lady when expected. She seized this chance to learn why the queen was here.

The queen entered. The baron followed obsequiously. She appeared much as she had before, the same powerful shoulders and hips, the same thick eyebrows and arctic eyes. The only discernible difference was that now she had a wide gray stripe running through her hair. She still wore a tunic and loose breeches. Briar chafed at the irony—she'd been punished and forced into heavy gowns, while the queen wore what she liked. This preference for clothes was the only thing they had in common. As for the rest, Briar was filled with the same disquiet and loathing she'd felt the first time she'd seen the queen.

Purpura's ruler stood by the hearth, blowing into her hands and rubbing them. "I find your mountain air too crisp for my taste, Baron."

"Perhaps some tea will warm you." The baron gave a majestic wave toward a lavish service.

A servant poured. When he'd departed, the queen stood by the fire and sipped. A hush fell over the room, but for the stark and occasional clink of silverware and teacups. The baron's waxed moustache twitched as he watched her.

She set down her cup. "This tea is already cold."

The baron bolted to his feet. "I'll have a fresh pot brought in."

She pointed to the hearth. "And see to that." A few reluctant flames peeked from beneath the log.

The baron apologized and called a servant in, who quickly refreshed the pot and then worked at the fire. Try as he might, the fire just sputtered and the flames rose up half-heartedly.

The queen drank for a minute from a steaming teacup cradled in her hands. She took one more sip and put it down, a look of disgust on her face. "No, I don't think I like your climate at all. It should be illegal." She gave him a wry smile. "Maybe I will make it illegal."

He echoed her smile. "Maybe you should."

She flung herself into a chair and, leaning back carelessly, thrust her legs out. "To the point: there's been a change in plans."

"A change?" The baron sat slowly, as if what he was about to hear could be delayed by the arrival of his bottom to the seat. His marionette smile was painted broadly on his face.

"Someone new. For your little peach."

The baron swallowed. "That may be difficult. She's grown quite attached to the young viscount."

"That's not my problem. Make it happen, Baron."

"Might I ask why?"

She laughed. "It's always about money."

The baron had paled. Now a bit of color returned to his face. "Who do you have in mind?"

"The young duke, Rupert Glodwell." Amusement quirked the corners of her mouth, and she watched his reaction. A strange current of emotions crossed his face, as if she'd jested or his ears had malfunctioned. Speechless, he worked his lips and licked them.

"Oh, I understand, Baron," she said. "Fear not for your daughter's happiness. With a paramour on the side and wealth to spend like water, there will be plenty to keep her amused."

With this callous view on love, the queen turned the conversation to other things. Briar only half heard. Mist, red and hot, fell over her eyes. Who was this woman who came and tossed Briar this way and that like a toy? What gave her the right? The baron was but a puppet. The queen pulled the strings and would laugh and laugh as she forced Briar to dance to her will.

Withdrawing from the window, fist clenched, Briar was filled with steely resolve. Her father had little means to control her now, and wouldn't. Under the law, she could marry whom she pleased or not at all. She fathomed little of the politics at play or why she was a pawn in them. All she knew was that she wouldn't be whipsawed like this. She would fight, tooth and nail.

The only question was Vance.

Why had his visits dwindled? Was he under the same pressure to marry someone else to suit the queen's purposes?

But one fundamental question superseded all of her

doubts and uncertainties: why had he not spoken the words a girl wants to hear from a spark?

A week later, the baron called Briar into his study.

He nodded toward a chair and smiled. "Sit, I'm almost done with this." He scratched at a letter. But his moustache twitched, and Briar knew he was pretending nonchalance.

She perched on the edge of the seat, a slow pressure welling in her throat.

"Another cloudy day?" he asked, still looking at his parchment. "I haven't stuck my head out all day."

"Gray as old soup." *Why doesn't he get to it?*

At last, he sprinkled blotting powder and blew it off. Again the moustache twitched. Again the smile. "I'll need you in three days."

This was code—don't go gallivanting in the hills; be dressed to entertain. Her heart began to pound. She knew this was coming. Not for one moment had she stopped thinking about the queen or the baron's reaction to Duke Whatever-his-name-was. Though she hoped it was Vance, her father's manner suggested otherwise.

"Who's coming?" she asked.

"Oh, one of the nobles," he replied airily.

That sealed it. It was the duke. She could have defied the baron then and there. She could have defied him when the day arrived and the duke's carriage rolled up. It would have been easy to take off on Dondle and avoid the whole thing— a confrontation with her father was nothing new. Curiosity kept her rooted to the front steps of the manse. What sort of person could make the baron friendly, almost apologetic, toward her? And when the queen spoke of the duke, her father had blanched and stared in disbelief.

The carriage revealed nothing about the character of the man who'd been chosen to make her life miserable. To be sure, it was almost as ostentatious as the queen's conveyance.

But that told Briar little. A dozen nobles sported fancy carriages.

A footman stepped down from the driver's seat, opened the carriage door, and announced, "The Dowager Duchess."

A woman descended, her gown hanging from her considerable frame like a circus tent. Dark ringlets framing her face were obviously dyed. Before gray set in, she had probably been blond. Her jovial appearance ended with her eyes, as sharp and piercing as a falcon.

"Lord Rupert Alamond Glodwell, Ninth Duke of Wakeley Court," the footman announced.

A pair of small pumps—too tight for the feet wearing them—stretched out and rotated, as if restoring circulation. A small hand emerged from the shadow of the coach's interior and closed over the edge of the doorframe for support. Three fingers of that hand were adorned with ruby rings the size of grapes, flashing in the sunlight. The hand itself was plump and framed at the wrist in white ruffles. With the assistance of the footman, the rest of the man, a youth of eighteen or nineteen, emerged. He stood blinking in the sunlight, looking dazedly about him.

He wore pantaloons, made all the more ridiculous owing to plump thighs. The waistline came almost mid-belly, which protruded like a large round kettle. His hair was a curly dull brown piled at the top of his head, except for two enormous side locks combed forward into upward curving hooks.

As the comical apparition advanced, Briar couldn't restrain herself. She laughed. At which the duke smiled, stumbled, and then, reaching out toward her with both arms, ran up to her.

"Jolly, Miss Briar, good to meet you," he said. "I mean, jolly good. Was there a joke? I hate to miss a joke."

His eyes were as wide and innocent as a calf's. Briar could do nothing but press his hands between hers and pat them.

"Only one my father just played on me," she replied.

"A prank!" He turned to the baron. "You'll have to play it on me. Oh, do, please! Everyone loves to, and I never mind."

The baron bowed. "I'll leave that to Miss Briar."

Briar took the duke's arm and led him into the manse. "There'll be plenty of opportunities," she said. "Let's get you settled."

When the duke had rested and dined, Briar escorted him on the same tour Vance had taken of the estate many years ago. When they got to the overlook of the servants' quarters, renovated and now kept in good repair, Briar asked, "What do you think of these huts."

Befuddlement clouded the duke's face. "By Jyd, I think they're just sporting."

"What is your policy for your own huts?"

He scratched his head. "I couldn't say. Others see to that."

"Do your servants appear content? Are they happy? Do they stay dry in winter? Do they have enough meat and vegetables for stew?"

A little fright came into those wide eyes as he turned them on her. "I shall look into it the moment I return."

He took up a brisk pace as they continued the tour and appeared relieved when they reached the manse.

The next morning at breakfast, Briar asked him, "Do you fence?"

His mother swooped in before he could answer. "Rupie displayed natural flair for the blade early on, a talent we assiduously cultivated."

"I should like to see that," Briar replied.

"Unfortunately, he has a strained shoulder." To the duke she said, "Are you applying that liniment, dear?"

He rose. "Nonsense, Mother. I shall display my skill now." He swung his arm in sweeping loops and jabbed the air. His momentum took him almost fully around. When he'd stopped, he wobbled dizzily. Seizing the table to steady himself, he spilled his plum wine.

His mother applauded, the pendulous dough beneath her arms swinging. "Well done, Rupie. You shall acquit yourself well if we're overrun with Turlians." She turned to Briar. "He has a mighty arm."

The conversation turned, and Briar was disappointed to not hear more about Turlia. While she was never allowed to visit the surrounding estates, many visitors had come over the years. Of late, the Turlian Claim was a subject of heated debate. She had learned much from Vance about the history and politics of Purpura. Turlia, just over the mountain from the baron's estate, contested the border. It was an old dispute going back centuries, and wars on both sides had made and remade the map until no one knew who owned what. Nonetheless, the queen's father, King Brodellorn, had returned a stretch of land in good faith and in exchange for peace. Many Turlians believed he didn't go far enough, that in fact, lands north of Einor—including those comprising the baron's estate—belonged to them. Hence, the Turlian Claim. On Brodellorn's death, the new queen fanned the flames of war, claiming that vast and rich expanses of Turlia belonged to her.

Sitting squarely amidst all of this, Briar was hungry for news of the outside world. And the queen's last words to the baron haunted Briar, for they sank in after that blur of anger had faded, and she reckoned big in them.

"We need this union, baron," the queen had said, and leaned forward. "My troops are occupied in so many places. I would hate to see your house go unprotected."

The baron's face had drained to the pallor of a corpse.

With all this in mind, Briar now asked the duchess, "Do you think it'll come to war?"

"I hope so. The sooner we're rid of Turlian riffraff, the better," the duchess replied.

"Doesn't it frighten you?"

"A couple thousand of Purpura's finest, marching under colorful banners, should squash 'em like bugs." The duchess reached for a bowl of whipped cream.

"Won't some die?" Briar said, as if she knew nothing about such things.

"Oh, not the important ones. There's talk of conscription."

"Conscription? For everyone?" Briar murmured. Vance leaped into her mind, and a heavy weight settled on her heart.

The duchess smothered a piece of toast with whipped cream and strawberries macerated in brandy, and then stuffed the whole thing into her mouth. "I believe so. Of course, the foot soldiers do it all. Nothing for our men to worry about." *Our* apparently meaning the nobles.

"Swords and lances pierce everyone, don't they?" Briar retained a mild voice, but it was all she could do to keep from seizing the fire poker and sending up a torrent of sparks.

"Our men will be officers," the baron observed. "Giving orders and all that."

The duke speared a sausage. "By Jyd, if I go to war, I'll have a big tent on the top of a hill and watch the battle from the best seat in the house. And have coffee and a big plate of this delightful sausage."

"Yes," Briar replied. "That's just where you should be."

Four days later, the visit was over—and not soon enough for Briar. She stood on the front steps with the baron, watching the carriage trundle away.

"Well, what do you think of the duke?" he asked.

"You must be joking, Father."

The baron pointed to the departing carriage. "Don't be hasty. He has many more of those, much finer."

"I don't want a carriage."

The baron gave her a sidelong glance. "He could buy you a hundred horses."

"Dondle's the best horse in Purpura. You said so yourself."

"Well, think on it."

"You must really despise me." Briar fixed her gaze on him before turning away, but he avoided her eyes.

Long and empty days followed. Briar wandered, never far from home or where she could not see the road, lest Vance came galloping along and she missed a single moment with him. He didn't come. Dondle hung his head, as though he missed their rides, or perhaps the great stallion sensed her dejection and was saddened. At night, she sat wrapped in a blanket before the highest window overlooking the road to the manse. For hours she stared at the night, as if sheer will could bring Vance back to her. When at last she returned to her room, she read and reread his letters by candlelight, feeling certain she would discover something she hadn't seen before—some hidden expression of his intentions. But there was no point in reading them—every word was memorized, and she found nothing new. Then she took up pen and poured her heart out. Her attempts ended crumpled and piled in the corner.

What if something had happened to him? What if conscription was more than a rumor and he'd been shipped off to war? Or brigands had fallen on him and left him lying in a ditch or a shallow grave?

Nearly mad with worry, she sought out Racca. The old woman was stirring her pot, the aroma of warm milk filling the air.

Briar dropped onto a stool and sank her chin between her fists. "What do you see in your pot, Racca?"

The old woman snorted. "I'm blind. What could I see?"

"Some word of Vance. Why hasn't he come?" *Will he declare his love? Will he ask for my hand?*

For a long time Racca stood, and there was nothing but the sound of her big stick scraping the bottom of the kettle. She gazed unseeing into the swirling steam.

At last, she stopped stirring, lifted her stick, and brought it down hard. The pot clanged like a bell. "You're caught in the middle of it like a fly in sap. Where can you go? Where can you run?"

"I could fly away on Dondle."

"The baron would haul you back, a horse thief. And don't think about going on foot. This place is too far, too isolated from another manor. Besides, 'tis the queen's land—every door would be closed to you. No one wants to swing from her gallows."

Briar raised a fist. "Then I'll climb over the mountain and join the Turlians in their fight against her."

"Ha! They've no love for Purpurans over there." Racca began stirring again, looking into the pot with her blue-blind eyes. "Only one thing to do—stay in it. Big changes. Big changes coming. Stay in it, little fly."

"And Vance?"

But the old woman removed her stick, laid it across the top of the pot, and sank into her chair. Soon she was snoring.

CHAPTER FIVE

*W*hen summer was finally summer, it came suddenly. Early-dawn warmth penetrated Briar's dream, rousing her. She rose quickly and threw open the balcony doors. With two quick steps she was outside and leaning over the vine-covered balustrade, inhaling the sweetness of the morning air. The sky was an endless blue, untouched by a single cloud. Birds were caroling in the trees. The shadows were cool and inviting.

The duke and his mother were back for a visit. That didn't stop Briar. She was out on Dondle before anyone stirred and spent the day sunning and swimming at Abunary Pond—her father's anger be damned.

That night, she was beginning to drift off to sleep when rustling came from her open balcony doors. Alert, on her feet in a moment, she reached for a vase she could use as a weapon. Wind stirred the curtains. Moonlight streamed in—dreamy, mysterious, brimming with passion. And a silhouetted figure slid into view and peered in. The next instant, just above a chorus of cicadas, someone softly calling her name stepped inside.

"Vance!" She rushed across the room and threw herself into his arms.

"Shh, you'll rouse everyone," he murmured against her cheek.

"I don't care. Where have you been? I've been worried."

"Don't be mad. I'll explain it all, I promise."

"Hush, you're here now." She led him to a loveseat and lit a candle. Then she was back in his arms. "Hold me. Don't let me go."

"Never ... never ..."

They rocked, he breathing her hair, she clasping him, melting into him. Thus they remained until the candle burned low. Then he was at the window again and promised to return in a few days.

That was enough for her. The whole time he hadn't offered an explanation. Now, she didn't need one. She floated. The queen's plots, the duke's silly comedies were all far below her, and she paid them little mind.

Two days later, Vance was back and nothing else mattered. They wandered in the meadows, holding hands, and she marveled, for it seemed she'd never felt hands before or noticed that his were both strong and soft. They sat in the shade and—cutting apricots, peaches, and plums lying ripe at their feet—slipped sweet slices past each other's lips. His head nestled in her lap, he read to her from a pocket volume of poems. The words shone a light where all had been dark, stirring her with passion and ideas she didn't know existed. Her mind soaked it all in like a thirsty nomad. But he could have been talking about selecting a vest or a new cane—it gave her a chance to linger on the man he'd become. He'd grown to the noble height of his father. His limbs were lithe, his fingers supple, and the muscles in his arms rippled with vitality. He had the same waves of silken hair, the same thoughtful brow of his youth, the delicate lips, the bold nose.

His eyes could be faraway and dreamy, yet at times they were piercing and roused with fire. But when they fell upon Briar they grew as gentle as a lamb's.

She walked in a glow of happiness, yet sometimes when she was dropping off to sleep, it occurred to her that trouble touched his brow. By morning, all her concerns were fled and forgotten, for she couldn't walk beside him without feeling peace and contentment.

The duke watched them like a woebegone puppy. After dinner one evening, Briar drew Vance onto the veranda, anxious for time alone with him. Beneath a bower of honeysuckle, she took his hands in hers and looked up into his eyes. He gazed back transfixed, his eyes sparkling like stars, and leaned slowly toward her lips. At that moment, the duke came bustling outside and trotted up to them.

"I say, Vance," he said, "do you have pointers? I've got a dandy bunch of 'em. Make the best birders."

With a sigh, Vance released her and turned to the duke. The ensuing conversation was as consequential as dust in the attic.

Whatever Vance did, the duke imitated. Vance poured her punch and the duke arrived with a second glass moments later. The number of times she had two slices of cake before her were too numerous to count. Once, stealing away with Vance for a walk in the garden, the duke hurried up to them.

"Capital idea. Lovely time for a stroll." He inserted himself between them.

Whenever Vance rode up for a visit on his bay stallion, the duke and his mother arrived soon afterward. Briar could never figure out how they managed it. What she did know was that the duke was a nuisance, his mother an annoyance, and Briar could tolerate both if Vance just proposed.

She couldn't help but tease him. "Better be careful, or the duke will sweep me off my feet."

Vance glanced at his competition—the luckless gentleman had managed to spatter his blouse with red wine—and then looked away, troubled.

The warm days begged for a picnic. Soon the families were out on blankets and clustered beneath giant yellow umbrellas. After food and wine, conversation broke into small knots. Briar and Vance retreated to where the others were but a murmur.

"Read to me," she said, and prepared to park her head on his lap, where she could listen to verses and find castles in the clouds.

"Not just yet," he replied. "There's so much I want to tell you."

Her heart beat wildly. "Tell me quick!"

He traced a finger down her cheek and was about to speak when the duchess called, "Vance, dear, I need you." And Vance was recruited to adjust the shade of her umbrella.

In frustration, Briar expelled a breath that sent a lock of her hair flying.

The baron added his own form of interference, calling on her to join them in cards or croquet when Briar and Vance were close. In private moments, he scolded, "You're neglecting our other guests." Publicly he simply glared.

Summer waned, and so did Vance's visits. A vague disquiet began settling over Briar. He gave no explanations; she didn't ask for any. She was jealous of anyone who distracted him from her or took him away, even for a minute. Greediness overtook her to spend every moment wrapped in his smile, his laugh, his eyes—for every moment to be filled with light and love, as if they would never have another. Why would she dim his visits with unpleasant questions?

When he came, they still took their walks in the country-side, read poetry, and swam in Abunary Pond—most often not alone but with the duke scrambling to keep up. Their long bouts of fencing had never stopped from when they were children. They seesawed back and forth as to who sent the other's sword flying. The duke was conspicuously absent from these exercises—claiming a flare up of his shoulder—which suited Briar fine.

Sometimes she prattled on and found Vance fixed on vacant space or staring off to the mountains. Once, when they were sunning after a long swim, he turned to her with darkened brow. "Briar, there are things I must tell you—"

"Yes!" She held her breath, her heart quickening.

Glancing at her, he appeared disturbed by her response, and turned away.

How hard could it be to tell a girl you loved her? But he was so disturbed she didn't have the heart to press him. Perhaps he felt as she did and didn't want to disrupt the bubble they were in. Her desire to stay in that bubble kept her from pursuing it further. She was relieved when the duke started floundering in the pond, and Vance leaped up with a curse and dove in to save the lad.

This wasn't the only time Vance started to speak of what preoccupied him. Something always interfered, and in truth, Briar didn't want to know. Not if it was bad.

Disquiet turned to foreboding, and it seemed that something precious, something she would never find again, was slowly slipping through her fingers.

A long gap followed in which Vance didn't come at all. She prowled the house like a trapped and half-starved beast. She snapped at everyone, the duke and his mother—who had practically moved in—appeared frightened of her, and the baron withdrew into his study for long spells. Pacing in front of the manse, Briar could see volumes of pipe smoke belching from his window.

At last, Vance came. Even the duke and his mother appeared relieved. Briar was at the bursting point. Almost from the moment Vance alighted from the carriage, she grabbed his arm and tugged him along with her.

"We're fencing," she said.

At the scene of their childhood battles, he barely had time to draw his sword.

She thrust. "Where have you been?"

He parried. "I promise, I'll tell you."

"Tell me now." Her blade came dangerously close to nicking his ear, and then she assailed him with a ferocious rain of cuts and slashes. He was too busy defending himself to reply.

For a moment, they were *body to body*, pressing close. She shoved him away. "Do you have something to say to me?"

"So much …"

"Then say it."

"Not here. Not like this."

She parried, blade up and to the outside. With a twist of her wrist, she sent his sword flying. She pointed her tip at his fallen weapon. "Get it."

He backed away. "Enough."

"Give me something new."

"I wish I could."

"There must be. Something from your fencing master."

He turned up his palms, imploring. "You've bested me. There's nothing more, I swear."

In disgust, she threw her sword like a knife. It sailed straight into the fence post, where it quivered.

By evening, Briar had simmered down. In fact, her mood completely reversed. He was here. He'd promised. Anticipation fluttered in her breast. At last, he would propose. They would be together, the shadow of war be damned. She could leave the baron, the cold walls of the manse, the sullen stares of the servants. The duke and duchess would depart from Briar's life forever, and she would no longer have to pretend with fake affectations and curtsies. Briar could be Briar. And the only person whose opinion she cared about wanted her no other way.

After dinner, Vance managed to draw her away from the party and onto the veranda. Conversation from the dining room faded. But for a lone bird, piping plaintively in the distance, the night was hushed.

He took a packet wrapped in decorative paper from his pocket. "A trifle, to recall our childhood romps."

"Could I ever forget them?" She pulled away the wrapping and found a crimson handkerchief embroidered with silvery eldara leaves.

"I know how much you love them," he said.

She tied it to the sash around her waist. "It will never leave me."

Taking both of her hands, Vance's gaze roamed over her face like he'd never seen it before. "You're so beautiful."

With the tip of her finger, she touched a small scratch her sword had left on his cheek. "Does it hurt?"

"Nothing from you hurts. Briar ..."

She looked up at him, her heart fluttering. "Yes?"

"There's so much I need to tell, must tell."

She waited in warm expectation.

He bit his lip, appeared to be searching for words. "These are difficult times—"

"We can weather anything together. We will."

"If that were all—"

"Your father! Is he ill?"

"No worse than ever. He asks after you."

"Tell him I won't stand for it. He must visit and help me fend off the duke."

Vance laughed. "Father loves you. Said not to let them push you around."

"I never will." Briar plumbed the depths of his eyes. "I know what I want."

The bird piped a note. Vance gazed off, listening, and the fire that often leaped into his eyes returned. "The world's in motion—shifting—churning with something new." He turned back to her. "You must know you're closest to my heart. But the queen—"

At that moment, a man emerged from the shadow of the trees and made a signal with his hand to Vance. The man was dressed in the simple garb of a peasant. His shaggy black hair and the coarse stubble on his cheeks would seem to reinforce that impression, but the long knife at his hip and a missing ear lent him a sinister aspect. A few of Vance's servants usually accompanied him on visits. If this man was one of them, Briar had never seen him. Disquiet closed over her throat.

"Who is he?" she asked.

But Vance quickly stepped from the veranda and spoke to the stranger out of earshot. Thirty seconds later, the man receded into the shadows. Vance came running back to her.

"I must leave."

"But you just got here."

"Can't be helped." He took up her hands, holding them so tight they hurt. "If I don't return, know that my heart is yours, wholly, completely. Never think it isn't."

"What are you saying?"

But he was already running to where the man had disappeared. A moment later they both emerged from the trees on horseback. With a crack from their whips, their steeds leaped and raced down the road.

Briar slumped against the railing.

The duchess came onto the terrace. "Briar, we need you inside—my dear, you're pale as a ghost!"

Briar was barely aware that anyone had spoken. Her ears were riveted to the fading drum of the horses, swallowed by darkness, until there was only the bird's lament.

CHAPTER SIX

The leaves burst with fiery crimson and gold, and then they browned and began dropping to the ground like unwanted children. One day, when the wind tossed and scattered them, a rider stormed down the road and up to the manse. From the purple and gray insignia on the back of his uniform—a winged helmet beneath two crossed battles axes—Briar knew he was the queen's messenger.

She didn't have long to confirm her suspicion that the message involved her. The baron called her into his study.

He nodded to a chair. "Sit."

She remained standing. "This will be a short conversation."

"You're going to be stubborn about it?"

"I am."

He stared at her, glowering. "You know what I expect."

"I do."

"Well, will you do it?"

"I've already told you. I won't."

The baron stood and at the same time, his fist crashed on

his desk, shaking his quills and fluttering papers. "Dammit, girl, you will!"

"You can't make me. Neither can the queen." She eyed a half-opened papyrus with the queen's seal visible on it. "What does she have on you?"

He sat heavily in his chair. "Stupid girl. She protects our border. Raise her ire and she'll leave us defenseless. Turlians will overrun the estate by spring—if the servants don't throw us out first. It's only fear of *her* that keeps them in line."

"What's that to me? Who are any of you to me? I would've been happier raised by wolves."

Staring at her coldly, he picked up a glass paperweight and tossed it from hand to hand. "Understand me, I can throw you away as easily as this." He turned and tossed the weight out an open window. The sound of it shattering came from below. "Do it, or I'll drive you out. You'll never come back. Food and shelter? Denied you. Clothing? You'll leave in rags."

Briar's blood turned to ice. "I understand you, Father."

As she strode to the door, he called after her, "I wouldn't go looking for your viscount. If he loved you, he'd have returned."

For once, she could almost agree with him, for almost two months had passed and Vance hadn't come back. It seemed he never would.

Briar tore off across the countryside on Dondle, her mind churning with doubt, apprehension, and a good dose of outrage. If she had never met Vance, it would be different. She would have given no thought to marriage. Though she was just shy of seventeen—almost past the marrying age— she could care less about the contempt and ridicule she would receive from the world if she lived forever a spinster.

But she had met Vance. If they married, they could start their life together, far from the baron, far from the pernicious influence of the queen. Up to now, love was only a promise, a seed. If they married, it would burst forth, full, deep, strong. Unassailable.

But Vance was missing, the queen overshadowed Briar's life, and the promise was disappearing like the leaves of the trees.

Briar rode Dondle until the stallion was foaming. When she returned that evening, she found the baron huddled with the duke and his mother. Briar gave them a perfunctory curtsy and went to bed early. She didn't sleep but stood at her balcony door, looking out on the night. Clouds moved in, bringing rain that pattered against the glass and trailed down in streams.

Next morning, as the servants cleared the last of breakfast, the duke stood with his hand over his heart. "Sir, may I have permission to speak with your daughter?"

The baron rose immediately. "By all means, my boy."

He and the duchess departed more quickly than the plates, and the door shut behind them. Briar looked to the window, but there was no escape. The storm had gone cold. Flurries of snow spun in pinwheels.

"Miss Briar," the duke began, his eyes as round as a calf's, "I would give up my best pointer, no!—all of my pointers and carriages, all of my, my—oh, I don't know what, but everything that means everything to me, if you will—"

Briar had been holding her breath, but now she exhaled. "Rupert, you're a kind boy, but—"

"Hear me out! I was saying … what was I saying?"

"Everything and everything."

"Yes, yes, I had it all memorized and now it's fled away. You do that to me, Briar. You take my breath away. You make me feel like a sick puppy. When I'm around you, I feel all gooey inside and my knees shake."

"With that terrible effect, it's a wonder you want me around at all."

"No! Listen! There are no other girls in Purpura. You're the jewel; they're the pebbles. Only you can make my heart sing. Only you can me happy!"

"Sweet little Rupert, you're the last person in the world I would want to hurt." She could feel him begin to shake. "I'm so sorry."

"Then ... then you're refusing me?"

"My heart belongs to another."

His faced turned to pale green chalk as he looked at her. He burst into tears and rushed from the room. Thirty minutes later, he and his mother bundled into their carriage, and Briar could hear him wailing all the way up the road, "She doesn't want me. How can I live?"

Briar stood beside the baron on the front steps of the manse. She was there for Rupert. She knew what it felt like to lose what you longed for. The baron was there because decorum demanded it. Now he turned to her.

"Wait in your room."

Briar considered her options. Her impulse was to defy him, to saddle Dondle and head into the hills. There had been a lull in the storm, but now the clouds were dark ominous mountains. The wind whipped her hair, and a few flakes began to fall. One slip on the slopes now would spell disaster for the stallion. But if she must go, she would go on her own terms. She strode into the foyer with the intention of taking the sword and dagger that hung there. The black-smith—bull-necked and barrel-chested—stood before the sword. The dagger was missing.

"Step aside," she said.

He folded his massive arms. "Sorry, Miss. The Baron's orders." He bared his teeth with a malicious curl of his lips.

Briar eyed the empty spot above him. "Where's the dagger?"

He shrugged.

With nothing more to be gained here, she headed for the kitchen to pack provisions. At the inner door, she found the head cook and scullery maid barring the way, the first bearing a rolling pin, the second a cleaver.

Briar's mind spun. Even with all the bad blood between them, she could hardly believe that her father would deny her food and weapons.

"Give me something," she said to the cook. "He'll never know."

"He'll know. And it'll be us where you're going."

"Where's that?"

The cook's smile—so much like the blacksmith's—made Briar's blood run cold.

"You'll know soon enough." The cook pointed upward to Briar's room. "Better get. That's his orders."

Briar reeled back the way she'd come and headed upstairs, her mind flooded with questions. Why to her room? What could he possibly do to her there? More importantly, what was his next move? And what was hers? Even if she had weapons, what then? Was she to hurt people she had grown up with, despite their animosity?

In her room, she went to her wardrobe and took out a heavy cloak, riding boots, leggings, and several pairs of pants and shirts. She had no idea where she would go, but at least she could be warm.

She folded the clothes and began arranging them in a bundle when someone tapped on her door. Outside, she found her chambermaid holding homespun breeches and tunic, the rough clothing the peasants wore, but older—little more than rags.

"He says you're to take off that gown and put on these. I'm sorry, miss."

"It's okay, Dolly."

"Do you want my help?"

"No. Just tell me what he's doing."

"He's givin' orders to everyone. I don't know what."

"That's okay. You can go."

"No, miss, I'm to bring you down when you're done. He'll take the skin off my back if I don't."

"Wait here, then."

Trembling, Dolly nodded. When the door was closed Briar took off the gown and laid it on the bed. She changed into the breeches and tunic, and pulled on her boots. A sudden thought sent her out onto her veranda. Why wait to see what the baron planned? She could slip out this way. But the tanner's son—a lad her age—paced below.

She called down to him. "We played pirates, Jak. Fought with sticks."

"You ruined one too many of my traps. Don't deny it! I know it was you, spyin' when I made 'em, watchin' when I set 'em. Besides …" He plucked a shiny two-pennig coin from his pocket and polished it against his jerkin. With a pat, he returned it for safekeeping. His father stalked up the path toward him, brandishing a quarterstaff.

Back inside, a trapped cougar paced the floor, glancing at the wardrobe—the hearth—the ceiling—the walls—seeking an escape route. But the furniture was silent, and the walls seemed to close in.

Heart pounding, Briar paused to breathe, determined to think this through. The baron had anticipated her every move—blocked all the exits.

But perhaps it wouldn't be so bad. This was just a demonstration of power; that he could keep her in her room as readily as the bars over her childhood window had. The clothes were an added humiliation, an attempt to force her to marry the duke. For all she cared, he could sentence her to a diet of bread and water. She would never yield.

The only thing to do was see how this would play out. From beneath her pillow, she took out the handkerchief with the silver eldara leaves Vance had given her, folded it carefully, and placed it in a pocket. After braiding her hair in a long rope that hung down her back, she took one last look at her room. There was nothing of any meaning here except Vance's letters. She slipped one beside the handkerchief—there were too many to carry—knowing that it would hurt to look at either of them. For a moment she thought of burning the rest in the corner hearth so her father wouldn't read them. But they were far too precious to destroy, and her father couldn't care less about them.

Resolved to see this through no matter what he planned, she tied her bundle, slung it over her shoulder, and opened the door. She found Dolly wiping away tears.

"It's cruel and unfair," cried the maid.

"Hush, don't let the baron hear you."

"Oh Miss! You can't take that." Fresh tracks poured down Dolly's cheeks, and she pointed to the bundle.

A chill wind stirred the curtains at the veranda. Briar pulled the extra clothes from her shoulder and stared down at them before tossing them back into the room, foreboding growing in the pit of her stomach.

Dolly escorted her downstairs and into the foyer. Briar gazed longingly at the sword, but its stalwart guard was patrolling below it.

They continued out through the front doors, down the steps, and on to the south lawn before the house. Snow was streaking down in earnest now. Servants were assembled in a semicircle, huddling close for warmth—but each held something—a pitchfork, a rake, a shovel, a broom, a fire poker. At the center of the radius stood the baron. Dolly led Briar to him and then melted back with the others.

The baron stared at her boots. "Those belong to me. Remove them."

Briar took a step back, but Jak, his father, the scullery maid, and the cook joined the semicircle, and several of the men raised their makeshift weapons. Briar would gain nothing by going for the sword. The blacksmith was conspicuously missing.

She tugged off her boots and flung them aside.

The baron scanned the assembled domestics and pointed to a washerwoman about Briar's size. "You, give her your sandals. You can take her boots."

The woman rushed forward like a harpy. After snatching up the boots, she retreated to the others, leaving well-worn sandals behind.

The baron's voice rang out. "Hear me! Henceforth, this" —he waved a hand toward Briar— "doesn't exist. If she returns, give no blanket, no porridge, no shelter. Drive her out. Anyone who helps her will dangle from that tree." He pointed to the great oak with its broad and sweeping arms. A soft murmur rippled through the crowd. Although Dolly wept silently, there were more than a few faces, who for years had scowled at Briar, that appeared pleased. Several were jostled aside, and Racca pushed past them and crossed the open space, the foyer dagger clutched in one gnarled hand. Snow fell in sheets and it seemed she walked in a cloud.

She didn't stop until she stood before the baron, proffering the knife. "Take it. You might as well kill her now as drive her out there." She tried to press the knife into his hands. "Do it, sink it through her heart."

He pushed it back. "Careful, old woman. I'm not above sending you with her."

Racca tossed her head up and laughed like a crow into the wind. "Coward. Give it to her. She'll die anyway."

The baron glowered but didn't stop Racca from handing the knife to Briar.

He waved his hand at the crowd. Brandishing their weapons, they took hesitant steps toward Briar to drive her out.

Snatching up the sandals, she turned to the baron. "You won't need them."

He held up his hand, pausing them like a frozen wave.

The wind shrilled. Briar leaned against it. As she trod up the road and then into the fields, a shroud of snow closed around her.

CHAPTER SEVEN

*B*riar plodded up a low hill. It was not much after noon, but the sky was as dim as dusk, and darkening. A terrible heaviness settled on her heart. As resigned as she'd been a short time before, as ready to turn her back on them all, she already missed her room, the idle conversation and laughter of the servants when they didn't know she was around, Dondle's excited whinny when she entered the barn. Even the sad and lonely visits with her mother were a loss, for the times her mother awakened from her daze were blessed gifts from the gods. Briar didn't even get a chance to say goodbye—curse the baron for all eternity—though perhaps it would have hurt more if her mother knew what was about to happen.

As Briar labored through the drifts piling around her, a stab of pain joined the heaviness; the places where she and Vance had walked were hard and frozen beneath her sandals, never again to be shared with him.

What would he say, what would he do if he returned, looking for her? At the thought, Briar was filled with a well of despair. She had no future but to leave footprints in the snow, and even those were fleeting. When she turned back, hoping for a last glimpse of the place she'd called home, her tracks were fading beneath the wind-driven flakes, and the manse had disappeared behind billowing sheets of white.

She strove toward the woods where she'd explored and played as a child, aware that she could easily be walking in circles. She could only hope that some inner sense guided her. If she could reach the trees she could use the knife Racca had given her and cut limbs to build a shelter; the trees themselves would provide protection, if only a little.

How long she battled on was hard to say. Cold bit her fingers and toes, and she knew she couldn't last much longer. She should have reached the woods by now. The slopes she traversed were unrecognizable to her, as though she'd entered an alien world bereft of all life except the tiny speck that struggled through it and the taunting cries of the wind.

She had to build a shelter of some kind. That, she knew. The where and the how eluded her in the bleakness of it all. But when she came to a long mound, too straight for a natural rise in the hillside, she stopped and began to dig with the knife, clearing snow, piling it on top of the horizontal ridge. The blade struck wood, confirming her suspicion she was tunneling by a fallen tree.

She worked quickly, but her fingers swiftly turned red and numb. Her feet fared no better. She sat a moment and began cutting lengths of cloth from the bottom of her tunic. The strips were then wrapped and tied around the sandals. More of it surrounded her hands in makeshift gloves. Then she set to work again and presently was able to burrow into the foxhole she'd made, where she shivered and hugged and rubbed herself for warmth, longing for a fire.

All that was left to her was to wait out the storm, to hope this was a sudden squall that would depart just as quickly. Her thoughts fled to Vance. Why had his visits fallen off?

What had taken him away so precipitously? He was not one to shirk responsibility. If he had been drafted into the queen's army, he would go. What seemed more likely is that the queen was putting some kind of pressure on him or his family. Her father's words haunted her: "I wouldn't wait for your viscount. If he loved you, he'd have returned." But he did love her. Of that she was certain. Who but her father and the queen could have kept him away? The other possibility was that he had, indeed, gone off to war. The queen had fronts other than Turlia she was embroiled in. Perhaps Vance had been shipped off to a distant land, far from Briar. Perhaps he was already lying on a field of slaughter, his eyes empty and lifeless.

The wind sharpened and rose in a torrent of angry wails. A second cry swelled with it, tortured, and Briar realized she was screaming into the teeth of the gale. All that had gone wrong pointed to one person. In that moment, she clenched her fist, vowing to bring vengeance on the queen, and the wrath coursing through her veins proved an antidote to the frozen walls of her new home.

Even that abated. Soon she was rubbing her hands and feet again. The sun must have sunk below the hills. Night drew an unwelcome cloak about her. Her eyes grew heavy. She knew instinctively that if she closed them she would fall into a slumber from which she would never return. Though her body protested, she wormed from her shelter and struck out again for one reason: it allowed her to keep moving, and movement meant warmth of some kind, though logic told her she was safer staying put. She struggled on then, wind and snow lashing her, and the grim reality of her plight drove home. She'd been born in a storm; she would die in a storm. But if that were her fate, she would die fighting. Now her laughter rose above the wind and mocked it.

She thought of the queen. There was no possibility of fire,

but wrath, wrath was a handy fuel; it lent her determination to survive so that she could throw the full force of that fury on the queen. The thought made her savage, and all of Budge's refinements dropped away like the dead and useless petals of a rose.

She battled into the stinging white, each step defying the baron and the queen. But even if she survived a while longer, what then? She had no coat, no boots, no real shelter, and this was the beginning of winter. Where could she go? How would she live? Racca's words returned: "No place to run. Not Turlia, not to another estate." The only option was forward into the storm, to the meadows and woods that long had been her true home. If not for Vance, she might have fled there long ago. On she forged, though she'd lost all sense of direction, with no idea where she was or where she was going.

Time was a vague companion. Heaviness returned to her eyes, and she no longer felt her hands or feet. Soon, though she must be moving, she lost all sensation of her legs, her arms. She was no more solid and real than the swirls of snow that came and went, and the world shrank. There was no ground, no sky, no left, no right. And the one who could tell was swiftly disappearing.

The only thing left was a face, sneering at her through the sheets of the blizzard. That face kept her going. She must reach it, take it into her hands and crush it. But even that began to fade. She staggered, fell, struggled up, took three more steps, and pitched face first into a drift.

She managed to roll over and made a last effort to rise, only to sag back down. She stared up at the falling flakes. Wind picked them up, tossed them like tiny fireflies, and then let them sift down to her face. Sleep tugged at her eyelids, yet some sense told her to look up—up through the snow awhile longer. Though the wind howled, though the snow spun and whipped about her, directly above was calm, and the flakes drifted down. Or maybe those were stars, way up there where all was black and sparkling. Far away and above, someone seemed to be crying. One of those tiny diamonds dilated, bright as the moon, though not so large. Not at first. But it seemed to draw near, and the sobbing swelled. The storm shrank back as if from shame, and now there was only this warm bright light descending slowly toward her. A few feet above her it hovered, a bright pulsing jewel, more fiery than an opal. She reached. If only she could touch it! But her arms were too heavy, and her eyes were too heavy, and just before she closed them, the jewel settled on her heart.

***

Warm. Soft. Gauzy heat. Wrapped in it like a blanket.
The jewel, radiating on her breast.
Drifting snowflakes.
Darkness.

***

Hands, reaching beneath her, lifting. Vaguely, she saw them, tall, ethereal, alive with light flowing through them. They peered down at her with bright emerald eyes, their hair of spun gold tossing in the wind and laced with falling snow. Gentle swaying as they carried her.
Darkness.

***

A bed of eldara boughs. A fire. A cave. The jewel on her breast, her hands cradling it. Salves rubbed into her fingers and toes. Hands and feet wrapped in fragrant leaves steeped in sunshine. The whistling wind fading beneath the murmur of singing—lilting, mellifluous. Though perhaps it was a dream....

***

Elixir, spooned past her lips, a pleasant burn as it flowed down her throat. She reached and found her knife beside her. Grasping the hilt, she fell again into a deep slumber.

***

Before she opened her eyes, she knew they were gone. But something was there—something large. She could tell from its breathing.

Sleep pulled her down once again.

***

Glue seemed to hold her eyelids shut. They parted, slowly. She made out the vague and blurry outlines of a cave, the lighter opening, the motion beyond of falling snow. The large presence was gone. She tried to rise on her elbows. Her arms trembled. The cave spun, and she sank back to the leaves and passed out.

She came to briefly, aware of a new presence—many pale discs staring at her through the opening of the cave. The discs grew. They were entering the cave, vague silhouettes of pointed ears, bushy tails, open jaws, sharp teeth. Wolves! Her hand closed on the dagger hilt. She could barely lift it. She drew back. The cave hummed with their growling. Deeper, terrifying, almost deafening, a roar sounded. The flames leaned. The pale discs scattered. A new silhouette leaped before the cave opening. Far larger in length and height than the wolves, it was four-footed, long and narrow of tail. It sat just outside the entrance and licked a forepaw. The rim of the moon rose beyond, illuminating snowflakes drifting down like tiny lights. Before sleep drew Briar into darkness, the beast—surely an immense tiger—lay down. But its head was lifted and turned toward the night, guarding.

***

The scent of blood drew Briar from sleep. The glassy eyes of a dead deer stared up at her. She recoiled. The deer's belly was ripped open. A growing puddle confirmed the animal had just been dropped there. She shot a glance to the entrance. The tiger was gone. Revulsion filled her, but her stomach rumbled—felt tight as a tourniquet with hunger—and her mouth watered. She rose slowly, determined to overcome the weakness that had been plunging her into darkness, and she struggled against a wave of dizziness. It passed quickly, and though her legs wobbled, she set about building a fire. She found tinder—bits of dried grass and twigs that had blown in over the years—and built a small nest. Wood, stacked against a broad log, had been left beside the fire pit by the strange beings who had nursed her, if they weren't a dream. With her knife, she sharpened the end of a stick and gouged an indentation in a slab of wood. Then holding the stick, its point in the hollow, she rubbed it rapidly back and forth between her palms. Soon she had an ember, which she slipped onto the nest, blew upon, and fanned into flames.

Next she worked on a spit, thankful that she had watched Jak the tanner's son broil a rabbit where he'd caught it. She searched through the wood until she found two stout branches. After trimming off the twigs, she cut them to a suitable height and then hammered them vertically into the ground with a heavy rock. Next, she carved a notch at the top of each pole. A straight stick lying across the two grooves would make an adequate spit.

The idea of skinning and dressing the deer twisted her stomach with disgust, but the alternative—starvation—compelled her to sharpen her blade on a stone and get to work. Presently, the deer was roasting over the flames.

The cooking took time, giving her a chance to examine her fingers and toes. There was no sign of frostbite, evidence that the haunting singers had been no feverish hallucination. Her thoughts turned then to the tiger. The beast had clearly saved her from the wolves. Briar held no malice toward them. They were driven by hunger, just as she was now with the deer, whose sizzling flesh made her mouth water. But the tiger—the tiger had stood guard, and she guessed it had left this meat.

She was too exhausted and weak to puzzle it out further. While she turned the meat, she considered the deer's skin. It was still snowing outside, and if she were to venture forth, she would need more than her father's rags to survive. Try as she might, she could figure no way to contrive a stretching rack without lumber, saw, and nails. Wind howled outside and tossed flurries across the threshold of the cave. Edging close to the fire, she rubbed her arms and legs, and cast about, seeking a solution. Fat dripped onto the flames and hissed. She turned the meat and then plopped down on the log in a brown study, her fingers digging into the bark. *It shouldn't be this hard*, she thought. *Just pin the darn thing down.* Then an idea dawned on her. Using sharpened sticks, she tacked the hide over the log and started scraping away the remaining flesh and fat.

With the skin stretched she sat before the fire, occasionally turning the meat, and considered her predicament. For now, she set aside the mystery of the tiger and strangers.

What troubled her was how to survive. She was uncertain how many days she'd gone in and out of consciousness. A peek outside revealed a thick blanket of snow on the ground and trees. And this was the beginning of winter. The cave was a blessing, would provide protection. But when this deer was gone, she would have to go out and forage. Her affinity for animals had kept her from hunting in the past. The thought horrified her. But without a doubt, she must hunt, or die.

Then what? There her mind stopped, for all beyond was as vague and indeterminate as the snow falling outside. No matter the weather, she must eventually venture forth.

Time on her hands, her thoughts turned to Vance, but the ache was so profound, so unbearable, that she focused instead on the queen. That hot burning inside fanned up in an instant. Questions of survival evaporated. She must survive to obliterate the power of the queen.

**

The deer was gone far too soon, and hunger drove Briar from the shelter of the cave. She made a three hundred sixty degree surveillance of her surroundings, and when she turned back to the cave she found herself staring at a blank granite wall. She rushed back to where the entrance had been. Reaching out, she found that a portion of the wall became semi transparent, and she could vaguely see the interior of the cave, her fire pit, the stretched skin, and the bough bed she'd lain on. Incredulous, she found that her hand and then her feet passed through the wall that wasn't a wall, and she was back inside.

Reassured that she could leave and return, she stepped out more resolutely and examined the location of the cave. With a start, she realized she was on the far side of the woods adjoining Abunary Pond, the place Racca had said was home to spirits. All she could think was that she had indeed met them, and that for reasons of their own, they had deigned to save her.

Certain now where she was, she explored more confidently, and with no fear of the snow. In the long lonely days before the deer meat had run out, she had fashioned crude but serviceable boots, gloves, and jerkin from the skin, knitting them with bits of wood for a needle and strings of hide and sinew for thread. She'd also contrived a belt and a scabbard for her knife. Beneath her tunic, the jewel that had floated down from the sky was wrapped in the handkerchief Vance had given her and tied with a string of rawhide around her neck, so they were both close to her heart. Finally, a pouch was slung over her shoulder. At various points in the woods, she left snares—simple loops made from rawhide, like the ones Jak made—and then she went quickly to the pond. Afterward, she returned to the cave and drank from the pouch as the ice melted.

That evening she checked her traps. Perhaps the one who'd sent the jewel was blessing her, or perhaps one of the forest spirits, but two of the traps had squirrels. After returning to the cave with these, she set about skinning and cooking them, as the woods provided much fallen fuel.

So the weeks passed. Skins were transformed into layers of clothing. Soon, the rags were no longer visible, and she was wrapped in a patchwork of fur, a hat crowning her head.

When storms swept down, she stayed warm and dry. No wolves troubled her. Nor did she see the tiger again until one day, when she was out hunting, she came upon an enormous white tiger in the burned out trunk of a great tree. It looked at her complacently, but its eyes lit in warning to not approach. Briar retreated behind foliage and watched. A short time later, the tiger threw back its head and let out a sound like a squeaking wagon wheel or the shriek of an injured hawk, and Briar realized it was in pain. At first, she couldn't tell what had happened. It didn't seem possible that anything could hurt this creature, not man, not beast. Then, with a cry of wonder, it struck her. The tiger was giving birth. Presently, cubs were nursing at her belly.

Next day, Briar returned to find mother and cubs gone, except one that had been left in the snow outside the hollow tree.

CHAPTER EIGHT

*B*riar searched the vicinity for the mother but knew she would find nothing. No footprints were visible in the snow. The cub mewled and flailed, digging itself deeper in the drift, burrowing its nose into cold, as though it might find cozy fur and glorious splashes of warmth shooting against its tongue.

She took the baby in her arms and brought it back to the cave. She dribbled water into its mouth and then sat back for a long think. She must find food for herself. More important, she must feed the cub. It was too young for meat. But where was she to find milk?

She found no answer except to go back out to search. She had little time. The cub would surely perish if it did not have nourishment soon.

It was snowing again. Not a harsh, wind driven, blinding storm, but a slow steady drifting down of flakes. She checked her traps. They were empty except one where something had torn the catch to pieces, staining the snow red and leaving enough—an ear, a part of a foot—to identify that the victim had been a rabbit.

Snow and wind no longer troubled her. She could stand in nothing more than skins wrapped about her torso, and the cold bothered her little. But now, looking down on the remains in the trap, something froze within her. She backed away, wary, and looked about. No eyes peered at her from the surrounding foliage.

Empty-handed, she returned to the cub. It raised its head from the skins she had swaddled it in and cried like a human baby. And then, all energy seemed to flee its tiny body, and it collapsed.

Briar dribbled more water past its lips. She mashed cooked meat she'd set aside and made a paste of it with hot broth. She tried dribbling a bit of the mixture into the baby's mouth, but it turned its head away. Desperate to get nourishment into it, she wiped the meal on its paws in the hope that it would lick it off. But the cub only dropped its head onto the fur skins. By nightfall, its eyes fell to half-mast and began to glaze over.

She must try foraging again, for her own store of meat was swiftly shrinking. A storm rose up, howling into the night. The sane thing would have been to stay snug inside and wait it out. But first thing in the morning, she struck out again, plowing through the whipping curtains and drifts, hope dimming with each passing hour. She made a circuit of her traps, which she'd reset. All were empty. Even if she caught something, there was nothing there for the baby tiger.

With a heavy heart, she began the trek home, wondering if she would find the cub alive. In the distance she heard wolves howling. Once more, she thought of the ravaged trap, and coldness gripped her heart. There was more than one hunter desperate for a meal.

For a time, the baying fell off, but some instinct told her they were near. She began looking from left to right, peering through the brush, casting her gaze behind her. Then she came upon a small clearing, stopped, and sniffed the air. The birds grew silent, and suddenly she tensed. She pulled out her knife and backed away to the broad trunk of a tree. The snow stopped. A hush fell over the glade. When they came, they came in a rush, a dozen wolves, running low, their eyes disks of gold in the waning daylight, their fangs catching the dying rays.

They quickly formed a semicircle. She flashed her knife, making it clear one or more of them would pay a dear price for making a meal of her. They would bring her down, of that she was sure. But they would get the fight of their lives. If they were hungry enough, they could drag off one of their fallen brothers.

The largest of them was a great she-wolf. She approached warily from the side, while two of her kin lunged and snapped at Briar's ankles. Her blade was a blur, catching an ear on her left, grazing the leader on her right. Back and forth she worked, giving them no opening, the knife nothing but whirling steel, presenting an impenetrable wall. They growled and cried in frustration and leaped back, yelping when her blade struck home. But they levied their own price. Soon she was bleeding from wounds on her legs and arms.

She knew it was a matter of time. They would tire her out. And then they would bring her down. Strangely, her only thought was for the cub in the cave; it would surely perish if she died. For a time, the thought renewed her strength. But all things come to an end, even the abundant store of energy that coursed through Briar's veins. The knife began to feel like lead, as though it were gradually growing larger or she was shrinking. Her head began to swim, her vision to blur, and she saw double. In a burst, she attacked phantom and wolf alike. They gave back, stunned. But then she sagged. Unable to lift the knife, it dropped from her fingers. A moment later she slumped to the bottom of the tree.

Even then, the wolves circled, wary, tongues lolling. Perhaps they thought it a trick. She looked no more at the pack but kept her gaze fixed on the she-wolf. It crept in, nose almost in the snow, grinning, snarling, its yellow eyes flashing in triumph.

In that moment, Briar held no malice. They were creatures like her, hungry, surviving in a harsh environment.

The she-wolf crouched, readying to leap. In that moment, a terrible roar sounded. A colossal white tiger sprang between Briar and the wolf. The wolf cowered back. One of her vassals sprang at the tiger, but it caught the creature neatly in its jaws and flung it into the brush. The next instant, the wolves scattered.

The tiger padded after them, but at the edge of the glade it looked back, as if beckoning. She hesitated, wobbled to her feet, and then followed, determined to see where this might lead. She was certain of one thing: this was the giant tiger that had given birth to the cubs, that had abandoned the one now dying in Briar's cave.

The tiger moved at a lope. From time to time it turned, as if to make sure she followed. Once she lost it among the dense trees. When she saw it again it melted away, and in its place a woman walked, a long white gown trailing behind her. The wind picked up the flimsy material and cast it out so that it swirled and was sometimes indistinguishable from the twirling flakes. Briar only had glimpses of her—tall, alive with light—and then at the next turn, she disappeared. Briar looked for footprints and found none, though paw prints pocked the new-fallen snow. But she went in the direction the woman had taken, and there, waiting—turned toward Briar in a small clearing—sat the tiger. A moment later, it took off again. Now they were both leaping through the brush. She was certain that she was being led. But where? And why?

She received an answer soon enough. They came upon a boulder. At the bottom, a rocky shelf thrust out, creating shelter. Further excavation had been dug beneath the shelf. Briar crept up cautiously and peered inside. Two gold eyes glimmered from the darkness, accompanied by a warning growl. Dimly, she saw the outline of the she-wolf, with five tiny bundles burrowing into her belly.

Briar backed away. Gripping her knife she peered into the surrounding foliage, expecting an attack from the wolf's followers. Perhaps they were out hunting. Perhaps the tiger frightened them off, for it sat nearby, staring at her a long moment. Then it loped off through the leaves.

After checking her traps once more, Briar returned to her cave and built a fire. Once more she tried feeding the tiger cub, to no avail. She flung the mixture into the flames and dropped her head into her hands. Her muscles were heavy from battle, but she barely felt it. The last hours swirled in her mind like snow, tossed in the wind, leaving vague outlines and images. Why had the tiger led her to the wolf den? Was the tiger one and the same as the woman? Briar was almost certain it was, and Racca's tales came back to her of a face changer, a great she-tiger that walked the hills, ruling all in sight. Now Briar was certain, the tiger and the woman were of the same beings that had saved her at the beginning of her banishment.

She began to wonder if the cub had been abandoned or left for her. That the tiger had saved Briar from the wolves was certain. But the mystery of the wolf den plagued her all the rest of the day and far into the night. An idea formed in her mind, a strange, wild idea, as wild as her existence in this harsh country. Next morning, she resolved to try it. Taking nothing but her knife, a string of dried meat, and an empty gourd she used as a bowl, she returned to the clearing before the boulder. Several wolves prowled nearby, none of them their leader.

Briar stepped from the foliage. "Let me pass." She moved toward the opening of the den.

They bared their teeth and barred her way.

On a hunch, she gave a slow wave of her hand, and this time they backed away. She crept to the opening. They could tear her to pieces from behind, but she was filled with certitude. If they were going to harm her, they would have already done so. She peered inside. Pale disks stared up at her, and a low menacing growl rose from the dim interior. Briar took out her knife, displayed it to the she-wolf and then placed it at her feet. Then she showed her empty hands.

"You've eaten from my traps. You must return something to me. I'm entering." She began crawling in. "Your pups are safe."

Outside, one of the wolves began to howl. Perhaps it was anticipating a meal. Briar paused. A light flared in the mother's eyes. Briar chided herself. This was no time to show weakness, and began crawling again. "I'm not going to hurt you. You know what I want."

Inch by inch she progressed, knowing any moment those huge jaws could fasten on her neck, and that would be the end of her. The she-wolf's growl rose, threatening, and then dropped to a whine. Briar was beside her now and, reaching out, stroked the great head. The mother lay back, presenting her belly. Gently, Briar worked one of the teats, squirting milk into the gourd.

When it was filled, she left the string of meat and backed out. The wolves outside crouched, their ears flat, their noses down in submission.

Briar laughed. "Come here." And one by one, they approached her for a pat on the head. "Next time, I'll bring you meat, too. But now you must hunt for her. There are cougars up here. She must stay with her pups and protect them. Go!"

With a bound they were off, crashing through the brush.

At the cave, Briar warmed the milk over a fire and then dripped it past the cub's lips. Day after day, it grew stronger. Soon it followed her outside the cave, where she played with it, and it slept pressed against her at night.

With food for the cub assured, Briar looked to her own survival. Her traps continued to yield little, leaving her dejected and despondent, but one day a surprising thing happened. She sat on a log, not far from where she and Vance had dallied by Abunary Pond, and sank her head in her hands, wondering what to do. A white-throated sparrow landed on a nearby rock, scratched through the snow, and then cocking its head at her, whistled.

"Did you find something, little one?

He whistled back, and then, having dusted away snow, he pecked at a few seeds, lodged in the cracks.

"You're cleverer than me." She waved her arm at the white landscape, barren of food. "I wish you'd find something for me."

It tilted its head left and right, eyeing her, and then winged off into the trees. With a sigh, she rose, dusted flakes from her hat, and began the trek home. She hadn't gone far when a flock of sparrows—all with white neckties—glided toward her. She stopped and watched in wonder as they fluttered around her head. She couldn't have said why, but she held out her hand, perhaps for the sheer joy of having one of them land on it. To her surprise, one bird after another dropped a seed into her fingers.

Over the next days, she listened to the warbles and trills of many birds, and learned to imitate them. Within weeks, she was whistling and chirping, or calling with the voice of the eagle or hawk. What's more, the birds brought her seeds, nuts, and bits of edible stems and leaves in sufficient volume that she could survive without traps or hunting, but for the cub. He seemed to grow daily, with an appetite to match. But then, it wasn't too surprising. The mother was a colossus; the son would be too.

The two of them wrestled outside the cave, rolling in the snow, the cub flicking her with its tail and then dashing off in a game of chase. Just as often it rolled on its back, Briar rubbing its belly, while the tiger licked her face.

By spring, he followed her on her circuit of the traps, and was big enough to hunt with her. Once, peering from a spray of forest leaves, they spotted a stag—majestic beneath a crown of antlers—grazing in a meadow painted with sedge, aster, poppies, and bluebells.

Briar whispered to the cub, "Go left and circle around." Then she was off and going to her right through the pines. Only when she was adjacent to the stag did she cut from the trees and dart into the meadow. The stag froze at her sudden appearance then took off in the other direction. At that moment, the tiger came racing from the trees on the other side of the meadow and charged at the stag. It would have brought the creature down, but Briar called, "Heel, Mirage," for that was the name she'd given him, and the tiger skidded to halt, allowing the stag to escape.

Mirage growled with discontent all the way home, but Briar told him, "He was too beautiful to bring down, and the mountain would be dimmer without him."

Still, she allowed him to hunt on his own. She could survive on what the birds brought. Mirage couldn't. But he always returned from his solo journeys, his muzzle clean of blood, and never brought her trophies.

From time to time, she dreamed that a boy with hair, white as snow, stood over her in the cave, and one night, after Mirage was old enough to hunt alone, she wakened to find the boy beside her bed furs. He made a small motion with his hand, and sleep drew her back into the underworld of dreams.

Three years passed. On stormy days, she stayed in the cave and practiced with a stick, rehearsing the thrusts and parries Vance had shown her, plus new tactics that sprang from her imagination, until her skin shone with sweat and the muscles beneath were as taut as steel.

Hot days or cold days, it mattered not, often found her high on a cliff top. She sang and the birds came, dancing and spiraling about her. She howled and far below came the answering bay of the pack. Soon they appeared, and together with Mirage, they streaked through pines and bands of sunlight, not to hunt but for the sheer joy of it.

During all this time, she felt no desire to return to her own kind, who showed her so little love or kindness, until one fall day atop her cliff, she looked homeward and saw a red glow and a dark column of smoke climbing skyward.

CHAPTER NINE

*B*riar shot along the trail from the cliff top, Mirage loping beside her. If she was right, if it was the manse burning down there, she would be too late. She'd once watched one of the servants' huts burn to the ground in minutes.

The sun was dipping toward the horizon when she left the trees and started down the first of the hills that marched toward her father's land. From this vantage point, she felt certain it was not the house that was burning, but one of the nearby pastures where the baron's cows grazed. It mattered not. Fires spread.

She hadn't thought much about the baron or the manse after the first days of life on the mountain. But now feelings welled up. The threatened land was her land, not from birthright but because ahead were her childhood haunts, the meadows she'd explored, the old oak she'd battled with sticks, the orchard where she and Vance had strolled arm in arm or lingered, reading hopes and dreams in each others eyes. And near the manse were walkways and paths, pools and fountains where she'd played. The fire was a terrible beast, come to destroy all she loved.

The thought lent power to her legs. She almost flew down the hillsides and across the meadows, the waist-high grass crackling as she passed.

Here was another threat. If the fire spread, eating the dry tinder on the hills, it would threaten her domain—the lands she shared with Mirage, the wolves, and the other creatures of the mountain.

Unable to keep up the breakneck pace, she paused and mounted Mirage, whose giant stride ate up the land.

She couldn't say she was frightened for the baron or that she felt anything about the danger he might be in. But there were her mother, Dolly, and Racca. What would happen to them?

Dusk set in. Ahead, a forbidding bronze glowed on the horizon. She urged Mirage on, to fly faster than the dark mass of smoke spiraling skyward.

How had the fire started? An accident? That was always possible. Grease spilled on a cooking fire. A tipped over lantern. Sparks from a chimney blown to a hayrick. But now the grumblings of the servants and their dark glances at the baron rose into her mind; and also the reports of rebels from Turlia, attacking over the border. If the fire was born from malcontent, if rebels had attacked the manse, how many would Briar find there? A dozen? A hundred? How could she fight them? The knife hanging from her belt was a meager weapon. Surely they would have swords, lances, spears, and arrows.

These questions plagued her in the moments before she arrived. By the time she reached a low hill overlooking the inner domain of the baron's lands, the situation was clear. One of the pastures and a corral were blazing. Flames shot ten feet from the hayloft of the barn and ran along the top edge of the roof. Roughly two score figures, silhouetted in the reddish glow of brandished torches, milled on the lawn before the manse.

People carry buckets of sand and tubs of water when there's a fire. No one waves torches.

Riding Mirage, she passed near the burning field. Flames snaked along the ground, consuming all before them, leaving blackened ground behind. She passed the barn. Smoke belched from the windows. Flames ran down one of the outer walls, which began to buckle and fall inward. It was beyond saving. She could only hope that the animals were out, Dondle among them.

Fire flickered in two of the manse's downstairs windows. One of the curtains ignited. A torch was tossed onto the gable above the front entrance.

The situation came into sharp focus. A man on horseback shook his fist at the manse, his cries angry. Briar didn't recognize him. But few of the tenant farmers owned horses. She doubted he was from around here, suggesting he was a Turlian rebel. The rest of the mob must be servants and other locals, turned against the baron.

With a shrill cry she was on them, her knife out and flashing in the flickering light. Dressed in animal skins, hair flying behind her, riding a giant roaring beast, Briar must have seemed a she-demon. They recoiled in fright. She leaped from Mirage and landed on the front steps.

Whirling, she confronted them. "Bring water or face me!"

"She's but one," shouted the man on horseback. "Brothers, sisters, this is your land. Take it! Drive the baron out!"

Briar pointed to the man with her knife. "Mirage! Take him!"

Mirage took off. The crowd parted, watching in wonder

as he raced past. The man spurred his horse. Almost upon him, Mirage leaped.

"Mirage, heel!" Briar cried.

The tiger sailed over the man and skidded to a stop, looking back at her.

"Make sure he leaves," Briar said.

Mirage replied with a roar and dashed after the horseman, fleeing up the road.

Briar turned to the crowd. "Where are the baron and baroness?"

"Inside," someone called.

"The baroness is dead," cried another.

Dead? How!

There was no time for answers. "Bring water, sand, and blankets!" Briar didn't wait for their response. She flung open the front door and dashed inside.

She found Dolly and several servants cowering in the foyer, which was beginning to fill with smoke.

Running toward them, Briar called, "Where's the baron?"

"Upstairs, miss," Dolly replied, clutching a piece of cloth to her mouth. "He won't leave."

"Go! Before the house burns down on you."

Dolly cringed against a wall. "Them outside will kill us for stayin' loyal."

"Not anymore. Go!"

Still Dolly hesitated.

"I promise, you'll meet no punishment," Briar cried.

Dolly pressed the cloth into Briar's hand. "Bless you."

Briar gave her a push towards the front door. Watching them leave, she paused to tie the cloth over her nose and mouth, then dashed up the steps.

Smoke was thicker at the top of the stairs and down the hallway leading to the baron's study. It was collecting along the floor. From above came the sound of windows shattering. A blast of heat rushed down upon her from the third-floor stairwell.

Briar pelted down the hallway. When she reached her father's study, she flung the door open. Flames ran along the ceiling beams. Her father was slumped over his desk.

She hurried to him and drew him upright. He appeared to be unconscious, but as she shook him, his eyes opened wide as if she were a phantom.

"You!" he croaked. "Come to take me to hell?"

"No, Father. To save you."

His eyes cleared a little. "Leave me. They'll flail me outside."

"They'll have to get through me first."

She pulled him to his feet. He tottered but allowed her to lead him, half sagging on her, to the doorway and then to the stairs. Flames jigged down the banister. The staircase ceiling began to sag.

She backstepped, turned, and steered him back down the hall. A roar rose behind her. She glanced back. Flames crawled down one wall. Smoke hung in a dark curtain before her, cutting visibility to a few feet ahead.

When she reached the study, she was in time to see her father's chair and carpets explode into flames, while at the window, fire leaped down the drapes.

She pushed on, crashed into a small statue, and then stumbled to the far end of the hall, where there was a spare bedroom. The door was closed. If the fire raged there as it did in the study, they were doomed.

Her hand on the doorknob gave her hope. It wasn't hot. She turned it and entered. Like her childhood bedroom, a tree climbed near the window.

She pulled the baron inside and shut the door, giving some relief from the heat in the hallway.

At the window, she kicked out the glass and urged her father out and onto the stout limbs of the tree.

"I'm too weak," he cried.

"Go or die. I can't carry you."

That convinced him. Down he went, Briar alongside, holding him steady while the fire roared in her ears.

No one waited below. They took three steps and collapsed face first onto a lawn.

Drinking in fresh air, Briar was the first to stir. She rose to her knees, heat from the house penetrating her back. She sank back to the grass, rolled, and looked up. Smoke belched from the study window. Fire shot like dragon's flame from windows closer to the main stairs. A minute later, yellow tongues crackled up the outer wall and then to the roof.

She wobbled to her feet. Latching onto her father, she guided him up and away from the house. Near a well, where the heat was not as intense and there was no danger of glass raining down on them, she crumpled to the ground.

When she caught her breath, she got up again and staggered to the front driveway, where the crowd watched the blaze in awe. They had abandoned their torches and stood with buckets glistening in the amber light.

Sand and water were useless now. With furniture, floors, and walls on fire; with the heat too great for anyone to venture near; there was little anyone could do.

She found Dolly and the servants who had remained loyal and directed them to see to the baron, checking for burns, dribbling water past his lips, and then carrying him to a makeshift tent to rest. Meanwhile, she sent half of the remaining crowd to dowse the servants' quarters and other structures, vulnerable to flying cinders, while the other half was dispatched with shovels and spades to keep the fire from invading more of the fields.

She would have joined them, but she could do little more

than sag on a bench and watch the house erupt into a pyre. Flames shot ten feet from the roof and waved in the night like supernatural trees, the smoke glowing.

Then it was no longer a building, but a leaping, quivering thing, consuming itself.

CHAPTER TEN

he next morning, wraiths of smoke trailed up from the manse, and embers burned like evil eyes in the ash. The house was a lonely shell of fireplaces and chimneys, scarred and fallen beams, soot-blackened floor flags, and blistered paint. The smell of smoke permeated everything.

Though charred and shattered at the top, the foyer wall where the sword used to hang remained standing. Briar recovered the sword among the rubble and ash below. She cleaned it off and found the blade to be straight and the metal unharmed. Even the edge was sharp, a testament to the sword smith's art. The handle would need new leather wrapping, and a new scabbard would need to be fashioned, but both were easy to obtain.

She spent a good hour searching for her mother's jewel box but could not locate it. At last, beneath the remains of the third floor, fallen into the ruins, she excavated the small silver casket. After carefully dusting it off, she held her breath and opened the lid. To her relief, she found her mother's ruby ring inside, along with a few gold coins. She closed the lid and put the little box in her pocket for safekeeping. The gold wouldn't go far, but she wouldn't part with the ring. It was all she had left of her mother.

Further exploration confirmed her fear that nothing more of value remained in the wreckage of the manse. The servants' quarters had largely been spared, and the field fire had been stopped, protecting the hillsides and mountain beyond. Dondle was nowhere to be found. Briar learned that he'd been sold the first year of her banishment, filling her heart with sadness. The other barn animals had been let out, and some of the servants were beginning to lead them home. Where home was for any of them was unknown. The baron might rebuild the estate, but could he hold it?

Briar found Mirage in a dense cluster of trees, unharmed by the fire. After telling him to stay out of sight, but watchful in case the rebel leader returned, she went to see her father, ducking into the tent as quietly as she could. He lay on a cot inside.

"It was you, then, not a nightmare," he said, his eyes still closed. "You smell like an unwashed dog."

She squatted beside him. "The wilds don't provide soap."

A full minute passed, then he said, "You've come back to gloat, I suppose."

"I saw the fire, or I wouldn't have returned at all."

He opened his eyes, glanced at her sharply, and then closed them again. "Now that you're here, what do you propose to do?"

This time she let him stew awhile before she spoke. She had thought on this long before but felt no inclination to reveal her plans. "How did you let this happen?"

He laughed harshly. "How? You dare ask that? If you'd done what I'd asked—"

"You had no one to sell for the queen's ambitions, and she abandoned you. A pretty beast to cozy up to."

"Be that as it may, the border has become lawless. Turlian rebels come and go as they please. Highwaymen rule the roads. I'm surprised I lasted this long."

"You could've defended without her."

"With what? I have no soldiers."

She leaped to her feet and paced. "I would've found a way."

He followed her with his eyes, which appeared to acquiesce in the face of her ferocity. "Perhaps you would. There was always something unconquerable in you. The gods know I tried."

She dropped to one knee beside him. "What happened to mother?"

"There was nothing anyone could do. She passed."

Briar saw it in her mind, a flower that slowly drooped and wilted and no amount of water revived it; day by day it dried and dried until it was nothing more than straw. Still, she asked, "Because of me? Because I was gone?"

"Don't flatter yourself. I doubt she noticed."

Another period of silence followed, during which an ache swelled in Briar's heart, one that hadn't abated the whole time on Einor. "What of Vance?"

He turned away from her gaze, as if it burned him. "No news."

"Was he drafted? Has he gone to war?" She swallowed. "Is he alive?"

"I know nothing."

"But Patrikka—she would know. She must've told you something."

Cold amusement stiffened his lips. "Ah, there's another one! After a suitable period of mourning, we married. Don't look so shocked. As I said, I needed protection from the queen, and it had the same advantages as your alliance with Vance once had."

Frost settled over Briar. "Where is Patrikka now?"

"Gone. Stole your mother's jewelry and ran off with an old Turlian flame. For all I know, he's behind last night's attack."

With a scornful laugh, Briar rose. "You used her; she used you. A pretty pail of fish the two of you make."

But it was the queen—her influence—her will—that cast its shadow over their lives, and the chill Briar had been feeling melted in the face of a slow burn. She walked the property, surveying the damage. The barn would need to be rebuilt. One of the servants' huts was lost, but the rest were untouched. The fences were easy enough to repair. The fields would recover with the first rains; by spring the hillsides would be awash with the hues of grass and flowers.

Racca was gone. Briar learned the old woman had disappeared a few weeks before the fire. Well, she always knew things before they happened. Perhaps she decided a hasty retreat during a fire didn't suit her.

The condition of the property, the faces of the servants turned to her for direction, did nothing to change her plans. Neither did her father's condition. He never rallied, and when Briar determined waiting wouldn't help, she went to his tent.

Dolly caught Briar's sleeve before she lifted the flap and drew her away.

"He's not the same, miss."

"What do you mean?" Briar asked.

"He's broken."

"Too much brandy?"

Dolly shuffled from side to side. "Ma looked in on him this morning. Apoplexy. What will we do, miss? How will we rebuild?"

Briar took her hands and gave them a squeeze. "Don't worry. Everything will work out." Briar started to turn away, but a thought made her stop. "All those years ago, when I was born, why did he want to throw me in the well?"

The habit of silence must have been strong. Dolly looked about to make sure no one listened. "Your uncle, miss—you've seen his portrait—with black hair and fiery eyes like yours. He raved about spirits and magic on the mountain. He was wild, defiant, in love with the untamed country and the mountain up there. He believed in the Turlian Claim and wanted to give the land back. The baron fought him, drove him into the snow as he did you that terrible winter. Then he forbade anyone to speak of it, or he would hang them from yonder tree." She pointed to the ancient oak with its spreading arms.

Briar could see it as though it were happening: a man with a heart as large as the mountain; his covetous brother turning on him; the fear and hostility of the servants; the little babe born with black hair, a daily reminder of a monstrous act. Now, none of it mattered.

"Thank you, Dolly. You're good and loyal. I couldn't have a better friend."

Briar ducked into the tent. The baron's face was as gray as the ashes of the manse. A shawl was draped over his shoulders. Another lay across his lap. He gazed about him, as though he was not quite sure what or where he was.

Briar took a deep breath. "I'm leaving, Father."

His speech was slurred, barely intelligible. "Leaving? For how many days?" He struggled to lift his hand, but it trembled and fell to his side.

There seemed no reason to be brutal now. If he was the same harsh unyielding man it might be different. She considered the softest way to put it. "For some time."

"Oh …" His eyes focused a bit. "Who will run the manse? Who will take care of me?"

"Dolly and the others know what to do." Hadn't they been

running things for years, growing food, tending livestock, repairing leaks? Even now, the carpenter and his apprentice were clearing away rubble to build a new barn.

What they would do after Briar and Mirage left was anyone's guess. But the baron hardly seemed a threat now, and what the servants had wanted all these years was possession of the estate. Now they could have it. Anyway, Dolly had promised he would have a spot in her cottage.

"You'll be back soon, won't you?" he asked. "Bring that handsome viscount with you. I always liked him."

Dolly brought in a tray of tea.

Briar poured him a cup and helped him sip. "Yes, Father, I promise."

The next morning she departed, a rucksack slung over her shoulders, the sword from the foyer swinging at her hip, and Mirage at her side. They avoided roads. Cutting through the countryside, they made a beeline for the queen.

PART TWO

CHAPTER ELEVEN

*S*everal weeks later, Briar strode through a forest, Mirage treading silently beside her. The chatter of birds, the squirrels scampering and leaping on the branches above, made her feel at home—as though she were back on Mount Einor—and many of the creatures marked her progress and followed, peeking at her through the leaves. She was loath to leave the green shadows for the world beyond. But neither Vance nor the queen were far from her mind, and the one fixed purpose that had occupied her for three long years lay ahead, pulling her to Freyclif, the capital.

The path was nothing more than a thread. That suited her fine. Mirage stood out with his white coat, black stripes, and size that dwarfed an ordinary tiger. He knew his job, sniffing for humans in the vicinity, and he always scampered from sight if any drew near.

The day was warm, the sun sliding lazily across an afternoon sky, when they came to the edge of the woods and saw a road unravel like a ribbon below them toward a small village. To her left, a lone mountain loomed. Forests hugged the lower levels, but the upper slopes were craggy and inhospitable, and the eastern peak was nothing but rock.

"Here's where we part," she said.

She knew he didn't like it. He didn't communicate aloud, but dream-like impressions flowed through her mind. The images were so distinct, the voice behind the thoughts so like Mirage, that from years of experience, she knew how to read him. She supposed that was how she was able to relay her intentions to Dondle and other creatures, large and small.

Now he was reminding her that the last inn she went to pushed her to defend her honor. If someone hadn't come to her aid, Mirage would have had to show himself.

"I wore a dress, thinking I would be treated with decorum," she replied. "It appears girls aren't valued in Purpura, and inn patrons assume you'll trade your body for a few coins. I won't make that mistake again. I'll go like this."

Mirage scanned her from boots to breeches to tunic, stopping at last at the lad's feathered cap on her head and the raven hair tied and tucked beneath her tunic. Her father's sword was at her waist. She kept the edge keen.

"Well? Am I convincing?"

Mirage bared his teeth, his gesture for a smile. *Like a lad of sixteen. I still don't like it.*

"We talked about it. There's no place for you to hide when we're in the open. Besides, I have something I want you to do."

Mirage sniffed sulkily and waited.

"Keep an ear out for word of Vance," she said.

How? You don't want me near people?

"You'll think of something. It's important. Please."

He gave her one searching look and then turned and started back into the woods, his tail flicking disconsolately. When he had disappeared, Briar left the trees and started down a hillside toward the road. Meadowland on either side was bursting with the colors of spring, lush grasses and wild-flowers and butterflies with harlequin wings. Below that stretched rolling hills of orchard and farmland. The unplanted soil appeared dark and rich, and the planted fields were green and bursting with vegetation.

Presently she struck out on the road, well-traveled and firm underfoot, making the hike easy. She was tempted to stop at an apple tree and fill her belly, but except for the sad incident Mirage had referred to, the two of them had lived out in the open since she'd left the manse. She wanted nothing more than to eat a home-cooked meal, kick up her feet by a fire, and drink a bumper of ale—after which, she planned to park herself for the night in the innkeeper's finest down bed.

A farmer and a lass Briar took for his daughter drove a wagon from one of the orchards and waved to her. The wagon was filled with burlap sacks, and one of them had spilled open, revealing ripe apples.

"Hallo, lad," he called. "Do you want a lift to Tubney village?" His shoulders were wide and powerful, and Briar had no doubt that he could pull a plow himself if his horse went lame. But he had a plain honest face and eyes as deep and brown as the earth.

Briar usually avoided spending time with anyone, lest they see past her disguise. For her singular goal, the less known about her appearance, the better. But she longed for that meal, and though the afternoons were warm, the nights nipped, and she wished to be settled before sundown. She climbed aboard the wagon and sat beside the daughter, who appeared to be about fifteen. Where her father was as sturdy and stout as an oak, she was comely and fresh, with bright blue eyes and roses in her cheeks. But she appeared shy, and stared at Briar with a mixture of interest and apprehension.

She hasn't seen past my disguise, Briar thought. *Good. Let's hope it sticks.*

"Where ya headed?" the farmer asked.

"Tubney, if there's a good inn there," Briar replied.

"They's a good'n all right, The Comb and Tap. I'm drop-pin' Reena there to sell apples. They make the best cider for miles around. I'll take you there. Are you settlin' in these parts?"

"I'm headed for the capital."

He gave her a sidelong glance and frowned. "Nothin' there for an enterprising lad." His voice dropped. "And you don't want conscription."

"They take you this young?"

The farmer's hands tightened on the reins. They were sun-browned and callused, with thick knuckles and fingers that looked handy. "If the queen wants you, she'll take you, mark my words."

"How goes the war?"

He batted away a fly. "No war goes well. People die." His daughter paled and glanced at Briar's sword.

The farmer gave Briar a thin smile. "You didn't hear that from me."

"My lips are sealed," Briar said. The girl's shoulders relaxed.

"I have no love for the queen," Briar continued. "You farm independent of a lord?"

"The last good ruler of this land, King Brodellorn, gave me this tract in return for a kindness. Better if he'd never had a daughter." He spat into the dust.

"A sick shoot can spring from a healthy tree," Briar observed.

"And t'other way too. My da was as mean as they came, took a belt to me from the time I was knee high to a grasshopper, told me I would amount to nothin'. Know how that turned out?"

Briar rubbed her chin, considering. "He died with yellow eyes and a swollen liver among a pile of bottles, while you raised a beautiful family and made out well." She nodded toward Reena. "Bet you never lay a hand on her."

The farmer smiled. "You're a discernin' lad."

"No, I had your kind of father. Someday I'll be like you and show him he was wrong."

"I like you, lad. If you want to work rather than …" His glance fell on Briar's sword. "I could use an extra hand."

"Kind of you, but I'm headed to Freyclif."

"Suit yourself. But watch your back. Besides the army, they's cutthroats and brigands about."

Briar nodded toward the mountain, which sat like the abandoned abode of an ancient god. "What's up there?"

"Nothin' but rock. They's a legend that an undying flame once leaped from the peak there—almost to the sky—like a beacon of hope."

"Do you think it's true?"

"Never thought much about it one way or t'other. They's a flat place like an altar at the top, and sometimes kids go up there and build bonfires. The fires always go out."

"Doesn't look too hopeful now," Briar said.

The farmer took a long gander. "I don't know. It always gives me comfort to look at it. It shelters the farms and all the lands below. Mount Toivara," he mused. "Means Hope's Flame."

"In the old tongue?"

He nodded.

"How far are we from Freyclif?"

"If I set out early, I can reach the marketplace there by midmorning."

They arrived at the inn and he drew up near the front.

"Give me an hour," he said to Reena. "I wanna look in on the widow Ede."

Briar helped Reena down and then unloaded a sack of apples for her to show the innkeeper. Then she shook the farmer's hand. As he grasped it, a new look came into his eyes, and he peered at her face more closely.

"Well, best of luck to you," he said, a note of worry creeping into his voice.

Briar thanked him and offered to carry the apples in for Reena, but she shrugged, saying, "I reckon I can tote 'em."

She was as good as her word and shouldered the load into the inn. She wasn't as fragile as she'd appeared, and surely fresh air and honest work had toughened her. Briar imagined that there was little on the farm she couldn't do.

The inn was a two-story building of mud and wattle with a wide front door beside a broad glassless window. The shutters were thrown wide, and the aroma of mutton, roast boar, and venison, mixed with the smoke of tallow candles and grease lamps, floated out.

Briar's stomach rumbled, urging her past the threshold. It was dim inside. A few candles and lamps threw wavering shadows, and most of the light came from a hearth fire, roaring in one corner. Her eyes quickly adjusted, and she made out a number of long plank tables, balanced uncertainly on barrels, and a score of three-legged stools. Reena had disappeared somewhere in the back, but a dozen patrons were scattered about, eating or playing dice. They glanced up as Briar entered but gave her no more notice. A lad of sixteen was inconsequential.

Seated in a far corner, she waved over one of the serving wenches, who took her order for cider, bread, and stew.

"Do you have a bed for the night?" Briar asked. One was available for three torlins. No room in this rustic inn was worth more than two torlins, but Briar was already dreaming of rolling up in a blanket—even if the mattress beneath was stuffed with straw rather than down—and paid to hold it.

While she waited for food to arrive, she took a closer look at the men in the dining hall. There may have been a few locals, but most were rugged and dirty, and kept to the shadows. She guessed some degree of illicit activity occurred here, as it did in most inns, smuggling of anything from tobacco and wine to wool or even silks, attracting men like these.

Briar's food arrived in a cloud of mouth-watering steam. The stew was tasty, though a bit salty, and the bread a rye and barley that could break teeth. But the cider was excellent, and she could well believe the farmer's tree-ripened apples had something to do with it.

Her meal finished, Briar pushed back in her chair, trying to catch conversation. Most of it was hushed and obscured by the general din in the place, but what she heard confirmed what she already knew: people grumbling about the war, high prices, and exorbitant tariffs.

With nothing more to be gained here, she thought she would settle upstairs with a bath, when six men entered the room. Something about them made her stiffen. Rather than wanting to maintain anonymity, they were loud and brash, drawing attention to themselves. In particular, one man's presence seemed to fill the room. He was tall, with the wide swagger of a sailor. His shirt hung impudently open, revealing sculpted muscles and a long knife scar. A large hoop dangled from one ear. His face—brazen, brown, and leathery from the sun—would be considered handsome but for the black patch over one eye, which lent him a sinister aspect. Briar wondered if he was a pirate. But how could he travel openly in Purpura if that were the case?

His eyes swept the room, sardonically humorous but also gauging, calculating, taking in the quality of weapons, the capability of each man. When his scan alighted on Briar, he moved on quickly, seeing nothing of import, danger, or use.

The dismissal both inflamed and suited her, but she focused on the latter to master the former. He overestimated himself and underestimated her, a mistake that could prove fatal.

For half an hour he and his boys threw knives into a wooden target, taking on bets from all comers. He was good; his blades formed a steel flower in the bullseye, and those taking his challenge paid a high price.

Drinks came. He quaffed a foamy tankard in half a gulp. When he banged the mug down on the table, Reena entered the dining hall from the direction of the kitchen. She surveyed the room and paused, her gaze falling on the knife thrower. The hesitation alerted Briar. Her hand edged toward her sword.

Reena started across the room, shrinking into the wall and shadows. But the knifeman spotted her. With the grace of a panther he sprang across the intervening space and cut off her exit. They exchanged words, inaudible to Briar beneath the din. But the man's grasping hands made his intentions clear. Never had hands seemed so ugly! He pulled her in for a kiss.

Briar leaped up, overturning her table, sending her bowl clattering to the floor. The commotion made the knifeman pause, turn, and watch as she strode straight at him.

"Poor man," Briar said. "She doesn't return your fancy."

"You're wrong," the man said, twisting his fingers through Reena's hair and pulling her close. "When you've got whiskers you'll understand. Run along, it's past your bedtime."

"When I've got whiskers, I won't force myself where I'm not wanted."

The man's face darkened. "You're forcing yourself now."

Briar smiled. "I know. Let her go, and you won't get hurt."

The man threw back his head and laughed, deep tones edged with poison. "There's a plot behind this very inn where they bury cocky fledglings. Leave now, and it won't have your name on it."

"I've seen it. It's about your size, not mine."

Aware that the man's cronies were creeping in, Briar edged toward the wall, so she wasn't surrounded. She told herself to stay loose. It was one thing to practice with Vance or the old oak tree, quite another to fight for real. Other than her encounter with the rebels at the manse, she'd never fought a battle where one could die. Sweat formed on her palms. The room had suddenly grown quiet, the only sound coming from the kitchen—plates clinking in a washtub and someone singing to himself.

The man shoved the girl aside and his hands edged toward the leather slings holding his knives.

"Coward." Briar stepped in fast, crowding him. "Throwing darts from a distance. Let's see what you can do with that." She nodded toward the rapier at his side. At the same time she drew Reena away from him.

The man squinted with evil intent and unsheathed his sword. Briar's was out in a flash. Customers pushed tables and stools aside, clearing space. Then the man struck with a barrage meant to dispatch his opponent in a few swift motions. Mindful of Vance's lessons, Briar focused on defense, using the first exchange to study her opponent's style. In the first flurry she saw all that she needed. He was self-taught but clever. Doubtless his technique grew from experience, picking up tricks from opponents and forming some of his own with a crafty brain.

The motions and rhythm of his attack were meant to confuse. She saw them all coming and realized with certainty that she could kill this man, leaving her strangely cold and empty.

Because he was unschooled, she unleashed an unschooled attack of her own, to drive him back and make him think he was dealing with a novice. Then and only then would she resume her disciplined style, honed from hours of practice in the firelight of her cave, exercise that left her gleaming with sweat despite the winter cold—and with muscles of hardened steel.

Confidence spread across his face. "There's the door," he said, delivering a ferocious attack. "Go home to mommy while you can."

Briar parried and returned a double thrust. "Not until you learn manners when you address a lady."

"That tart? She's had a dozen men."

"I think not, else you wouldn't have to force her. Unless that's the only way you can get a woman."

Anger and outrage flared in Briar with the same heat she felt toward the queen. And why not? This was someone strong riding roughshod over someone weak, for his own gain. She wanted to wipe that smug expression from his face, to make him feel what it was like under someone's boot.

The ringing of their swords filled the room.

Two of his comrades crowded near, trying to slip behind her. Briar was torn. The wall offered protection from a rear attack, but hemmed her in and didn't allow for the retreats her technique accustomed her to. So she followed when he backed away from the wall, taking the battle deeper into the room, allowing herself to be surrounded. This wasn't about her own neck. Reena's safety came first. No help would come from the onlookers. They watched as though this was a match between pit gladiators, and a weasel-faced man had started taking bets.

Briar shifted and glided, moving in and out of range, but always rotating the fight like a wheel so that she could watch his cronies. She marked all but one, lurking somewhere behind her.

"Eighteen notches, boy." Her opponent tapped his sword belt, where slanting strokes scarred the leather.

"None of them will stop my steel from running through your heart."

His eyes flashed with mirth, and the confident grin widened, exposing tobacco-stained teeth. Briar noticed a weakness in his form, a dropping of his guard after feinting, and wondered if it was a trick. She decided on caution. Better to watch and see if it was a ploy.

The tide of battle was taking her deeper into the room, leaving Reena vulnerable. But Briar parried and defended with ease, and she was dictating the pace now, driving him back, leaving him off balance and focusing on defense. Perspiration beaded his brow. She could hear the hiss of his breath as he strained for air. The end was near. The arrogance on his face started to erode, and his eyes widened in the recognition that he was outclassed, with no quick road to victory.

Desperate, he leaped on a table and then kicked off, sending it flying toward her. He grabbed a tankard of ale and flung it at her eyes. He overturned stools and chairs. She dodged them all neatly and pursued him with relentless blows.

The innkeeper entered from the kitchen, scowling, brandishing a club. Reena's father rushed through the front door. One of the cronies grabbed Reena, and she screamed.

Back on a table, the knifeman leaped off and charged at Briar, backing her up. Her foot slipped on a portion of the floor, shiny with grease. Thrown off balance, she was forced to defend.

But his guard dropped, and even as she retreated she lunged for the opening to his heart. Before her blade struck home, pain exploded in her head.

The room tilted, spun, and faded from sight.

CHAPTER TWELVE

*P*ounding at the back of Briar's head roused her from darkness. The to and fro brushing of a curtain came from her right, bringing with it a cool breeze bearing the fragrance of fertile soil. Someone stirred nearby. A moment later the aromatic scent of pipe smoke drifted over to her. She opened her eyes and took in a small room, dim in the light of a single candle that was strangely steady in the wind. The candle sat on a table of simple workmanship and threw the warm shadow of a man on the wall. Seated on a wooden chair, his expression might appear placid but for worry crinkling his brow. Briar couldn't place him, though he looked familiar. He and everything else of the past hours —or were they days?—whirled in confusion: strange faces, a girl, a fight, a man with a black patch over one eye.

She tried to rise from the narrow bed, and a sledge-hammer wreaked havoc inside her skull. She reached to the back of her head and found a bandage, slightly damp beneath her hand. When she looked, her fingers glistened with the faint stain of blood.

The man pointed with the end of his pipe. "Best stay put."

Briar lay back, and the pain subsided somewhat. "I know you."

"My daughter and I picked you up a few miles south of Tubney. I'm Juniper, Juniper Donyman."

It all came flooding back to her: meeting the farmer and his daughter, eating at The Comb and Tap, the sword fight.

"What happened?" she asked.

Juniper puffed away, considering her. "One of Diglan Crosse's men hit you with a pitcher. Cowards, every man jack of 'em. After threatenin' to bring the bailiff, the innkeeper and I chased 'em off. Then he helped me carry you to my cart, and I brought you here. You're heavier than you look. All muscle and whalebone. And from what I heard about the fight, nerve too."

Briar searched beneath the sheet covering her and found the linen of a nightgown. She glanced about the room and saw her tunic and breeches folded over a chair. The burn of a blush spread across her cheeks. No doubt now. Juniper knew she'd been disguised as a man.

She eased up a little and looked for her other things. Her sword leaned against one wall; her money pouch hung from the hilt, bulging as it had when she'd loaded it with her mother's silver casket. Briar knew with certainty that neither coin nor ring had been taken.

Juniper leaned forward. "My wife and daughter bathed and changed you. Your business is your own and none of ours. We'll not breathe a word."

Gratitude welled in her heart, and she tried to rise with the intention of paying him.

He removed the pipe from his mouth. "I've had my noggin hammered a time or two. Stay put a few days, take it easy, and you'll be right as rain."

She settled into the pillow with a sigh, and presently sleep overtook her. But Briar was a fast healer, and the next morning she felt able to sit and stand. She was unused to kindness and charity, and her first inclination was to leave, to not burden the family further. Besides, Mirage was out there somewhere, and though she had sent him away, she knew he wouldn't roam far. If he tried to find her, he might frighten these people, and that was no way to repay their kindness.

After breakfast, she gathered her things, but seeing her sway with dizziness as she strapped on her sword belt, the farmer urged her to stay, rest, and do nothing strenuous for a few more days.

There was wisdom in his bearing and more in his plain-spoken speech. Briar acquiesced, and from their porch, she watched them go about their work—the wife and daughter doing as much as the farmer—while Briar contemplated her plans. Without these people, Crosse and his cronies might have dumped her in a ditch, a meal for the worms. She owed them her life, and she needed to find a way to repay them, but the face of the queen still loomed in her mind, and her mission with that monarch called to her, though she was uncertain how to realize it. She had left the manse with no certain plan, only the idea that one would present itself at the right time, and still no plan had crystalized.

That evening, she offered to pay them for their trouble. They refused.

"Do you think we could take a pennig after you saved our Reena?" Joia Donyman asked. She must have looked like her daughter when younger, but where Reena was shy, her mother's smile and sunny disposition filled the room.

Briar looked to Juniper with hope, but he said, "She's right. It would be a poor kind of gratitude to take your money. No price can be placed on our little jewel there. She's the light of our lives."

Reena blushed, but she smiled at Briar. "We'd have taken care of you anyway," the girl avowed. "No one in these parts has any love for Diglan Crosse."

That settled it. After a few days Briar felt well enough to leave, but something about these people reached out and embraced her. She told herself she would leave tomorrow, and when tomorrow came, she bargained for the next day and the next. She slipped into their lives as though she belonged there, had always been there. And she relished the simple pleasure of the work: the warmth of the sun, the flash of the scythe, the lowing cows, milk squirting into pails, chickens scurrying for seeds, the threshing of wheat and barley, the scent of the soil mingled with her sweat. Days, then weeks, passed. It seemed an idyllic time, and even the humming flies carried the lazy music of eternity.

Best were the meals, when bread came steaming from the oven and slices were lathered with butter churned that day. And after the dishes were cleared, washed, and put away, they spent evenings dancing and laughing, first the farmer, then his daughter, sawing out tunes on the fiddle while Briar spun around the room with Joia or Reena. For the first time, Briar felt what it was like to be accepted in a family where she was loved, for Juniper treated her like a second daughter.

Though spring work was heavy—pruning trees, fixing fences, delivering animals, and planting cabbage, lettuce, and peas—Juniper often stayed up and talked with Briar about the sorry state of Purpura. Briar was grateful. Three years on Mount Einor had left her behind the times. The queen's war with Farfaeron was not going well. She'd promised swift victory and was now dug in—as much to save face as for victory. Everyone from the highest to lowest was bearing the price of her pride and ambition.

Briar was most interested in the resistance, the self-styled Fellowship of the Flame she'd been hearing about since leaving the manse.

"Maybe they're good, maybe not," Juniper said. "They say they're for the serfs, peasants, and slaves, but what serf or slave has the freedom to run midnight missions from one end of the land to the other?"

"They're against the queen, aren't they?" Briar asked.

"So they say. If they overthrow her, who will sit in her place? How will they rule? No one's clear on that point."

"What's their stand on the Turlian Claim?"

"The Fellowship? They support their brother rebels, I suppose. Why wouldn't they? They both fight the queen."

"Then the blackened lands, the burned houses, the ashes of people's lives scattered across the border—both groups lay claim to that."

"So it seems. I've little time to ponder it." Juniper lit his pipe and blew a gray stream toward the ceiling. "It all can go spinning around me. The land must be worked, or my family starves."

"What about Diglan Crosse? Is he in the Fellowship?"

"Hardly. He cares for no one but himself. He sells his sword to the highest bidder and calls dark alleys his home. I'm of the opinion that he and his boys hold up travelers on the road, from time to time. But like all snakes, he prefers slitherin' in the shadows. Stay away him from if you can. He'll croon to you by day and slit your throat by night."

The turn in the conversation gave Briar a chill, and she guessed that Crosse rather liked throwing his daggers from those shadows. It came as a surprise, then, that he showed up at the farm one day. She'd been folding manure into the soil of the north field. When she returned to the farmhouse, she saw Crosse talking to Juniper across a nearby fence.

Her first instinct was to charge between them, her sword

out and itching to complete what it had started. But if Crosse knew the family harbored her, it might put them in danger. Still, she would keep a close eye on the conversation, and if necessary, come to Juniper's aid.

Before she was seen, Briar ducked into the barn and peered at them through a knothole. Crosse sat his horse with one leg thrown carelessly over the saddle. The smile creasing his lips made Briar clench inwardly. Juniper stood his ground, his crossbow leveled at Crosse's heart.

The knifeman lifted a placating hand. "That's downright unfriendly, pointing that thing when I've come courting that pretty daughter of yours."

"She's not interested," Juniper replied. "March yourself off my property pronto, or I'll show you what this can do."

"Easy, partner. I've no quarrel with you. Can't a man pay his respects?"

"Where he's wanted. You're not." The farmer jerked his weapon, signaling it was time to move along.

Crosse ignored him and scrutinized the fence, which had recently been repaired, and the garden, free of weeds and bursting with lettuce, onions, and other vegetables, all things the extra pair of hands from Briar made possible. His eyes hardened, and he leveled them on the farmer. "You haven't seen that lad, have you, the one I played that little farce with?"

"Long gone, I'm sure. Now get. And don't come back."

Crosse trotted off at a leisurely pace, whistling a tune, but the farmer sent an arrow whizzing by him that got him moving fast enough.

When Crosse was gone, Briar joined Juniper, who stood squinting across the field where the horse had gone.

"Will he come back?" she asked

Juniper hefted the crossbow. "Won't be no conversation, if he does."

"Maybe I should leave. I don't want to bring trouble."

He put a hand on her shoulder. "Come and go when you like, but don't let a rat chase you out of your burrow." He grinned. "Besides, we've got a field to plant."

Things settled back to normal, up before dawn then work long after sundown, as regular as the rhythms of nature that abounded in every breath of the orchard, every shoot that burst green and new from the soil, every calf or foal that was born. Crosse didn't show his nose again, but one gray afternoon, after a chilling rain, a greater threat trundled in a wagon down the muddy road to the farmhouse.

All morning the storm had kept them in the barn cleaning stalls, for no matter what the weather, the farm gave them no break. But they'd stopped for lunch, leaving their mud-caked boots on the porch, tramping inside to rub their fingers before the hearth, then sitting down to steaming bowls of stew.

When Juniper had scraped the last of the juices with a crust of bread, he pushed the bowl aside, his face beaming. "I got an announcement. We got an extra pair of hands comin', though they'll be little 'uns for a while."

Joia smiled while Briar and Reena stared from one parent to the other.

Reena was first to figure it out. She rushed to her mother and threw her arms around her. "When!"

Her mom cradled her belly. "Six months."

"I'll make mittens and booties and a nice woolen blanket."

Joia shook her head. "You work hard enough as it is. Anyway, I kept some of your things."

"I can do it at night after my chores are done. I want to! A baby! We're going to have a baby!" And Reena started capering around the room like a foal.

Joia would work to the last, but the baby would slow her down, and Briar started enumerating in her mind all the things she could do to pitch in. As far as she was concerned, her debt to this family was still unpaid, though she was sure none of them would agree. It had nothing to do with saving Reena, Juniper told her, when she brought it up. "It's what neighbors do. If I lose a pig, they give me their fattest one. If they lose a good milking cow, they get my best."

Juniper took his fiddle off the wall, and they celebrated the new baby with a jig. As they danced round and round the kitchen table, Briar spied someone coming down the hill toward the house. She didn't like a thing about him and stopped short.

The farmer joined her at the window. "Leave this to me," he said.

Her sword was in the anteroom she slept in, but she reached for one of the kitchen knives. "There's strength in numbers."

He glanced at her weapon. "I've dealt with him before, and we want you incognito, no?"

She couldn't disagree, and he walked out into the yard without his crossbow. She watched from the edge of the window, feeling suddenly cooped up, longing for action.

The man pulled his wagon to a stop before the farmer. He was a small man with sharp little eyes, pointed ears, and mean little hands. He wore no hat, despite the gray and dismal sky, and his hair was shaved close to his scalp. The whole way down the road he'd worn a sour expression. It didn't change now as he faced Juniper. Briar had seen his kind before. Whether her father's relationship with the queen waxed or waned, tax collectors still came to the manse, and they all looked like this man: nasty and waspish.

Juniper stood before him, legs braced apart. "You're early."

The man set his jaw and squinted at the new corral fence,

the east field ripe for spring harvest, and an enormous pig waddling into a puddle. "Things look good here."

"This isn't a social call. Get to the point."

The man turned his button eyes on the farmer. "Another payment's due."

"I just paid you."

"By order of the queen: a quarter of your crop or payment in coin. You have three weeks."

"It's highway robbery."

"Three weeks, or she'll seize the farm."

"Bad weather killed last year's crop. We've enough only for ourselves. If I pay you, we'll starve."

The man shrugged. "Have it, farmer Donyman, or find another occupation." He flicked the reins, and the wagon went bumping back up the road.

The joy of a few moments before evaporated. The next days were as grim and drear as the rain, which returned, stinging and bitter. Juniper appeared to take it stoically, but he bit hard on the end of his pipe, and when his gaze wandered to his wife's belly, as it often did, his brow wrinkled.

Reena threw herself into work, rising early, skipping lunch, and stopping when it was dark. She ate dinner almost as she fell exhausted into bed. Joia would have done the same, but no one let her, and she was wise enough in the laws of childbearing to know where her priorities lay. But she called them together, and the family talked, thinking of what they could sell. There was little to spare. What they had would not pay the tax.

As for Briar, the happy bubble she'd been living in burst. Nothing was changed. The tax collector was only the arm. Behind it was the queen. Briar seethed as hot as when she'd been driven from home into a blizzard. Her debt to this family still hung heavy on her. Now they needed her more than ever. But how would she find the money to pay the tax? The few coins in her purse were hardly enough, and the Donyman's would never accept her selling her mother's ring.

One thing was certain, she couldn't help them staying here, and a plan sprouted in her mind.

CHAPTER THIRTEEN

Standing before the great drawing room door, Skyla pressed the terrier to her breast, her heart aflutter. How long had she waited for this moment to come face-to-face with the queen of Purpura?

She glanced at the footman to her left, trying to gauge from his demeanor what kind of reception she would receive beyond the stately door. His gaze was fixed forward, his expression stony. He was too well trained to reveal anything.

Certain no man could resist her, Skyla gave her blonde locks a toss and arched an eyebrow at him. "How do I look? Ready to conquer a kingdom?"

He stiffened and reached for the doorknob. "I will just announce you," he murmured.

She laid her fingers on his forearm and felt a tremor go through him. "No one is here. No one will see. Tell me quick, how are they within? Will I compare?"

The poor man glanced furtively around. Skyla thought it a sad sort of business for the servants here, for she guessed—not just from this man's demeanor but from every other servant she'd seen in the castle—that they all moved about their work as if an invisible fiend watched them. From rumors she'd heard of the queen's sorcery, perhaps that's just what was happening.

Skyla drew a gold piece from a purse, tied at her girdle, and pressed it into his hand.

He glanced up and down the empty hall again before pocketing the coin. He probably didn't see that much in a year.

She nodded to the door. "Are the other girls as pretty?"

He looked at her squarely now, his gaze sweeping from her slippered feet to the soft locks of her hair, especially lingering on her eyes and lips. "If it's not too bold to say, miss, no lass in Purpura matches your beauty."

"La, it's never too bold to compliment a lady. What of the queen's mood?"

"She's fuming at your tardiness. Be cautious, miss."

"But you see—" She laughed gaily. "Caution's not in my nature. Announce me, good footman."

The next moment he swung the door open, stepped into the room a pace, and announced, "Miss Skyla Silsken, of the kingdom of Marendel."

Skyla swept past him. At any other time the drawing room would take her breath away. The size of it, the ornate gold-trimmed walls, the arched ceiling—painted with mythological figures and almost lost high above—were like nothing she'd ever seen before. But her attention was on the figures arranged at one end of the room: two pretty girls, perched on their seats like little society finches about to flutter away. And why not? Beside them, Queen Naryfel of Purpura regarded Skyla with a stormy brow.

Skyla tripped across the room with the lightest of steps. When she was before the queen, she curtsied. "Is it so very late? I just couldn't get my hair right. And I couldn't find Foofy's ribbon." She held out the terrier for all to see. A ribbon tied in a bow to the long hair between the dog's ears looked quite ridiculous.

The queen, eyeing an enormous jeweled ring on one of Skyla's fingers, suddenly brightened. "We're pleased to have you at whatever hour your hair dictates."

"We better not, Your Majesty. I'm afraid a tea like this might not start till suppertime. If I'm not fussing over my ringlets, then I'm fussing over gowns or sashes. Does it suit?" Skyla twirled so all could see her dress and fuchsia-colored sash, which matched Foofy's ribbon.

"Perfectly," said the queen. She indicated an empty chair. "Please."

Skyla sat, and the little dog promptly curled up in her lap. While a footman served tea and orange-brandy tarts, she made a quick appraisal of the two girls, introduced as the Orendale twins, Wilona and Lysette. Sitting with their delicate fingers folded in their laps, they were as thin and stiff in their heavy satin gowns as one of the standing candleholders in the corner. But they were comely enough, despite a touch of melancholy in their eyes.

The queen stood in sharp contrast to the sisters. She kicked her feet out before her, displaying loose breeches—which matched an airy cotton blouse—and polished riding boots.

Skyla sucked in a breath and brought her fingers to her lips in dismay. "I've worn the wrong thing." She plucked up the dog and gave it a little shake. "Naughty Foofy, you didn't tell me to dress like the queen. Next time I must come in pirate pants, just like her highness."

The dog raised a sleepy eyelid, regarded the queen a moment, and promptly fell back asleep. The queen's jaw tightened but relaxed again as Skyla played absently with the giant ruby on her finger, as if she were now imagining wearing such an outfit.

"Really, Your Majesty, I had no idea this was the style in Purpura," Skyla said.

"It isn't," the queen replied coolly.

Skyla plunged on, either reckless or unaware of her faux pas. "No? Well it should be. Look how that outfit suits your hips and shoulders."

The queen studied her, as though trying to determine if this was a compliment or an insult.

But Skyla, rotating her feet, had already moved on. "See? These silk slippers do me no good outside the salon. What if I wanted to lawn bowl?" She leaned forward, and gave a confidential wink to the twins, who stared at her as though she were either mad or very foolish. "Or if I wanted to meet a handsome count by a stream, why, they should quickly become quite muddy. Now what's the use of that? No, Your Majesty has the right idea with those boots. But of course, as queen, who's to tell you otherwise? I'm quite envious. You're smart, and you've thought it out thoroughly."

The queen's eyes sparkled. The sisters relaxed in their seats, and surely a disaster had been averted. More delicacies circled around—crab and paper-thin slices of smoked boar on wafers, saffron buns, lilac cookies—and the conversation turned from gowns to skin.

"Your complexion is perfect," Wilona said to Skyla. "And how do you get your hair to behave like that?"

Skyla picked up an empty silver dish and regarded herself in it. Pretty blonde corkscrews fell to her shoulders, framing skin that would be as white as alabaster but for the rose touching her cheeks and the deep blush of wine on her lips. Large eyes gazed back at her with the innocence of a doe.

Skyla flipped the curls with her fingers. "If I wanted them to do otherwise, I should be at a loss. Sooth, I'm hopeless with everything else. Daddy tells me I'm a bit of lace and bubbles." She giggled a he-he-he, like the call of an annoying bird. " 'Good for little, and little good to anyone,' he says. He's right of course." She laughed again.

The queen winced at the sound. "But you've come to find a husband in one of our nobles, I understand, so not totally useless."

"Well, there's that, of course, but little else." Skyla sighed. "But how am I to find one when the roads aren't safe? I hear there's a bold highwayman who hangs men and ravishes women."

"He wears a black mask," Wilona said, a dreamy look in her eyes. "Even so, they say he's handsome, with a voice that seems to sing."

"Does he really ravish them?" Skyla asked, almost hopefully. "The terrible highwaymen in my country compromise the ladies and roast the men over a fire."

"No, never a hand on any of them, though he disarms the footmen and guards with a flick of his sword."

Skyla nibbled thoughtfully on a cookie. "It would be both frightening and exciting to meet him … I suppose my future husband will have to wait. Such dangers dizzy my mind."

The queen shrugged. "He'll swing from a gibbet soon enough. Anyway, I have the perfect match for you."

Skyla clapped her hands. "You do? Oh, tell me, please!"

"The Duke of Glodwell." The queen shot a look at Wilona and Lysette. The sisters paled but nodded back with pasted-on smiles. "I shall bring him here, and you will judge for yourself."

Skyla picked up her dog and shook him. "Wake up, Foofy, I'm to marry!" But then her shoulders sagged. "Other perils stalk the countryside."

The queen's face darkened, far more than when Skyla

first entered the drawing room. "What perils?" the queen asked, her voice suddenly strained.

"Some sort of fellowship."

"The Fellowship of the Flame," said Lysette. "They operate in secret, forming bands of peasants, robbing granaries and warehouses of food and clothing, stealing gold and jewels from the nobles."

"That's a silly idea," Skyla replied. "If they hurt the nobles, who will rule them?"

The queen sat forward, her eyes cold and bright. "Don't ruffle your feathers. I'll squash them like flies. They'll dangle soon enough beside the highwayman."

Despite her confident tone, her face remained dark. She rose. "I have affairs of state to attend to. Please, stay as long as you like." With that she strode from the room, her boots ringing decisively on the marble floor.

The tea ground on. Skyla grew bored with the twins' chatter. Once or twice her chin sagged to her collar, and she roused from snoring sounds from her nose.

The third time this occurred she stood and stretched. "I'm no good to you now. I'm going to crawl into my little bed and dream of your highwayman."

With that, she swept from the room. With unerring steps she went down several flights of stairs and found the main artery of the palace. No one paid her any mind. Noble gentlemen and ladies, soldiers, guards, and servants streamed both ways in the crowded corridor. Soon she'd passed through the tall double doors leading out of the castle and was quickly walking through the city.

She paused to glance back. More a grand old mansion than a castle, the conical red-shingled rooftops and lone tower were partially obscured by fog rolling in from the bay. It was an inviting and comfortable old building that belied the beast that occupied it.

Turning away, Skyla continued through the city. The roads narrowed. The houses turned from estates to ill-kept buildings with peeling paint and sagging rooftops. By the time she turned into a deserted alley, the sun had fallen from sight, and long shadows cast a gloom on walls grimy with age.

She stopped at the end of the alley and put down the little dog. "Keep watch," she whispered.

The dog trotted to the opening of the alley and disappeared into a shadow. Satisfied that he was hidden and that no one observed her, she stepped past a jumble of old boxes, empty wine bottles, garbage, and other throwaways to a discarded straw mattress, leaning against one wall. Behind the mattress, a portion of the wall had broken away, leaving a gap large enough for her to enter the building beyond. The soot-blackened walls, the scattered rubble, and the remains of a fallen staircase told the story of a devastating fire. The building had been looted long ago. All that remained were a legless table and an armoire, too large to pass through the gap in the wall. Other than her own, no new footprints disturbed the blanket of dust on the floor tiles.

She opened the armoire and removed a lantern, which she lit. Then she quickly unbuttoned her dress and pulled it over her head. Petticoats and chemise soon followed, and she pulled off the slippers.

From a crate inside the armoire, she retrieved tunic, pants, boots, cape, a few handkerchiefs, a bottle of poppy oil, and a mirror. She put the clothes on quickly. Sitting on the crate, she took up the mirror. Her fingers slipped beneath her blonde hair and the next moment she pulled off a wig. A mane of black hair tumbled free. With one of the handkerchiefs and the oil, she began to wipe off powder and face paint. As she worked, the eyebrows went from light to dark, the skin from pale alabaster to sun bronzed.

When all the makeup was gone, she folded the gown and undergarments, placed them in the crate along with the mirror and slippers, and returned them to the armoire. A moment later, she trod like a cat up the alley to the street beyond, the little dog nothing more than a shadow in her wake.

CHAPTER FOURTEEN

$\mathcal{C}$ louds veiled the stars. The moon was a distant lamp, glowing faintly behind a curtain. All was dark silhouette, but in the dimness, a road turned through a wood. Trees gathered thickly on both sides and formed a dense canopy above. Near where the road bent, a giant rock loomed like a crouching beast. No birds pierced the silence, no wind stirred the leaves, no twigs rustled beneath the tread of a puma, if any passed through the underbrush. The night held its breath.

For a moment, the clouds thinned and parted from the moon. If anyone had been present, they might have seen a motionless figure leaning against the rock, head cocked and listening, a cape tossed carelessly over the shoulders, hair as black as night tied behind, a mask across the eyes dividing the face into light and dark. One hand rested on the hilt of a sword, jutting from beneath a tunic. The other held the reins of a horse that seemed nothing more than a deeper shade of the surrounding shadows.

To all appearances, it was a man of medium height who stood there. No one would guess this was a woman. No one would guess this was Briar, working toward vengeance.

The first thing she'd done when she'd resolved to help the Donymans was to locate Dondle with a tip from Dolly. She didn't consider it stealing. The horse simply jumped the fence and came to her as soon as she whistled. Later, after her first forays as the highwayman, she'd sent more than ample payment for his value to the owner. Though as to that, no price could be placed on a steed like Dondle.

His ears tipped forward, nostrils flaring.

"Yes," Briar whispered. "Now it comes."

Far away, a murmur rose and gradually drew near. She mounted, and the only sound was the creak of the saddle.

A rhythm like beating rain drifted to her and grew to a steady clip-clop, accompanied by jangling.

"They've entered the wood," she muttered. "It's dark … they slow—the trees are phantoms, hovering over them. They peer about, eyes wide with apprehension. The high-wayman has never attacked here, they think, but wouldn't this be just the spot for him? Yes, it would." She grinned mirthlessly.

Now the beat of hooves sounded on the hard dirt. She leaned a little in the saddle. The horse, with no signal from its rider, left the shelter of the rock and stepped into the middle of the road as a carriage rolled into view, its lanterns casting an eerie glow.

The driver yanked on the reins. The team reared, neigh-ing, their eyes rolling in fright.

Briar regarded the driver silently. He stared at her, frozen in his seat. Beside him, a guard reached for his sword. Briar lifted her finger and, with a slow back and forth motion, told him no. His sword slipped back into its scabbard.

Dondle walked forward until he was nose to nose with the team's leader, whose ears lay back in fright.

From within the carriage a man cried out, "Why have we stopped, dammit, is something wrong?"

The coachman appeared about to speak, but Briar put her finger to her lips. Her horse moved on, making almost no sound until it stopped within arms reach of the guard. He yanked at his sword. Before it was halfway from its scabbard, Briar's steel flashed out and was pinned to his heart.

She shook her head. "They're not worth it." Her words floated on the air as softly as a moth.

His sword dropped back home.

"I say," came from within the carriage. "Are you deaf? What the deuce is going on?"

Briar ignored him. "Remove your weapons," she said to the guard and driver. "Then into the trees with both of you. Run. Don't stop running. If you're within five miles of here, I'll find you."

The men hesitated, seemed to weigh the chances of two against one. But Briar pointed to the close-gathering trees, where the shadow of a great beast moved. A growl issued forth, low and menacing. With haste, both men unfastened their sword belts.

Briar pointed to the dirt. "Leave them there."

With their weapons in the dust, they took off into the gloom.

The man in the carriage swore. "Of all the confounded nonsense," he said. The carriage rocked, the door opened, a ponderous man emerged. His cheeks swelled, as though stuffed with plums. His wig sat unevenly on his head and flopped over one ear. "I tell you, man, if we arrive past midnight, I'll—" He stopped and his eyes flared when he caught sight of Briar in the moonlight.

She pitched her voice low. "Do me the courtesy, sir, of watching your language. My horse has sensitive ears." She walked her ride toward him, her sword resting on her shoulder. "How many within?"

"I … I'm alone," he stammered.

"I don't think so. Ho!" she called. "Out with you, or I'll skewer this pig and roast him."

Voices argued under their breaths within. Then a man and two young ladies stepped from the carriage. Briar recognized Wilona and Lysette, her late companions in the salon of the queen. They regarded her with a mixture of fear and fascination.

But Briar turned her attention to the man, shrinking unsuccessfully from the lantern light as the girls crowded him. Gentlemen were usually trained swordsmen, and it was her habit to appraise opponents at the outset. This man was tall, with a narrow waist that slanted up to shoulders that, while not broad, might contain power. Short dark hair topped his head, giving him a boyish quality. His nose might have been bold, but for a bulbous tip. His hand rested on a sword hilt, while he worked his jaw, drawing attention to a prominent wart on his chin.

"I say," said the fat man, "What's this all about?"

"I find myself short of coin for ale," Briar replied. "And I never seem to quench my thirst for the stuff."

"But see here, you can't stop the queen's citizens. She'll hang you from the nearest tree."

"Mayhap, but before she stretches my throat, the back of it would be quenched. Now then, let's make a small donation for the highwayman." She plucked a leather bag hanging near Dondle's shoulder and tossed it to the feet of the quartet before her. "Rings, pins, brooches, purses—nothing's too much for the thirsty traveler."

Wilona gripped the tall man's arm. "Defend us, Lord Quale." Her breast heaved, and her eyes glowed like she wasn't certain she wanted defending.

Lord Quale edged away and looked over his shoulder as though to locate an escape route.

"Good god, Wilona," said the fat man. "Careful what you say. The man's the very devil. He's spirited away the guard and driver, leaving nothing but their swords."

"But Daddy!" she complained.

Daddy pointed, and the others looked to the dust, where the swords lay.

Wilona gasped. "How…? I heard nothing."

Briar shrugged. "Perhaps they were as thirsty as I and decided to try an establishment up the road. Now then, quickly, that bag awaits your generosity."

"Lord Quale?" Wilona's voice rose.

Quale's fingers wiggled nervously. "Perhaps it would be best to do what he says."

But Lysette behind him, said, "Defend us, sir!"

At that Quale drew his weapon. "Off that horse, black-guard, and fight like a gentleman."

"If I were a gentleman …" Briar dismounted and faced him, her sword still resting causally atop her shoulder.

Quale stirred his sword in the air, as though awaiting her first move. The grip, the awkward stance, the forward position of the body spoke volumes, and for a moment, a pang of grief shook Briar as she thought of Vance's smooth lines and practiced elegance.

Quale lunged like a schoolboy, projecting his intent, so that Briar could have defended while eating an apple. Steel rang out two, three times, and then Quale's sword went flying.

"Now—to my ale coin," Briar said.

They began to deposit their wealth in the bag, but when they were done, Briar pointed her sword at the father's midsection. "I believe you would deprive me, sir."

He stepped back, but reached inside his shirt and threw

down a pouch, which jingled as it hit the ground. Briar felt no remorse. Before setting foot in the royal drawing room, she'd learned that the twins' father had made his fortune arranging the capture and enslavement of Turlians. The girls were no better, endorsing their father's plan to match them for financial gain. Briar knew nothing of Quale, but as a rule, the nobles supported the queen. This one appeared as pampered as his traveling mates.

"You," Briar said to Lysette. "Bring the bag here."

With the bag tied to Dondle, Briar told the four to empty the contents of their traveling trunks, throwing shirts, cravats, and gowns of fine silk onto a canvas sheet, which she bundled to her saddle. Then she directed Quale to unhitch the horses. With a swat on the rump, they dashed down the road, and the beat of their hooves faded away.

"But it's miles to the nearest inn," cried the father.

Briar shrugged. "Wait in the carriage."

"Good god, man, it's not safe."

"Safe? Of course it's safe. Who would rob the queen's citizens and risk having their neck stretched?"

With a bow and a laugh, she rode into the night.

CHAPTER FIFTEEN

*D*isguised as Skyla, Briar sat with the Orendale twins in the queen's drawing room. The queen had not yet entered, perhaps to drive home the point to Skyla that two could be late, and the ruler of Purpura was more important than a minor noble of Marendel. The only sign that Skyla was disturbed by having to wait forty minutes was frequent yawning and staring out the window—though she had demonstrated both behaviors in her prior visit—and listless running of her fingers through Foofy's fur.

The twins made no notice. They fluttered their fans and were full of chatter about their encounter with the high-wayman four days ago.

"I'm surprised you returned here at all," Briar said. "It must have been terribly traumatic."

Wilona clasped her fan to her heart and looked upward, as though the highwayman were grinning down on her from the chandelier. "Nay, the more I think about it, the more extraordinary he was."

Briar pulled a loose thread from her sash. "If I should ever meet this rascal I'm sure I would—I would—oh, I don't know what I would do. But I wouldn't let him make love to me as he did you."

"Oh no!" Wilona replied. "He didn't make love to either of us. But the way he looked at me ..." Her face warmed with the glow of a teenage girl swooning over the cameo of her latest heartthrob.

"The way you go on about the highwayman," Skyla said, "one would think there are no men left in Purpura. How am I to find a husband if they're all in the war?"

"Not all of them," Lysette replied.

"Good, because my chambermaid—she's quite a gossip— told me of several desirable bachelors: Count Kerrain, Lord Mouel—and what's his name? Dartee, I think it was."

"You must mean Viscount D'Arté."

"That's it." Skyla studied her fingernails a few moments before lifting her eyes to Lysette. "What of him?"

"Quite handsome," Lysette replied. "But no one knows what happened to him."

"Was he lost in the war?" A lump rose in Briar's throat. The room—which a moment before had brightened at Vance's name—dimmed.

Lysette shrugged, and Briar could get no more out of either of them. Instead, the twins chattered on about the highwayman.

The queen strode into the room. "My apologies, I was delayed by affairs of state." She cast a meaningful look at Briar. "Do go on. You were saying about this highwayman, Wilona. Was he the dashing rogue you hoped for?" The queen flung herself into her chair and slouched in it, feet thrust out, like she was already bored of the conversation.

Wilona blushed deeply before replying. "Handsome, a ferocious fighter, but a perfect gentleman. A light burned in his eyes, did it not, Lyssette?"

"If there is magic in the world, then he commands it."

Lyssette perched on the edge of the chair, her fan aquiver. "A ferocious beast aided him. That's how he disposed of the guard and driver."

The queen eyed her narrowly. "Magic? I doubt it. He probably had a confederate or two hidden among the trees. There's enough superstition among the commoners to convince them that demons haunt the woods and byways." She reached for a strawberry scone from a nearby serving tray and ate with gusto. "Anyway, we'll soon hear a more sober account. Lord Quale is joining us momentarily."

For reasons Briar couldn't identify, she felt herself stiffen. She didn't think Quale would penetrate her disguise any more than the twins had. People saw what they expected, and no one expected anything from Skyla Silsken, beyond a pretty face and silly prattle.

The queen glanced at her as though she sensed Briar's discomfort. But Briar smiled and tittered with the awful he-he-he and fluffed her doggy's fur. The queen, a line of irritation between her eyebrows, glanced at the door as it opened. The footman announced Lord Haywood Quale, of the house of Dundridge.

Quale stepped in servilely, each foot pausing as he set it down, as though he were tiptoeing into the room. Briar decided that her snap judgment of him during their nocturnal encounter was correct. He was as limp and ineffectual as a noodle. Perhaps she was unfairly comparing him to Vance—they had the same height and build. But there the similarity ended. This man's eyes shifted about the room with the insecurity of a boy entering school for the first time.

He bowed low to the queen, presenting the top of his stubby head, and held the position far longer than required.

"Sit, Quale," the queen said at last, or the fool would have bobbed on one knee a minute longer. "We were just speaking of your encounter with the highwayman. What's your opinion? Does he use magic?"

Quale seated himself, one hand on his sword hilt. "He may, the way he sent my sword flying. I gave a good account of myself, mind you. I thrust and parried and would surely have broken past his guard. A full three minutes we fought, and I could see the sweat on his forehead, glistening in the moonlight. A few more seconds and I would've had him. But my sword seemed to fly from my hand as though some force had taken hold of it. I don't believe, as I think on it now, that his sword had contact with mine at all."

He glanced at Wilona and Lysette, seeking confirmation, but both girls giggled behind their fans.

"What about a beast?" the queen asked. "Did you see or hear anything in the woods."

"No, Your Majesty. If there was anything there, it did not reach my attention, which was bent on protecting my two charming companions and their father." He inclined his head toward Wilona and Lysette. Both girls lowered their fans and smiled back, somewhat stiffly.

"In any case," he continued, "I hope you will rid the roadways of the menace so that lovely ladies may travel in the style and safety to which they are accustomed." As he said "lovely ladies" he turned to Briar and smiled. An odd look came into his eyes, wistful, melancholy perhaps, and for a heartbeat they hardened and seemed to probe her features, only to return to their former merriness. "I have not had the pleasure …"

The queen tossed her half-eaten scone on a plate. "Miss Skyla Silsken, of Marendel."

Again the servile bow, this time to Briar. Despite the man's height, he seemed to have shrunk to the size of a rabbit.

"A pleasure, miss. I hope this talk of brigands and high-waymen hasn't upset you."

"Why should I be frightened," Skyla replied, "if there are bold men to protect us?"

Quale placed his fist over his heart in the pledge of a soldier. "You may count on me to lay down my life. But let us hope the opportunity never arises," he hastily added.

Briar twiddled Foofy's fur. "Let us hope. It would be a shame to see such a gallant sacrifice himself."

He adjusted the lace around his collar. "'Tis a gentleman's duty, miss."

Briar sighed. "It's a terrible thing to see a man shirk his duty and hide behind a woman's skirts." She glanced at the twins, and they colored perceptibly.

"May you never see that nor ever be in need." Quale leaned forward, and for the first time he seemed sincere, not puffing himself up. "If he is not careful, the rogue will find himself dangling from one of her majesty's gibbets."

Wilona dropped her head into her palm. "I suppose he must be hung."

The queen shrugged. "I'm not concerned about your highwayman. While he was robbing you of a few baubles, the so-called Fellowship of the Flame looted one of my granaries —taking a large quantity of corn and barley destined for my army—before burning it to the ground."

"Right you are, Majesty," said Quale. "We can handle the highwayman."

Briar yawned. "Did you fight in the war, Lord Quale?"

Quale averted his eyes. "I would, most assuredly, but my feet are quite flat. They could not handle the strain of marching."

"Can you not ride?" she asked. "A talented sword like yours must always be needed on the front."

"Ah yes, but as her majesty noted, she must focus on this

flimflam Fellowship. It's up to us to protect the citizens of Purpura from marauding gypsies and brigands."

The queen smiled. "Not so, Quale. It's true I'm protecting my supply chain, but I'll start sending patrols out tonight to guard the highways. They'll ride in intervals. Maybe your highwayman can spirit away a driver and guard. Let him try it with six trained soldiers."

Wilona's fan froze midair. "Then ... you'll hang him?"

"Alongside the leaders of the Fellowship." The queen's eyes hardened. "Though for them I plan a special treat first. They'll beg for death before I'm through with them."

Lord Quale shook his fist in victory. "That's the spirit."

A messenger came into the room and handed the queen a note. She glanced at it and rose. "You must excuse me. Fear not, friends, Purpura will be free of them soon."

After the queen left, Wilona and Lysette tried to draw Quale into further reflections on the resistance and the high-wayman, and whether they would ever be able to travel safely again, and did he think they would ever see their precious rings and brooches, because those belonged to their mother, and father had taken to his bed after the attack, poor dear, and his gout had become much worse. They thought him quite traumatized.

All the while, Quale stole puppy-dog glances filled with longing at Briar. But Briar was yawning, an act she didn't have to work at, for the tedium of these gatherings —which had sent her flying into the fields as a girl—overtook her with as much power now as they ever had, and a terrible throbbing came from the empty place in her heart Vance once filled with the warmth of his smile.

Quale was standing, demonstrating the technique he'd used to almost disarm the highwayman, when Briar's dog suddenly scampered off her lap and through the doorway, which had opened to allow servants to bring a fresh supply of rosewater cookies and jelly tarts.

"Naughty Foofy," Briar cried, rushing across the room after him.

Quale called out, "Must you go?"

"I shan't be a moment; I'll just see to the little imp." She glanced back at him.

His shoulders drooped. "Do return soon."

Outside the drawing room, Briar spied Foofy skittering down the main hallway. She picked up her skirts and trotted after him, up a flight of stairs and down another corridor. When guards or servants passed, she giggled and pointed to the offending pet. "Disobedient puppy. I shall give you a spanking when I catch you."

But when she reached an empty hallway and followed Foofy to a partially open doorway, she whispered to him, "What have you found?"

The room had a long table and diamond shaped floor tiles. Paintings on one wall were of kings and queens of Purpura. From the artists' depictions, they were kind and benevolent, not like the tyrant who now sat near the long table. Beside her was a man with dark hair, a trim moustache, handsome features, and an eye patch. Briar's pulse quickened at the sight of Diglan Crosse, the man she'd fought defending Reena's honor. He exuded strength and confidence, though, as before, arrogance burned in his one eye. She had to admit the devil was handsome, but perhaps she wouldn't have thought so had she not just left Lord Quale.

The queen was studying an old and weathered papyrus spread across the table. Briar took the opportunity to whisper to Foofy, who trotted down the corridor and disappeared around a corner.

There was a perfect understanding between them. If anyone came, Foofy would alert her.

The queen looked up from the parchment. The smile on her face was dark and sent shivers down Briar's spine.

"Well done, Crosse."

"Perhaps you'll add a bonus in gold," he replied. "It's what you seek?"

"Almost." The queen sat and scrawled on a piece of paper. "Follow these directions. You'll find it. And Crosse? Absolute secrecy. Do it alone."

He spread his hands, palms out. "Something now, to defray expenses."

She withdrew a pouch from a nearby chest and tossed it jingling onto the table. "Double the reward if you return within a fortnight."

He bowed and turned to go. Briar scooted into a room across the way and listened from behind the door, left open a crack.

"And Diglan," the queen said. "Don't play me false."

"That's never good for business," he replied. His footsteps faded down the corridor.

When the queen didn't emerge, Briar started to leave the room, but Foofy appeared, rose onto his hind legs as though listening, glanced back at her, and disappeared back the way he'd come. A moment later, Briar heard footsteps approaching. Presently, a balding man appeared and entered the room Crosse had just quitted.

Briar crept back across the hall and listened by the doorway. She could see them within.

"Have you assessed the damage to the granary?" the queen asked.

"Ruined," the man replied. "We'll need to rebuild, top to bottom. But it's worse than that."

"What could be worse?" The queen rolled up the parchment and locked it in the chest from which she'd taken the sack of coins.

"They raided another granary early this morning."

"And the condition of that one?" the queen snarled.

"They emptied it."

She dropped into a chair, glowering. "They're smart, I'll give them that. Attack my granaries and my armies starve. My armies starve and the expansion of the empire goes ill."

"You should concentrate on meeting the needs of your people, not making war on other countries."

"When I need advice, my dear steward, I'll ask for it."

The steward steepled his hands and tapped his fingertips. "Then heed it now. Your people are starving. This Fellowship is handing out bread."

The queen stared at him blankly. "Bread?"

"All around Freyclif. It showed up on doorsteps. An unmanned table was set up in the market square, a mountain of loaves piled on it. If they keep this up, their support will grow."

His feet stirred, while she stared at a vacancy in a corner of the room.

After a period of silence, she said, "There will be no support when the people hate every last one of them."

"Hate? Not while they're being fed," the steward replied,

"They won't be fed much longer. Put a guard on the granaries, warehouses, and ports. And as for the Fellowship, I have something special for them."

"What do you propose?"

Her eyes turned frosty. "Soon, my good steward, soon you will know. And when you do, all of Purpura will hold its breath."

CHAPTER SIXTEEN

a short time later, Briar slipped through the streets of Freyclif. Fog rolled in from the sea, leaving vague lines of buildings, fore and aft, and the scent of the ocean. It thickened as she went, and once or twice she stopped and listened. It seemed that someone followed, but perhaps it was just a flag or someone's laundry flapping from a window. As she continued down a narrow lane the sound returned, a soft shuffle, as from stealthy feet.

She glanced at Foofy. He looked up at her, but did not appear perturbed. Still, she muttered a few words and he took off into the fog.

The queen's comments in the drawing room left Briar disquieted. The queen was crafty. What she shared publicly was one thing; what she planned and schemed on her own quite another. Relays of troops on the highways were meant to pacify the nobles. But the queen likely had other plans, other servants she commanded. The dashing Diglan Crosse must be one of dozens paid to do her bidding.

Was one of them following Briar now? Had she slipped? She reviewed the last two meetings with the queen. Nothing seemed out of the ordinary. She'd been careful leaving the castle and careful traversing deserted streets under cover of dark. Still, spies could be all around the castle. She would have to be vigilant in the future, and have Foofy make a full reconnaissance before they entered or exited the palace.

She stopped and listened. No sound drifted through the fog. She hurried on and turned into her alley. By the time she'd removed her disguise and changed into the highwayman's clothes, Foofy hadn't returned. She whistled softly, but still he didn't show. She had no concern that something had happened to him. He could take care of himself.

Waiting was unnecessary. He would find her, would never leave her unguarded for long. After gathering a few supplies, she started back up the alley. For the next few minutes, she slipped like a wraith through side streets, pausing, listening, for it still seemed she heard the faint echo of footsteps.

She jumped a fence and made her way through a narrow yard, thick with weeds. At the far end, a mountain of old wagon wheels and broken hitches rose into the fog. As Briar passed the heap, she heard a sound and turned back. A figure leaped from the rubble and landed in front of her. In a flash, Briar drew her sword. Mirage leaped through the fog, roaring. At the sight of him, the figure cowered against the junk pile.

Mirage, heel!

The tiger drew back but kept his yellow eyes fixed on the figure, a girl of about nine by all appearances. She wore tunic and hose—ragged, frayed, and covered with grime—and a battered yellow hat that flopped down. Her limbs were as wiry and scrawny as a monkey.

Briar pointed with her sword. "Why are you following me?"

"I bring a message. From the resistance."

"Hand it over."

The girl tapped the side of her hat. "It's in here."

"Tell it then and be gone."

"We want to talk to you."

"Why?"

The girl grinned, her teeth surprisingly straight and white. "I'm just the messenger."

"Then message this. I'm not interested."

"One meeting. That's all we ask."

Briar chuckled. "We? You're part of the Fellowship?"

The girl stood tall. "I am, as anyone with a heart would be. The queen starves us and whips us till we bleed. Maybe you've seen 'em, kids sleeping on the street, begging in the marketplace for a scrap. The queen and her ugly war are killing us all."

Briar considered these words, while the girl eyed Mirage apprehensively.

"What is it?" the girl asked.

"A tiger." No use explaining Mirage's tricks. The less anyone knew of how he masqueraded as Foofy, the better.

"Never seen a tiger before. He's trained?"

Briar smiled mirthlessly. "He's his own man, free to come and go as he likes."

"But he follows you."

"For now. This meeting—where and when?"

"You know the Shady Bone?"

"I've heard of it."

"Good. Be there in an hour."

"How will I know who to meet?"

"Look for a man in a black cloak. He'll hang one glove off the edge of the table."

With that, the girl melted into the fog. Mirage looked at Briar, asking whether he should follow.

"No," Briar said. "Let her go."

At the edge of the city, in a copse of ash trees, Briar found Dondle. As she rode, she considered the situation she was going into. The Shady Bone was a tavern on a lonely stretch of road a few miles from the capital. Its reputation rippled through the countryside as a place for desperate men, working nefarious ends. She'd thought it a prudent spot to avoid.

Now circumstances were doubly troublesome. Someone knew about her. The queen didn't seem likely. Someone affiliated with the resistance must have followed her from the castle. That presented problems, for now she didn't know whom to trust, or whether it was safe to return to the castle. She could continue her night missions, robbing nobles and playing the gnat to annoy the queen. But her primary reason for masquerading as Skyla was to learn something of Vance. All this time, she'd heard no word, found no clue as to his whereabouts. All signs pointed to her worst fears: he was dead, a victim of the queen's war.

Though years had passed, the loss still pierced her heart, and once more the rage that had kept her alive through the long cold winters of her banishment rose within her: she would have vengeance. And from what Briar had seen, no one would weep for this monarch. Her people hated her. And those who served her feared her.

The fog thinned as Briar rode, and by the time she reached a hilltop overlooking the tavern, the mist was gone. Mirage had traveled through the countryside. Though not far away, he always kept from sight. Rumor of his existence surrounded the highwayman. But as yet, until tonight, no one had seen him beyond a shadowed hulk in the moonlight.

Dondle pawed the ground uncertainly. Briar patted his shoulders. "Shall we see what the fare is like?"

Snorting, Dondle shook his head and refused to move. She knew what he meant. A trap might await them down there. The girl messenger could've been nothing more than a servant of the queen.

Briar dismounted. "Suit yourself. Don't blame me if you miss a good meal."

She started down the road. Not too many steps later she felt Dondle nosing her backside.

"That's better," she said as she mounted. But Dondle flicked his ears, his way of telling her he didn't like it, not one bit.

She let him graze in a nearby field and stepped inside the smoky interior of the tavern. The faint light of tapers flickered on a few of the square wooden tables, and she had the sensation that she was still in the fog. She discerned the outlines of a bar, wooden chairs, a stone fireplace, and embers glowing on the hearth. Her eyes adjusted soon enough. A pair of men huddled near one of the walls. Neither wore a black cloak. A plump man wearing an apron was clearing a table. He looked up as she entered. Otherwise, the tavern appeared empty. She stepped further into the room, peering into dimness. Presently the pair rose, flung down a few coins, and departed without a glance at her. Then she saw him in a shadowed corner, his face lost beneath the hood of a black traveling cloak, one riding glove hanging off the edge of the table. Candlelight barely penetrated that part of the room. Even so, he sat with his back to the tapers. It was a clever stratagem. When Briar sat, the light would be behind him. It also placed him nearer to a window, allowing him a quick exit should the need arise.

Carrying a load of dishes, the aproned man disappeared through a doorway. Briar crossed the room, her boots soundless on the straw-littered floor, and dropped into a chair opposite the hooded man. Her guess was right; shadows were layered over shadows, and she could make nothing of his features. She waited, one hand resting on the pommel of her sword.

He called the party. Let him make the first move.

At last, a low chuckle came from beneath the hood. When he spoke, his voice was little more than a raspy murmur. "You're playing a dangerous game."

"And you aren't?"

The aproned man came out bearing a tray with a tankard and two pewter mugs on it. These he placed on their table. He didn't glance at the man opposite to Briar, but his eyes took her in. "Anything else, governor?" This to the hooded man.

Her tablemate lifted his hand toward Briar. "The mutton here is excellent."

She poured ale from the tankard, sniffing it before she drank. She still didn't know where this was going; the possibility of a sleep potion or poison was remote but real. "I've eaten."

The aproned man left. Her tablemate leaned forward. "What's your goal?"

She laughed. "When do thieves need to explain themselves? As your messenger said, times are hard. She looked like she could use a meal, by the way."

"She can. As could anyone not blue blood." He continued to pitch his voice low.

"You steal from the queen's granaries. Feed her."

"Have you seen the slaves toiling under the sun and the queen's lash? They eat first."

Briar had heard of the slave camps, and from a distance had seen teams of men and oxen dragging massive blocks of granite to build a defensive wall around the castle. But her role as Skyla did not allow an inspection of the slaves' condition, and she did not encounter them in the forest where the highwayman wrought his crimes.

"How did you find me?" she asked.

"It doesn't matter. If we can, the queen can."

"Let her try."

"You don't know her—"

"I know all I want to know," she spat back.

"Then join us. We can use a good sword, a clever mind."

She drank and put down her cup. "Not interested."

He poured ale and then swirled it thoughtfully in his mug. At last he took a sip. "You need to stop. You put our missions at risk."

Briar stared at him, trying to penetrate the shroud of darkness enveloping him. "Never."

A long pause ensued. "You won't get what you want," he said.

She snorted. "I thought my motives were a mystery to you."

"She's already set her hounds on you."

Briar pondered whether to share what she'd learned from the queen's interview with Crosse. For the time being, she decided to keep it to herself. "She wants you more."

"Don't be fooled. A rogue brigand is a terrible itch to her. She won't resist scratching, won't stop until you're gallows fruit, rotting in the sun."

The air seemed to have turned cold. Briar glanced at the hearth, wishing a blaze was roaring there.

He rose. "Think on it. You'll gain nothing against her, and you interfere with our work, confuse the people we're trying to rally to our cause." He pulled the hood lower and took up his glove. "Wait five minutes. I've a cordon of men surrounding the tavern. They'll allow you to pass unharmed. But if you try to follow, it won't go well with you."

Then he melted into the gloom, snuffing out the candles as he passed.

CHAPTER SEVENTEEN

On a cold autumn morning, a man stood in a cart, hands tied behind his back with a rope that cut into his wrists. The cart trundled along—two horses drawing it—accompanied by a squadron of the queen's soldiers. Clouds cast a pall across the sky. A few peasants lined the muddy road, a little-used byway with heath and boulders on both sides—a rough country good for little but to reach somewhere else.

Despite the desolate landscape, the soldiers, a grim lot, glanced apprehensively about and gripped their halberds, a testament to the daring, courage, and tenacity of those they feared.

If the man in the cart was concerned, he didn't show it. He stood erect, gazing ahead. A light burned in his eyes, such as seen in one who looks beyond a short existence, who sees the long pattern of pavement stones stretching far behind and far ahead, who knows with certitude that whatever happens this day, others will follow—and the march of many feet will stamp out a way to a land where the sun shines bright, even if now blood must sprinkle the dust.

The soldiers and even the captain of the guard looked upon him with awe, for no one can gaze upon a man who bears himself with iron conviction and not feel dread and wonder.

The procession passed into new terrain, fields where serfs—lean, hungry looking women and men—reaped hay and piled it in mountains. They paused in their work and collected at the roadside to watch, their faces inscrutable as they peered at the stony visage of the condemned man, who looked only onward, as though the thunderheads had parted and he beheld a sun-drenched land rich with the fruit of the soil.

The road turned from the fields and passed into a little dell, with close-pressing trees and overhanging boughs. Now the soldiers gripped their weapons tight and peered apprehensively into the dense green about them. If any attempt were made to free their cargo, this would be the place, and in truth, the man standing like a god in the cart appeared to smile.

The first to fall was a soldier to the right of the cart, an arrow clean through his neck. The next moment, cries filled the glade. Men swung from the trees. Horsemen charged in, cutting off escape fore and aft. But the queen's soldiers were trained and seasoned. And outnumbered the small band attacking them. They raised their shields. Their captain barked orders. And soon they were charging, sending the would-be liberators flying into the trees, at least, those that survived. A dozen of them lay slaughtered in the dust, and those that lived and tried to crawl away, were executed on the spot. This was not done out of malice. The queen had personally ordered it, should an attack occur.

After seeing to their own wounded and dead, the procession continued on, until at last, it came to a sole tree overlooking a lonely field. No peasants labored there. No abodes overlooked the spot. No travelers journeyed on the road. Such was the wish of the queen that here, in this place that time seemed to have forgotten, this leader of the Fellowship of the Flame would be executed with no one to see, no one to mourn, no one to cry out in grief and anguish.

He was taken from the cart to a gibbet beside the tree. His expression never changed. To those watching, there might have been a multitude surrounding him, a roar of protest sounding, such was his manner—placid, but never losing the fire in his eyes.

In truth, only buzzards, gliding in lazy loops above, witnessed what passed, and after the deed was done and the soldiers marched on, they began a slow circling descent.

Perhaps witnesses along the road spread the word, or perhaps it was the soldiers—awed by the ardor in the condemned man's eyes—that passed on rumor of what occurred, but the tale spread quickly to every corner of Purpura.

Some saw it as a message from the queen: this is what befalls traitors. Others saw it as a call to rise up.

Whether the ranks for the Fellowship swelled with new recruits is unknown. But that redoubtable organization retaliated with fresh attacks on the queen's warehouses and granaries. Her majesty, outraged at the defiance, was not finished. She levied a terrible tax on wheat, rye, barley, wine, and other foodstuffs, until all of Purpura groaned under the weight of it. She issued a proclamation: stand with me, dismantle the Fellowship, string every last one of them up on the gallows, man, woman, and child—for it reached her ears that even children were used on missions against her—and you shall eat. Defy me, and you shall feel the wrath of Purpura on your backs.

And the people answered. Where the condemned man had hung, a torch burned. Where men had been slaughtered in the dell, a flaming brand stood. Others took up the symbol and it spread like a wave across Purpura. In the secret hours of the night they stole across the land: weavers, tailors, and those who threshed flax for thread, bakers and barbers, cobblers and cartwrights, millers, plowmen and potters, farmers and furriers, yeomen and drapers, servants and serfs, and even the lowly gong farmer scouring the privies. These, the toiling souls from every corner of the land, left torches burning like beacons, like the brightest stars in the heavens. They shone along roadsides and hilltops, in fields and atop gibbets, for while there is darkness, there is still a light that cannot be extinguished.

From a tower window high in the queen's castle, she looked out as, one by one, spots of light appeared all over Freyclif, down along the harbor, in the slave shantytown known as Desperation, and out upon the foothills and knolls beyond.

She threw back her head. And those in the castle that heard swore that a fiend bellowed and gnashed its teeth in the highest chamber.

aryfel's boots sounded strangely hollow on the stairs leading to the castle's tower. Her mind kept straying to the drawing room. The Orendale twins had each other, and soon someone would snap them up. That silly Skyla would go even faster, if not to the duke then to that spineless Quale, who would adore and fawn over her. Even the male servants couldn't help but look with gooey eyes at the child when they offered her sweets. Whatever her want in brains, the girl would never lack for rich and hand-some lovers. And such would satisfy her.

With a frown, Naryfel paused at the top of the stairs, a hand at her chest. She puzzled over the feeling there. If she was honest with herself—she prided herself on being ruth-lessly so—she would have to admit she'd borne the sensation many years.

"Loneliness. That's what it must be."

There was but one thing to do, she decided, and she stiff-ened her back. She could satisfy physical needs at a whim, and on occasion did so, discarding paramours as easily as stale bread. Diglan Crosse would do, if she were looking for that. But no, that would not fill this hole inside. She needed an equal.

Since none existed, she banished the notion from her mind and stepped briskly into the tower. A minute later, a servant entered with a box. She took it from his hands and dismissed him, bolting the door. No one was to see what she did here, not even the steward. Perhaps especially the steward, who challenged and thwarted her at every turn. No matter. There was nothing he could do as long as she operated within the parameters of the law. What she did tonight, then, was not for his eyes. Not that it was outside the law, though perhaps it was, but because no one need know until she was ready to offer a little demonstration.

She put the box on a long table, where beakers of various sizes were suspended over candles. Bubbling came from within the glass vessels, and liquids of various hues emitted steam, carrying an odor like rotten eggs that drifted out a window. On the hearth in the corner, a low fire crackled beneath a pot, and more steam curled up the chimney. In another corner, a small collection of black leather-bound volumes leaned on a shelf. A book lay open on the table, along with several crumbling and faded parchments.

Naryfel opened the box and one by one removed and examined the contents: spider-tongue root, hellebore, crypt lichen, and various other roots, herbs, and evil gemstones. These she placed in the compartments of a specimen cabinet, taking care to label each tiny drawer. However, she retained several ingredients for her current use, setting them out in a row. Beginning with the herbs and roots, she ground each into fine powder with a mortar and pestle, from time to time assessing her work to determine the consistency of the grind. When she was satisfied, she stored several of these in a marked drawer, but retained one that she carried to the kettle at the fire. These things needed to be precise. With a measuring spoon, she sprinkled the powder into the pot. Immediately, the steam turned black. She stepped back, a little daunted, but soon the color dissipated, and she took up a large wooden spoon and stirred, her eyes closed, all the while muttering words of dark enchantment.

Words alone were not enough: she focused on her goal and on hate, letting them flow like ingredients into the potion. The room disappeared from her mind. The spoon was a great broom, and she saw it sweeping across Purpura, sending her enemies flying like dust.

A horrid stench spewed from the kettle, but slowly it faded. When she could no longer detect any odor, she stopped stirring and ladled out a single cup of the mixture, like stew swimming with islands of fat. She deposited the brew into a silver bowl and then added several drops of a tincture from one of the beakers. All the while she muttered a strange chant, an incantation in a language long forgotten.

Slowly, like ink, a black shape rose from the bowl, spreading out into the vague form of man, but with no surface contours, no features, no reflection of light, as even obsidian might cast. The room seemed to darken, as though some of the radiance from the candles had been absorbed.

More invocations poured from her lips, and she made a motion with her hand as though she were directing the flow of air. The phantom floated across the room—a low screech, barely audible, going with it—and then descended on the fire. The flames sputtered and winked out. But a moment later they shot back up again and the specter evaporated with a shriek.

Naryfel stared, her brow furrowed and dark. Slowly, her fingers curled into a fist, and she slammed it down on the table, sending the beakers flying and shattering onto the floor. The resulting steam rose up and enveloped her. Dizziness overtook her, and she seemed to wander, lost. But then fresh air blew in from the window, and she dropped into a chair.

Never one to accept defeat, she was soon up again. She boiled water on the hearth and brewed tea. When it was strong and dark, she sat in her chair, stirring and stirring, and then took up one of the dusty volumes beside her. She thumbed through the text, running her fingers down the pages, searching.

Not finding what she sought, she took up one of the decaying parchments. A word there had crumbled away, but she guessed what it was. That's what she needed. That and only that. If all went well, Crosse would bring it.

CHAPTER NINETEEN

*A*t Juniper Donyman's farm, Briar was up and pacing before dawn, her mind a jumble. Her thoughts kept returning to her encounter with the Fellowship of the Flame, first the little girl—as hard and determined as Briar had been as a child—and then the man hidden in the shadows of the Shady Bone. Both left Briar unsettled. The past years she'd had a single focus: vengeance on the queen. Then why not join the resistance? Didn't they share the same goals? But what were the Fellowship's ultimate objectives? What was their stance on Turlia? Were they to blame for the destruction of the manse as much as the queen, forming alliances with the Turlian rebels?

These questions seemed unfathomable. Briar liked simple and straightforward—something she could run a sword through. Nothing about Purpura seemed simple. Vance could have teased it out; it made Briar's head ache.

But alone, what could she really do? She had no illusions about overthrowing the queen. She could interfere, weaken the queen in small ways, and mock her. Naryfel was just the kind of person who would react to such things. Underneath, she was a spoiled child, unused to being thwarted, to not getting her way. Any little setback ignited rage. She could not stand defiance, disagreement, or opposition of any kind. She expected obedience. The highwayman should have gotten under her skin. But she seemed indifferent, her sole focus on crushing the resistance.

At least, that's how Briar saw it. The man in the Shady Bone saw it otherwise and had urged caution. The queen did not like to show her hand, he'd said.

The man was presumptuous, almost scolding in the way he spoke, suggesting Briar was being rash and foolish, treating her like a child. Briar clenched her fist. She didn't need his advice. She could take care of herself.

But there was more to it. It wasn't just his ironclad conviction. She sensed that he possessed such conviction not only regarding her, but all things—as though he possessed an inner compass that guided him infallibly—and it filled Briar with disquiet.

No closer to resolution than she'd been an hour before, she gazed out the window. Night gave way to gray. Reena was a silhouette, crossing the yard for her morning chores. Pots clattered in the kitchen as Joia prepared breakfast, humming a little nursery rhyme and pausing from time to time to rest her hand on her belly. Juniper was already in the fields, harnessing an ox to till the soil.

These were good people, feeding her, giving her a room when she'd recovered, letting her come and go as she pleased, without question. After one foray as the highwayman, she'd left an anonymous donation to cover the queen's farm tax. Juniper wasn't fooled, but said nothing. He refused to take more than a few pennigs for room and board, though Briar sometimes tried to repay him by feeding and currying the horses, and seeing to other odd jobs about the farm. She would offer more, but Skyla's hands must be free of cuts and scrapes, though those same fingers, if anyone looked closely —as that damnable man in the Shady Bone would, if he saw her in daylight—they would see calluses from years of swordplay and living in the wild.

Restless, Briar took another turn about the room. She needed to do something. The highwayman worked at night, Skyla by day. Soon the afternoon would come, bright with promise. And time for another trip to the queen's castle.

***

Sun streamed through the windows as Briar, ringletted and ravishing as Skyla, tread lightly along on slippered feet down a castle corridor. A servant glanced at her apprehensively as she passed. Well he might. This was the area of the castle the queen used for private business.

"Have you seen my little terrier?" Briar asked him. "The naughty thing ran this way, I'm sure."

The servant pointed down the hall and then hurried on without a backward glance. Whatever his errand, he was no more welcome here than Briar.

She stepped to the end of the corridor, which terminated at a long hallway running perpendicular to it. She lingered a moment, watching, waiting to see if anyone traversed from either direction. Satisfied that the area was deserted, as it had been on prior visits, she retraced her steps and stopped at a door just up from the queen's audience chamber. The door was locked, but in a few seconds she picked the lock with a small file and entered the room beyond.

It was little more than a closet, and dark except for faint light coming through a pane of glass set into one of the walls. After shutting and locking the door from the inside, she stepped to the glass. It afforded a view into the queen's audience chamber. Briar had discovered it quite by accident as she wondered one day if she might hear anything from an adjoining room. She could only conjecture on how or why the spy room was there. This didn't seem like something the queen would want, though perhaps she used it herself to observe people she might deal with. More likely, a prior ruler had deemed it helpful to have such a chamber, and now it was something the queen kept secret and locked for her personal use.

In addition to the glass, the room had another curious feature. A system of vents carried sound from the audience chamber to the spy room. Though speech sounded a bit muted, every word was intelligible, and Briar had listened here once or twice before.

As she'd hoped, the queen was already within, studying an ancient parchment, perhaps the same one Briar had seen before. Someone knocked, and the servant Briar had passed earlier entered, bearing a tray of refreshments—a decanter of wine, sliced pears and apples, and cheese.

"Diglan Crosse to see you, Your Highness," the servant said.

"Show him in," the queen replied, without looking up from her examination of the parchment.

The man bowed, and presently Crosse swaggered in.

The queen eyed him as he entered. "You've a spring to your step, Crosse. Does that mean you've found what I want?"

Crosse poured himself a glass of wine and downed half of it. "The next best thing." He paused, smiling at her, evidently relishing that he could play with her a bit.

"Don't mince words. What've you got?"

He smiled. "It's coming."

Her face darkened. "I told you to trust no one with it."

"The owner wouldn't release it. Seems he wants assurance he'll be paid."

"You had the money."

"But not the face. Mine disturbed his confidence." Crosse snickered, and the handsome mask he wore slipped off. Briar saw him for what he was—a soulless heartless sword for hire that would sell his own daughter if it profited him.

The queen laughed. "Even a bag of gold can't overcome a black heart."

Crosse tossed a pear slice into his mouth. "Seems not. Anyway, he's coming."

"When?"

"One week hence. You might want to secure your roadways. Your highwayman may prove a problem."

She pondered that. "Are you still in contact with the owner?"

"By carrier pigeon."

"Good." She spread out a map of Purpura and waved Crosse over to the table. "Do you know Rimril Road?"

He nodded. "Little used. No reason for the highwayman to loiter there awaiting riches."

"Nor the resistance. Have him take that route. When he reaches our border, send scouting parties through the area to make sure it's clear. Be discreet, but never far from him. If an attack comes, they must squash it. And Crosse ..." She fixed her gaze on him. "If anything goes wrong, kill him and bring me what I want. I'll pay you double."

Crosse sipped his wine. "I may just kill him anyway."

"If you thought you could, you would've already." Her eyes turned cold. "Don't fail me, or you'll end up dead yourself."

He tossed down the rest of his wine and laughed uproariously. "The price of dealing with the devil. What do you need the damn thing for anyway?"

She studied him a long moment, then shrugged. "It won't be a secret much longer. It's the missing ingredient I've sought for years. The Nyctarix. With it I'll brew something neither the resistance nor its supporters can contend with."

"A weapon of some kind?"

"You might call it that." She gazed off, her eyes aglow, as if she were seeing it already.

CHAPTER TWENTY

*B*riar spent the next days riding the Purpura stretch of Rimril Road. Deep cart ruts, narrow passages, trees and thick underbrush that hemmed in from both sides—in combination with the desolate countryside, where no farms, orchards, or pastures existed—made the way little used. The road itself was in disrepair. At times it was washed out from countless floods; at times bridges had crumbled away. In the latter instances, drivers had to walk their horses across a dried streambed, for while winter was in the air no rains had yet drenched the thirsty soil in this part of the kingdom.

A bridge might have been the perfect site for Briar to hold up the carriage, but they were all built in open country, where she and Mirage would have little place to hide. A patrol could easily spot, track, and chase her down.

Instead, she found a location in dense woods, not that she liked it any better. Though it seemed perfect for a surprise attack, the dense stand of trees filled her with foreboding. She tried to shrug it off, but in the waning daylight, the stooping trunks and twisted branches, with long beards of lichen hanging down, looked like witches reaching down to snatch her. Sticky spider webs clung to the limbs, and more than once, as she awaited the arrival of the carriage, she killed a weaver the size of her hand, descending from above.

The redeeming quality of the spot was that, unlike farther ahead and behind, the undergrowth thinned. For someone on the road the mass of saplings, shrubs, vines, and ferns appeared to be an impenetrable barrier. But where Briar stood, and across the road from her, the brush gave way to a maze of paths, probably laid down over the years by deer and other forest animals. As a result, Briar and Dondle had a secure place to hide on this side of the road, which she could make out through the foliage. At the right moment, he could jump the brambles. As for Mirage, he would scour the territory for sign of the queen's patrol, as he was doing now, and would leap in and warn her, if necessary.

The waning sun left the wood dim and ghostly. Through the leafy canopy, clouds burst into flames. When orange and pink gave way to a hue like blood, Briar heard carriage wheels and the jangle of harnesses, for a trick of the trees left all hushed until the carriage was almost in sight.

Four white horses appeared around a bend, trotting at a leisurely pace and drawing a long-distance coach, bouncing and swaying and covered in dust. The driver looked warily at the gathering trees, his fingers wrapped around a military horn. Another man sat beside him, and even in the gloom Briar recognized Diglan Crosse. He sat with arrogant nonchalance, his feet thrust out, and he was singing a little tune. Nonetheless, his hand rested on his sword hilt, and his daggers were ready for a quick draw beneath his arms.

Briar backed Dondle up, and then he charged forward and leaped over the brush. As he landed, another horseman sprang over the shrubs on the opposite side of the road. He was hooded and dressed in the uniform of the queen's patrol.

Where's Mirage! All Briar could think of was that he must be trailing a patrol elsewhere in the woods. Perhaps a small contingent had split off to protect the carriage.

Whatever the reason, Briar had little choice. Sword out, she charged at the opposing horseman. His sword flashed from its scabbard.

The driver lifted the horn and blasted a note that would summon the dead.

Crosse was yelling, "Drive! Drive!"

Briar's sword swung in a wicked arc that would terminate at the horseman's shoulder. Her one thought was to dispatch him as quickly as possible, though she had no desire to kill him. She'd encountered one or two of these patrolmen before. They were ill trained and knew nothing of the fine art of dueling.

To her surprise, the man caught her blow with his blade. With a deft motion of his wrist he almost dislodged the sword from her hand.

"You make a terrible mistake," he cried, as she rained a torrent of blows on him. "This isn't your territory."

"My prize is wherever I take it," she replied, and thrust and double thrust, trying to break his guard, which seemed as impenetrable as a shield. This was no farm boy conscripted for the queen's use, but a seasoned fighter, and Briar guessed she'd run into another highwayman, though none were known to her. Perhaps she'd inspired a copycat.

"You pick a strange spot to profit by," he said. He was tall and lean, and tensile strength and suppleness spoke in the fluid motions of his arms, in the subtle twists and turns of his body. He was nothing more than the shadow of a tree swaying in the wind as he turned his ride left and right, presenting sharp angles and no good target for her to strike.

"Then you won't mind leaving the sorry pickings to me."

He retreated from her onslaught, drawing her to his side

of the road, and suddenly, to her dismay, she heard the coach slip past behind her.

"It does you no good," he said. "Leave it to us."

Briar was tired of the debate. The prize was getting away!

Reading her mind, Dondle wheeled and dashed after the coach. They could fight over the spoils later.

No horse could match Dondle's speed. He seemed to gather the ground beneath his hoofs and draw the carriage back to him. When they were alongside the rear wheels, Briar leaped from her saddle. For a moment she could see through the window, where a man in a gray robe cowered in a corner, clutching a jeweled casket to his breast. He gripped a curved knife with a giant sapphire on the hilt, and Briar had the impression of eyes drawn to slits.

She caught the top edge of the coach. The idea of flinging open the door and seizing the casket flicked through her mind. She dismissed the notion the next instant. With the horseman without, along with the driver and Crosse, she'd be caught like a rabbit in a trap. Instead, she swung to the roof.

The coach careened down the road, bumping, bouncing, threatening to shake her off. She teetered her way forward. All the while the coachman numbed her ears with blasts from his horn, and suddenly Crosse rose up and turned, knife drawn.

"Think you can stop me with that pin?" Briar laughed, and thrust her sword forward to demonstrate her longer reach and the inadequacy of his blade to reach her. Crosse grinned in reply, and his eyes glinted with deadly intent.

Horsemen of the queen's patrol leaped the brush on one side of the road. Another group of them vaulted in from the other side.

The hooded man was riding alongside the carriage now. He called up to her. "Jump! Jump while you can!"

Distracted by the arrival of new fighters, Briar missed the quick movement of Crosse's hands. When she turned back to him, his knife was up, and the next instant his arm snapped like a whip. In the dull light the blade was a blur. Briar twisted. If she hadn't, the knife would have sunk into her heart. It struck her shoulder instead. She tottered to the side of the carriage. There she swayed, with Diglan Crosse, grinning, stalking forward, another knife already in his hand.

She tried to lift her sword. It felt as though it had grown to twice its size. Something hot and wet was blossoming beneath her tunic. She tipped and crashed to the ground, white-hot pain shooting through her.

Then there was yelling. The clang of swords. The blur of men and horses straining against each other. The carriage fleeing down the road. And the face of the first horseman appeared above her, hood flung back. His features swam before her, two of him, three of him. They blurred and merged together, and for an instant it seemed Vance gazed down on her, his brow knitted.

A warm thought rose up: Vance had come to lead her to the land of the dead, where they could abide together.

The world was dimming. The man picked her up in his arms. Now she saw the difference. Vance but not Vance. For the horseman's face was thin and careworn, and Vance's golden curls were missing.

A terrible roar sounded. A white and black blur streaked from the trees.

"Heel, Mirage," she muttered, her strength ebbing fast. "Heel …"

Everything faded.

PART THREE

CHAPTER TWENTY-ONE

*P*ain brought Briar back to consciousness. The horseman was bending over her, drawing Crosse's knife from her shoulder. Dark figures huddled around her. She tried to rise.

"Don't move," he said in a hushed voice. "You'll lose more blood."

She sank back down, head swimming. For a time, she passed in and out of consciousness, with vague impressions of being tied to a litter, of being carried through the night by a band of grim men, of rain falling in dismal curtains.

Then they were camped beneath a rocky outcropping. A fire crackled nearby. The huddled bodies of sleepers were scattered about, rolled in blankets. A lone sentry was silhouetted against a backdrop of drizzle.

She attempted to lift onto her elbows, but weakness and searing pain in her shoulder pulled her into darkness.

When next she awakened, all was white. She felt hot and chilled and hot. A woman knelt beside her, and Briar thought she was back on Einor in the blizzard, and the spirit people had come to help her. All else—her career as an outlaw, her time at court—was a dream, a delirium born of hunger and weakness and wandering in the snow. But the woman came into focus, and Briar saw they were inside a tent.

"This will sting," the woman said, her sun-browned features rough but kind. She poured from a bottle onto a cloth and cleaned the wound. It burned. The scent of wine filled the air.

Briar drifted in and out of sleep. The times she was awake, she was on fire, her heart stampeding, her breath as shallow and fast as a panting dog.

Her wound was cleaned and dressed often. From the smell, Briar guessed yarrow and sage were being used as poultices—plants she knew well on her mountain—and later, rose petals. Her tunic had been removed and she lay beneath a rough blanket. Whoever these men were, they had left her jewel at her breast, wrapped in its handkerchief and tied onto the leather necklace.

At times she muttered and raved at visions. Despite her fever she was aware that the horseman came often and talked with the woman in a corner of the tent, the man's face obscure in the dimness of the single candle. Her nurse called him Tich, an affectionate sobriquet that meant "friend" among the peasants—revealing nothing of his identity. But from his cloak and his voice, she recognized him as the man she'd spoken to in the Shady Bone.

"The wound is red and swelling," the woman said to him with a shake of her head. "Her neck's bulging too."

"Is there anything you can do?" he asked, voice tense with worry.

"It's beyond my art. There may have been poison on the knife."

Briar could believe it. Instead of getting better, energy drained from her, as though the spirit that animated her body was ebbing away.

Shortly after this conversation, a young man with long white hair glided into the tent, his iridescent robe whispering about his feet. The woman shrank into a corner of the tent in fear. When he reached Briar he bent over her.

"Mirage," she murmured.

He smiled and took up the jewel, placing it on the wound. Then he laid his hand over it, and it began to pulse and glow. Light streamed through his fingers and warmth penetrated her shoulder.

Briar squeezed his hand. "Stay close."

His eyes twinkled, and he passed from the room.

The next period floated by as in a dream. She was aware of being moved, of traveling through a rain-veiled world of shapes that emerged and disappeared like phantoms, elusive and deceiving.

She awoke in a bigger tent. Rain pattered outside, less fiercely now. Later, when it stopped, she heard the music of a stream.

***

A breeze lifted the tent flap, and the flickering light of a campfire leaked in. The woman who'd care for Briar was gone, leaving the tent empty. She tried to rise. Pain commanded otherwise. But she was grateful to be alive and that it was not the shoulder of her sword arm that had been injured.

Her throat was as dry as a scab. A pitcher of water and a cup stood on a table nearby, but her wound thwarted any attempts to reach it.

The horseman ducked inside, his hood pulled low. When he spoke in soft tones, Briar recognized him as the resistance fighter from the Shady Bone.

"I warned you to stop," he said.

"It would've gone fine if you hadn't shown up."

He pulled up a stool and sat, still keeping to the shadows. "Because of you our quarry got away. What were you after?"

"Something the queen wanted. Small enough to fit in a casket."

"What were you going to do with it?"

"Give it to you." She laughed bitterly. "Why did you save me?"

"We don't let people die." Then in a different voice, he said, "I won't let you die," and he pulled back the hood.

"You!" Briar stared at him. At first she thought she was still in the grip of delirium. The dark short-cropped hair, the bulbous nose, the wart on the chin, identified him as Lord Quale, the buffoon she'd met in the queen's court. But the eyes were strangely different: mild, tender, bright—not foolish as she remembered—and his face was leaner and lined with worry.

He smiled, reached for the wart on his chin, and removed it. Then he stroked the end of his nose and pulled away a lump of flesh-colored putty. Then she knew. Him but not him. How the years had altered those dreamy and philosophical features, for now he bore a burden on his shoulders.

"Vance!"

He chuckled. "Two can play at subterfuge."

"You knew it was me? In court?"

"Dearest, I would know you anywhere. I knew you on the road, hooded and hidden in the night's shadows."

"Dearest! You dare call me that!" She reared up to grasp him, and if the pitcher had been closer she would have sent it flying like a missile, but a hot brand stabbed her shoulder and tore out an oath instead.

"Easy." He tried to coax her back down.

She slid away from him. "Don't touch me. Fetch that woman. I need to get up."

"It's too soon—"

"I'm going. I'll mend elsewhere." She tried to ease up, to slide to the edge of the bed, and managed to get her feet on the floor.

"Let me explain," he said.

"Oh, I see it clearly; I'm not a fool. Except to love you. All that's over." She tried to stand, and this time she swayed from weakness, and the room spun in dizzy circles. Her hand closed on the pitcher.

He caught her, kept her from falling, and guided her back to the cot. "You don't understand—"

"No," she snapped. "You don't understand. I thought you were dead, moldering on a battlefield. It tore my heart apart. All this time you could've sent word that you were alive." Her heart hardened. "That's not love. Get out. I never want to see you again." She threw the pitcher. With a graceful twist of his torso—a motion she knew well from their battles as children —it sailed harmlessly by and shattered on the hard earth.

***

The day wore on, and Briar had plenty of time to stew. It had been Vance all along. Vance on the road. Vance at court. What was his game? She couldn't reconcile any of it with the Vance she knew, who had always thought of her foremost, even when they were children, taking her punishment, finding ways to help her escape the manse because he knew she was happiest running through the countryside and with her animals. One thing was certain: he didn't consider her trustworthy, otherwise he would have confided in her, told her he was a member of the resistance.

Oh! If only he had! She would have gone to him in an instant. They could have been together all this time, compan- ions of the heart, in life, sharing the same vision for the future: a future free of the queen. Why couldn't he see that? Didn't he know what was in her heart?

But that gave her pause. What could she say about what was in Vance's heart? As she thought back on earlier times, he'd never declared his love, never expressed a single tender sentiment concerning her.

Perhaps it was all an illusion, this picture she'd formed of him, an impression as false and untrustworthy as the disguise he'd worn. Nothing more than a mask.

If Briar had been well enough, perhaps she would have left the rebel camp, and that would have been an end to it. But though her energy was slowly returning, she was still weak, and could stand or walk for short periods only.

No greater torture could have been devised for a girl always on the move and with her wild instincts, for though she was as feeble as an old woman, desire still roared and leaped in her veins. The one redeeming thing about her current circumstance was this: she couldn't stay angry forever, and little by little she went from a boil to a simmer.

Vance peeked in on her every few hours, but her response must have told him she was still too hot to touch, and he ducked out of the tent with furrowed brow and the eyes of a scolded dog.

The next day, she was well enough to walk about the camp, and on the following morning, she allowed him to accompany her for a stroll beside the stream. It matched anything on Einor for beauty, with the water chuckling over rocks polished smooth by time, with the lush growth of ferns —as green as emeralds, rearing up like miniature forests along the shores. Trees sheltered the path, and sunlight cool and sweet filtered through the leaves. Bathed in peace and beauty, the whole place seemed idyllic, a small land unto itself, floating and timeless, separate from the world's troubles.

How could she remain angry here! She allowed Vance to accompany her, ostensibly so he could catch her should she suddenly weaken and stumble; but really, all enmity had melted away, and she began to feel that old familiar flutter in her breast when he was near.

However, she wasn't ready to let him know that. Not yet. She had questions that needed answers.

They crossed a little footbridge, where she leaned against the railing and watched the water swirl and plash and toss up a fine mist, while an egret stood motionless, meditating on the magic of it all.

"Your father's well?" she ventured.

His hands tightened on the railing. "He passed two years ago."

"I'm sorry. He was a good man. I loved him dearly."

"He thought of you as a daughter."

"And your mother?"

"Never far from the other half of her sentences. She joined Patrikka in Turlia."

A sparrow whistled plaintively in the leaves. Far away another took up the call. The egret stirred, stretched its wings, and took off.

"You should have gotten word to me," she said at last.

"Word of your banishment from the manse reached me. I thought ... I thought I'd lost you. People said you perished in the snow. Once, I sent a messenger to the manse, but Dolly replied that a storm took you."

Briar pushed away from the railing, and they walked on, turning onto a new path that plunged into the trees.

"But you must have heard the manse burned to the ground," she said. "That I returned and threw the brigands out."

"I heard a tale of a wild raven-haired fury and a giant beast that descended on Turlian rebels. I could hardly credit it. And I was tied up with missions for the Fellowship." He paused, gazing down at her with those eyes—as dark and deep as two wells—that had won her heart as a child. "Still, I suspected—hoped—some of it might be true."

"But why didn't you reveal yourself sooner? Why the disguise at court and the tavern? Why the subterfuge?"

"As a leader of the Fellowship, I can't follow my heart. I must think of the men, women, and children under my command, of their safety. I needed to understand your motives and whom you supported. You made it clear that night at the tavern you weren't joining us. And ..."

She turned on him sharply. "What?"

"That you were on your own fool's mission."

"That's how you see it!" But she knew he was right. Compared with his work, hers had been rash, ill conceived—with no over-arching goal beyond revenge. It led nowhere.

On they walked, across thick carpets of moss and clover, while in the boughs above, a wood thrush trilled like a flute.

"But before the baron drove me out, why didn't you let me know of your life sooner? I would have joined you. You knew I was a pawn in the queen's schemes and bait for the duke."

He sighed. "I tried. Something always interfered."

"Not hard enough. You could've sent word."

"It wasn't the way to tell you. I can't put a word of my work in writing outside the Fellowship. But there's another reason. I can hardly admit it to myself. That ..." He paused, watching a second thrush swoop in with a twig for a nest, joining the first one. He sighed. "That if we were together in this, my love for you might interfere with what needed to be done. Now that has come to pass. I let the casket escape to save you." He turned to her and took her in his arms. "I couldn't let you die. Who knows what terrible price the queen will make us pay for following my heart."

Briar reached up and touched his cheek. The lines there seemed suddenly deeper, his eyes more careworn. "Swear you won't do that again."

"I don't know that I can." He pulled her close and his lips found her, softly at first, then matching the hunger in hers.

***

The days passed, Briar wrapped in a hazy dream. Her recovery progressed slowly but surely. Soon she challenged herself to adopting a dueling stance and took herself through a ballet of thrusts and parries. But her stamina was slow to return, and she was quickly fatigued and out of breath. Vance told her to allow time for healing, but she would have none of it, and twice a day challenged herself with drills. Day by day she lengthened her fight routine; day by day her endurance grew.

Vance was often away on business of the resistance, but when he returned, they resumed their walks. Now they held hands, read to each other, or dropped fruit into each other's mouths, lounging together as of old. At these times, they never spoke of his work but reminisced about their romps at Abunary Pond and the tales that seemed to play before their eyes in the swirling steam of Racca's pot.

"I still long to see Misty Cove and the secret cave and the Golden Gull rocking like a cradle in the moonlight," she said one day.

The strain on his face melted away, replaced by wonder. "It would have been grand," he said. "Sword fights across the deck."

"Pirate battles."

"Buried treasure in the gold and emerald sands."

Briar sank into the vision, but then it dissolved. She was seized with a sudden foreboding that the happy bubble they were in would burst, and she would lose him forever. She seized his arm. "Take me there now! Let's escape all this. No shadows. No intrigues. Nothing to separate or hurt us. Only you, me, and the wide sea before us." She took a deep breath, and it seemed she inhaled the tang of salty air.

His eyes sparkled. His face flushed with excitement, as though he saw the waves dashing and spraying against the rocks and heard the gulls calling.

But he turned toward Freyclif, the lines of worry returned, and the weight of command settled back on his shoulders.

She released his arm. Pushing the fantasy from her mind, she never spoke of it again.

At first, she was not permitted to attend meetings that took place at the camp. Some of the resistance fighters treated her with suspicion. She was certain that her interference with securing the jeweled casket was foremost on their minds, and more than one of them wore a face as wrinkled with worry as Vance's. But Falcon, the girl Briar had met in the capital, was there, and she often looked from Briar to Vance and back again with a knowing smile.

It was after one such encounter with Falcon that Briar confronted Vance.

"Why am I not allowed in the meetings?" she asked.

He avoided her eyes. "It's too soon."

"Too soon for what? A nine-year-old girl is admitted before me?"

"Everyone is tested, proves their loyalty."

"And she did?" Briar said, incredulous.

"In spades."

"Give me a chance. I'll show them what I can do."

He glanced at her shoulder.

She rotated it. "It's better daily. I'll be able to fight soon."

He beamed. "Good. When you can disarm me like you

used to, then I'll speak for you. Briar, I don't doubt you for a moment. The boldness of the highwayman, the disguises, the spying in the heart of the queen's lair, you've more than demonstrated your mettle. They should be begging for you to join us. And they will. I swear it."

This gave her encouragement. After going through her usual moves, bending her knees, thrusting, slashing, shifting her feet in the dueler's dance, she grasped the sword and took it through a series of slow motions. Because she used her whole body, pain coursed through her injured shoulder, down her arm, and radiated up her neck, making the muscles swell and burn like hot irons. But each afternoon she bathed in the coolness of the stream, and whether it was the temperature or some healing property of the water, she couldn't say, but it quickly restored her. In a few days she added lifting stones, heavier than her sword, to her routine, to strengthen both arms.

Soon she felt ready to test her recovery with a bout with Vance. This wasn't the fierce battling of old, but the kind of training sessions he'd had from his fencing masters: drilling feints and blocks, feints and blocks, lunges and parries.

All the while, she felt Mirage nearby. She knew that if he worried about her for any reason, he would come. He lurked in the forest like a shadow, though occasional sightings of a white blur stirred up wild stories around the campfires at night, and both Vance's and Falcon's gaze would fall upon her.

"He's yours?" Vance asked, during one of their duels.

Briar's blade flicked out, catching his on the haft and whipping it aside. "A friend."

"What is he? He's too large for a tiger."

She frowned. "You're going easy on me. Put something into it. Who cares what he is. All that matters is that I love him and he loves me. I would've died on that mountain without him."

"You always had a way with animals but … will he harm the company?"

"Never. He understands I'm with you now." She lunged past his guard and the tip of her sword pressed against his breast. "I am with you now, aren't I?"

He stared at her, stunned. "You're better than before."

"Good. Bring me into the Fellowship."

He nodded. "I'll speak for you tonight."

Joy rushed through her, and for a moment she felt a little lightheaded. She stood back and holding out her sword, rotated it at the wrist to offer another bout. "Now show me how you disarmed me on the road."

That afternoon, five women rode into camp. All were young and fierce-eyed, but one stood out from the others, with grizzled hair that fell in thick waves to her shoulders. Pillowy flesh draped her body, belying a foundation as solid as rock. She tossed her reins toward two men that stood gazing at her, starry-eyed. One of them sent the other tumbling so he could see to her horse.

"Who is that woman?" Briar asked Falcon.

"Irem." In awe, Falcon watched the woman duck into a tent with Vance, followed by the other women who had accompanied her into camp, longbows slung over their shoulders. "Our top leader after Makken."

Briar regarded Falcon in astonishment. "I thought Vance was number two."

"He is. But Irem streaked like lightning through the ranks. Vance insisted they co-lead. He says that she sprouted from the soil, a farmer's daughter and a farmer's mother. Makken's the lion, Vance the flame, she's the heart of the Fellowship." Falcon pointed out a pony. "She brought me that gypsy to use on missions."

Briar didn't see Irem again until late that afternoon. With the women who habitually flocked at her heels, she stepped up to Briar and, taking up her hands, plumbed her eyes. Irem's fingers were calloused, her eyes gray, with wisdom lines beginning to set in at the corners. Briar underwent the scrutiny like a soldier, but inside she felt like she had as a girl, when Racca peered down to the depths of her.

Irem studied Briar's hands, turning them this way and that, and again looked into her eyes. Finally, what might have been a smile curled the woman's lips. "Strong. Powerful," she said to herself. "Woe to anyone that raises a hand to oppose this one." She gave Briar's hands a squeeze and strode away.

Neither the squeeze nor the smile filled Briar with much hope, and she paced the camp for hours on tenterhooks. At last, she took refuge in the woods, where she and Mirage raced through the trees and the lengthening shadows until they were both exhausted.

That night Vance kissed her and whispered a few words of encouragement before going into a large tent, where Irem, her bow women, and other high leaders of the resistance already waited to debate Briar's fate.

She sat on a flat rock near one of the campfires, Falcon beside her, and waited. A few more fighters ducked past the flap, men who had fought when she'd fallen, and who had helped carry her to safety. Their faces were stony, now and before, and she never felt an ounce of sympathy or acceptance from them.

Falcon picked up an acorn and tossed it into the fire. "Don't mind them. As soon as you're in, they'll hug you like a sister. That one with the missing ear, Old Joe, he carries me on his shoulders like I was his daughter."

Briar felt a lump rise in her throat. "Everyone here loves you like you're family."

"The only one I have."

"What happened to yours?"

A shadow fell across the girl's face. "Killed. By the queen."

"I'm sorry. Who raised you?"

"Me. Out there." Falcon jerked her hand out to indicate the world.

"No one should face that."

"No one."

Loud voices rose from the tent, arguing. Vance's might have been among them, and perhaps Irem's, but the tent was some distance away, and all sounds mingled with the music of the stream.

Falcon took Briar's hand between her two small ones in a gesture that was almost maternal and just as comforting. "Don't worry, Vance won't let you down."

"Some of them don't like me. I botched their mission."

"You didn't know we'd be there. It's not your fault. Anyway, the resistance can always use another fighter, and you're the greatest swordsman in Purpura."

"Vance said that?"

"I've got eyes. So does Old Joe. And he's honest. You've got more than one friend in there."

Briar could only hope that was true, but the night dragged on, and the stars wheeled above, and little Falcon fell asleep against her breast. Arguing no longer came from the tent, but muffled voices stole across to her from time to time. At last Vance emerged with several other men and women. They shook hands, and everyone but Vance headed into the night, Irem and her companions mounting and riding off, others seeking tents and bedrolls. Old Joe winked at Briar before going to the perimeter of the camp to take up watch, and Vance stepped over to her, smiling.

He gathered Falcon into his arms. Briar followed him as he carried the little girl to a tent and laid her on a bed of animal skins. He kissed her forehead, and she rolled over with a murmur, pulling a blanket with the crossed-torch crest of Vance's family over her ears.

When Briar and Vance were outside, he led her to the bridge. The water sang softly below. Somewhere a nightjar called. The air was cool and filled with the scent of the pines.

"She's the sweetest thing in the world," Briar said.

"And the fiercest. Reminds me of you when you were her age."

"I didn't have it half as bad."

"Nor I by a thimbleful. But it hasn't daunted her spirit."

"I'm surprised the Fellowship allows children."

"For a long time, we didn't. She and others like her—what the queen calls throwaways—proved they have a place in the organization. We couldn't deny them."

"And me?" Briar swallowed, for if he said no, she knew that soon they must part, he to carry on his work, to be forever separated from her; she to go … where? Now that her sorties as the highwayman had proved a false strategy, what was left to her? Return to the manse and her addled father? Return to Einor and a life without the company of others? Or Vance? With bitterness she felt that perhaps her father's estimation of her had indeed proved true. She was a wild thing that had no part in society, doomed to live forever cut off and alone.

His eyes sparkled. "You're in. Understand, the Fellowship does more than steal food and clothing for the needy. We're an army. No single one of us can topple the queen. Our power lies in fighting as one."

"I know that now. Without discipline and organization, we will fail."

He turned to her and took both of her hands. "I know your heart and mind. And your worth. But some of the others—not many—need to trust you. Prove that you'll follow orders and you'll rise quickly through the ranks."

A gust of wind shook the trees, echoing the turbulence she'd felt all day. "And Irem? Does she believe in me?"

"She and Old Joe stood for you as much as I did."

The wind died away with a sigh, and the leaves grew still. "Then it's the others I need to prove myself to. Give me a mission, anything, no matter how dangerous, so I can show them they can count on me."

"You have more fire than any of us. Temper it, as you did when we fought with sticks, and no one will oppose you."

"Then you think I can? Tell me quick. Don't think about it."

He took her head in his hands and touched his forehead to hers. "Yes. Because whatever you put your stubborn mule of a mind to, you accomplish."

She laughed. "Where do I start? I can try to get the casket back. As Skyla I can poke around the castle without anyone suspecting me."

He pondered that. "We do need to know why she so desperately wanted it."

"I thought you knew."

"No, we got drift that something was coming, something she needed, but not the purpose," he said.

"She told Crosse it's for a weapon."

"Then we must know what it is, or we won't be able to fight it."

"Then I'm your girl," she said, adopting the silly voice of Skyla.

That settled it. But first, he told her that she needed to enter the first level of the Fellowship, so that she understood how it worked and what their goals were. Meeting after meeting followed, some all day, some late into the night. She was caught up in a kind of ecstasy. For the first time she felt that she was part of something and belonged. Whatever enmity some of the Fellowship might have borne toward her lifted away. She was one of them, and now they smiled and laughed and teased her like an old comrade of many missions. She learned of their vision for Purpura, their view of the queen, of how the struggle would unfold. Their commitment was sealed in blood, knowing that for each fighter that was lost, two more would spring forth and take up the cause.

Bleary-eyed from these talks, she and Vance would tumble into his tent, and their bodies fused in waves of passion. Afterward, drenched in perspiration, they swore never to be shut off from each other's lives again. His work was her work; and her work, the taking down of the queen, could only be accomplished with the people of Purpura beside her.

They vowed as sleep overtook them; they vowed upon awakening: companions in life, one life to share, one life for the freedom of Purpura.

So the days passed, a glowing dream, a glowing future, but chill winds from the west began to toss the trees, clouds cast a pall, and one day a bird fell dead and frozen from the sky.

CHAPTER TWENTY-TWO

Clouds raced across the sky. Geese winged south, loudly protesting the change in weather. A frosty wind whipped Briar's jacket as she sat astride Dondle atop a hill. Far below, on the main road to Freyclif, soldiers marched in a long line, like ants. The big stallion snorted and stamped impatiently.

Briar patted his great neck. "Patience, my friend. We must bide a bit longer. Battles will come. And when they do, you'll show them what you're made of."

They started down a switchback trail. Before she carried out the mission she and Vance had planned, she wanted to see the queen's army, returned from war. Near the capital, she left Dondle in his hiding place in the trees, with instructions to fly if anyone drew near. She wasn't worried. As yet, he'd never been discovered, but if he had been, he might be recognized as the highwayman's steed. Though as to that, rumor had it that the highwayman was dead. Briar thought Diglan Crosse might have started the tale, and he was welcome to the notoriety. For the time being, Briar had no need of the highwayman, and since her injury, he had retired.

As for Mirage, he was her shadow, separated sometimes by leagues, but following, always following her. He listened to conversations at the oddest places—a roadside well, a tavern, a noble's keep, a barn, a kitchen, a dining hall, all places Briar couldn't penetrate—and was a good source of information for the Fellowship. That was how she'd learned of the returning troops and the grumbling among nobles that the queen's war was costing them dearly. Juniper was right. From the lowest to the highest in Purpura, everyone paid the price for her ambition and quest for power.

At the main road into the city, Briar slipped into a crowd of onlookers and watched the troops pass with their hollow and sunken eyes, their haggard and drawn faces. As bedraggled a crew as can be imagined, they limped by, though several swung on crutches, propelling forward on one leg, the other left behind on a battlefield. Their uniforms were torn and stained with grime and blood. The queen's insignia was faded or rubbed out from their shields, and the metal dented. Their swords were notched, their sandals tied on with bits of yarn, rather than leather. Many wore no sandals at all.

Here was the queen's army. Returned from victory? It hardly seemed so, but of course, the official proclamation would be that they'd sent the enemy running from the field. But the overriding impression was this: war was expensive, and the queen was struggling to keep it up.

Briar turned away and hurried through the empty streets —the population gone to see the returning soldiers—and for the first time she questioned her long-held passion for fighting. There was nothing romantic about it. Every one of these men had someone— mother, father, sister, sweetheart—who held an agonized breath while lists of the fallen were called out in the marketplace. Every one of these men for the rest of their lives would be haunted by the clash of swords, the boom of the battle drum, the cries of the fallen. It was written into their faces, in their eyes; and all their proud pennants were trampled in the mud.

With a sigh she turned into the alley where she kept her disguise. Mirage, in the form of an imposing dog, awaited her there.

"Keep the alley clear," she said.

When he was pacing near the entrance, she ducked into the abandoned building, changed, and put on her makeup. A small mirror satisfied her that she was as transformed as Mirage. After wrapping herself in a cloak, so it was unclear whether she was servant or lady, she left the alley. The growling guard dog lingered in the alley a moment more, then came scampering up in the form of Foofy.

Briar swept him into her arms. "You naughty thing," she scolded, "making mommy worry. Don't you run off again like that, or I shall spank you."

Foofy whined. He was as good as she was in dropping into his role. Probably better.

She made her way to the marketplace. It made her sick to eat or drink anything from the queen's hand, and she could use a cold drink and a slice of bread to brace herself for the task ahead. Besides, the square often supplied useful information, with its milling customers and rows of vendors hawking wares beneath colorful awnings. Acrobats and musicians strolled through the marketplace, bringing the only liveliness, for half as many people as usual bartered before the stalls, and more than one merchant stared out from his booth with a worried expression.

Briar stopped before a beverage stand and tossed five pennigs onto the counter after ordering ale.

The proprietor quickly swept the money up. "Sorry, miss, it's ten today."

"That's robbery," she replied, but laid down the balance.

He shrugged. "Taxes and tariffs drive up prices."

Briar quaffed the mug in a few gulps. Though it tasted watered down—the man had to survive—it washed road dust from her throat.

She fared no better at the baker's stall. The bread was stale and hard, the price jacked up almost beyond what anyone but a noble could afford. When she told him it was worth a fraction of what she'd paid, the owner grumbled, telling her to take it up with the queen.

"Shortages everywhere," he said. "The war's draining us dry."

Briar heard the same grumble of discontent throughout the marketplace, though most spoke with furtive glances over their shoulders.

Nothing more to be gained, she took a shortcut to the castle, crossing an area called Three Hills, which formed a semicircle around a flat valley. Two of the hills were relatively bare. The third was thick with elm and box elder. A different kind of tree, a manmade gallows, stood stark and black on a stage built in the valley, along the diameter of the semicircle. A stone wall and holding cell for condemned prisoners bordered the back of the stage. But what drew Briar's attention was a burly man in a black mask, which covered his face down to his neck. He practiced before a chopping block, whirling a giant sword with such speed that it whistled as it cut the air.

Sickened, Briar hurried on, her fingers at her neck. Few passersby gave her a glance as she proceeded to the castle. Near the front gate, certain she was unobserved, she discarded the cloak, rolling it up and hiding it beneath a bridge. Then she proceeded past the guard, who smiled with moonstruck eyes at Skyla, well known to him.

Let him dream, she thought.

Ill-used and poorly paid, he had little else to live for. Unless he joined the resistance. It filled her with purpose, and now she fought for something noble.

Perhaps the guard would join the Fellowship. Recruits from among nobles, the queen's servants, and even her army were not unheard of. Maybe a few of the courtiers, diplomats, housemaids, footmen, and guards streaming in both directions through the front entrance of the castle numbered in those for the cause.

Lost in these musings, she almost ran straight into a tall man. It was only by a deft twist that she avoided colliding, for he was eyeing a buxom serving wench in the other direction. When he turned toward her, she saw that it was Diglan Crosse.

Surprise, then lust, flared in his eyes as his gaze swept up her figure. When he reached her face, his arrogant leer froze. He squinted, searching her features.

"Oh dear," she squealed. "You almost crushed poor Foofy." She thrust the little dog in his face. "Apologize to him, you naughty man." Foofy made a low growl, far more menacing than what would be expected from a creature his size.

"My pardon, miss," he muttered. "You left me hypnotized."

"Humph." Briar stalked off, but when she glanced back, he was staring after her with a puzzled brow.

If he'd penetrated her disguise and recalled their encounter at the Comb and Tap, the jig was up. Skyla would have to return to her father in Marendel, posthaste. But Briar would welcome the chance to balance the score and run her blade through Crosse's heart. If the coward would come out and fight like a man rather than throwing poison darts.

Wilona and Lysette were already in the drawing room

when Briar was announced. Two footmen stood ready at the tea buffet. No one else had arrived.

Wilona glanced up with a woebegone expression, on seeing Briar's gown. "I wish I had a rich father who could keep me in new dresses," she complained with a pout.

Briar felt a pang at having taken the twins' clothing that night in the forest. They were silly, but they were people, suffering under the weight of the queen's war like the rest of Purpura.

"I'll send you to my dressmaker," Briar said. "She's a dear and will make you both look like princesses."

"That's sweet," Wilona replied. "But father won't allow it."

"You misunderstand—it's my treat. You both wore those same dresses last season. If it's one thing I can't stand, it's last season's dress."

"But where have you been?" Lysette asked.

"I sent word to her majesty. Didn't she tell you? I was caught in a downpour. My physician was quite concerned about my fever. But it seems the cure was worse than the malady. He let out so much blood, I was weak for weeks."

That seemed to satisfy the twins. They turned the conversation elsewhere, babbling over how no one was throwing balls or planning picnics or soirees, and when was this silly war going to be over. The only use Briar could think of for their presence was to keep Skyla amused, for there seemed little else the queen could extract from them, now that their father had fallen on hard times like the rest of the nobility. As for Briar, the queen was only interested in money, namely, an alliance with her fictional father in Marendel.

Vance entered a short time later in the guise of Lord Quale, with plum nose and wart-decked chin. He bowed awkwardly, staring with infatuation at Skyla, showing not the slightest flicker that less than twenty-four hours before, they'd plotted strategy for this tea and then spent the rest of the evening in his tent, making a blanket toss and quiver.

"Miss Skyla," he said, "you're more beautiful every time I see you."

Briar held out her dog. "You haven't said hello to little Foofy." You sounded like oo. Little like ittle.

Vance withdrew an arms length and began to sniffle. "Are you sure he won't bite my head off?"

"Silly Quale. See? He's wagging his tail at you."

"Just to lure me in. I believe he's quite jealous. If he were a tiger he would bite my head off."

"He'd do no such thing. Now say hello to him, or I shan't speak to you for the rest of the afternoon."

Vance reached for Foofy's head, but was suddenly seized with a fit of sneezing. When it was over he gave the dog a hesitant pat, while Wilona and Lyssette rolled their eyes. All Briar could do was shrug back at them.

A chill swept through the open windows, the fire burned low, and the usual hour for tea was drawing to a close when the queen entered. Her face was haggard, her shoulders more stooped, her hair tired and limp. Deep lines pinched the corners of her eyes. She seemed distracted and spoke little, allowing the conversation to eddy around her.

At last, Briar said, "Are you unwell, Your Highness?"

"A bit tired, perhaps," was the reply.

"But the army was victorious, were they not?"

The queen eyed her, as though trying to determine if Briar was mocking her. "My armies swept the field. You can count on it."

"I hope they finish sweeping soon. I'm tired of war. No one will host a ball."

"We'll have to keep you amused here, then, won't we?"

Vance arched his eyebrows at Briar. "I will too."

"Sorry, my dear Quale," the queen replied, "but I have

other plans for our little confection." She turned to Briar. "I promised you a duke, remember?"

Vance drew back. "I hoped a different arrangement might advantage us both," he said stiffly.

The queen ignored him, but leaned toward Briar. "Have you written your father? I thought he would be here by now."

"So did I." Briar sighed. "But daddy is a scatterbrain. He would lose his nose if it wasn't attached to his face."

"Write him again, dear. It would be in everyone's interest. Things are about to move swiftly for you." The queen rang a bell sitting on a side table.

A footman entered and announced Rupert Alamond Glodwell, ninth duke of Wakely Court. In tripped the duke, stumbling across the floor, his face pink and plump, his eyes wide and innocent, blinking as though the world was a new and bewildering place, but enchanting nonetheless.

One by one, the queen introduced him to the party, whereupon he bowed with a grand motion of his arm. But when he came to Briar he stopped short, his head tipped, and his eyes grew larger and flickered with recognition.

Briar gave an almost imperceptible shake of her head. "I hear you love a jest better than anyone in Purpura."

His face brightened with understanding. "I do, Miss ... Miss Skyla is it?"

Briar touched her fuchsia-colored fan to his chest. "*You* must call me Sky. Can you do that for me and never forget?"

"As long as you wish it," the duke replied, staring back and forth from Briar to the fan, as if one or the other held an important secret.

"Then I'm the happiest girl in the land."

The conversation turned to soirees, to marriages, to the disappearance of the highwayman—causing both of the twins a pang of sadness—to talk of war. All the while, the queen grew listless and sat downcast, staring vacantly at a point on the floor.

At last, her gaze lifted to Briar's ruby ring. "Do you play triumph, Skyla?"

"It seems all the rage," Briar replied. "But I'm lost at cards. It must be all the feathers between my ears."

The queen's lips pressed into a satisfied smile. "Nonsense. I'll teach you."

Briar clapped her hands. "Will you? Then I'm sure to have the best teacher."

The duke appeared nonplussed, perhaps thinking of the many games played at the baron's manse, but a moment later he giggled. "Oh, do let's." And then he winked at Briar. Fortunately, the queen, busy ordering a deck of cards from a servant, didn't see.

When the cards and a game table arrived, the queen explained the rules. There were four suits—swords, wands, cups, and coins—with numbered cards two through ten, plus Page, Knave, Queen, and King. In addition, there was a triumph suit, running from lowest in value, the World, to highest, the Fool. The first player begins with any suit but a triumph card. The next player can only play a card of that suit or a triumph card. The highest card wins, called a trick, and the value of each card captured is added up.

"It's all so confusing," said Briar, when the rest of the game was explained.

"Don't worry," the queen said. "I'll help you." She reached over and patted Briar's fingers.

"Then I'm in good hands." Briar had to stifle the impulse to recoil from the queen's touch, which sent shivers through her with its iciness. "But how marvelous for the Fool to be the most powerful."

"Isn't it?" said Rupert.

"See, my dear?" the queen said to Briar. "I promised that you and the duke were compatible."

"Don't be so sure." Vance said. "There's more to Miss Skyla than meets the eye."

"Don't be jealous, Quale. I'll find another girl for you."

"But how, when my heart belongs to another?" Vance looked directly at Briar, and for a moment the doltish and simpering Quale act dropped away.

"Don't be silly," Briar replied. "There are lots of girls who would jump at the chance of marrying the handsome Lord Quale. Wilona or Lysette, for example." The twins went crimson, and not from embarrassment.

The game proceeded. For the first few rounds, the queen teamed up with Briar to teach her the game. At first, Briar purposely suggested bad cards, while the queen had her make decisions that led to her winning.

The queen won the first game, and by her majesty's contrivance, Briar came in second.

Vance swore and flung down his cards. "Beginner's luck."

"Natural talent, my dear Quale, bestowed by the gods," Briar replied. She caught Vance's eye to show she understood: the queen was trying to inflate Briar's confidence; he wanted Briar to take the bait. "Another game! I shall win this time."

"Let's make it more interesting," the queen said, "and bet something?"

"Capital idea," said the duke. "I'll wager my two prize bitches. Best little hunters for ferreting foxes."

Vance offered his silver cufflinks.

"But what could I wager?" Briar asked.

The queen nodded toward Briar's ruby ring. "How about that little trinket?"

"Mommy's ring?"

"Your father will buy you another. If he's as rich as you say," she added darkly.

Briar studied the ring, turning it so that it caught the light of the many candelabras. "Oh, very well, it's too heavy anyway. I don't know how you men lug around those big heavy swords. It makes me tired to think of it. But what will you wager, Your Highness?"

"I'll throw you a ball."

Briar gazed at her ring. "No, something equal to this. You must have its twin in your treasury."

For a long moment, the queen's jaw pulsed with tension. "Very well."

"And a tour of the castle." Briar rocked the ring so that it flashed and sparkled. "It's a glorious old building, and you haven't let me see it all."

Not looking at all pleased, but seemingly hypnotized by the crimson sparks shooting from the ruby, the queen acquiesced.

Round after round followed. Coming into the final hand, the queen led. Briar was second, but she pretended to not know her score, allowing Wilona or Lysette to assist her in keeping track.

The duke shuffled the cards and after dealing, led with a Knave of Wands. "I hear the highwayman was killed."

"Let's hope not, sir," Briar replied, glancing at Lysette and Wilona. "He would leave too many broken hearts."

Vance tossed down a King of Wands, the first time it had been played that afternoon. Before anyone could reply, Briar swept up the card and examined the illustration. A man stood in a driving rain, wearing a crown, holding a torch that blazed and illuminated the landscape, despite the torrent falling around him.

"A valiant king," she said. "With inextinguishable fire."

"No ..." The queen stared off, the glow in her eyes as

strange and unsettling as the change in her voice, as if someone else sat there. "You can douse it, you can choke it, you can quench it. You can stub it out." She glanced down at the fan of cards in her hand, plucked one out, and threw down the Hanged Man.

Then she leveled her gaze at Briar, the helpful tutor gone from her eyes, leaving them as opaque as frosted glass.

Briar tossed the Fool onto table. "My trick."

CHAPTER TWENTY-THREE

"*N*ext time, I'll win your fuchsia fan," the duke said to Briar.

Briar touched his arm with it. "I hope you shall."

With a wink to her and a bow to them all, he excused himself, the Orendale twins trailing in his wake.

The queen conducted Briar and Vance through the halls of the castle. Flickering flames from candelabra shone on the cold flagged floor. Despite a quantity of tapers, the light did little to breathe warmth into the many large marble statues, human and mythological, nestled in alcoves along the way. The tour began in proper in a large rotunda—high-domed with a frescoed ceiling—where dignitaries and nobles swept by in silks and satins and colorful gowns and capes.

They made there way up the many stories. Views from balconies, of the city to the east and the coast to the west, might have been spectacular but for thick fog that swaddled the palace. Briar sighed, disappointed once more in not viewing the sea. For the hundredth time she wondered if she would ever hear waves, feel sand as fine as sugar beneath her feet, or rock to sleep aboard the Golden Gull in Misty Bay, wrapped in Vance's arms.

On the top floor, Briar nodded to stairs that she guessed led to a tower. "What's up there?"

"Nothing of interest." The queen forced a smile and tried to hurry them on.

"Is there a tower up there? I should like to see the view above this dreadful fog."

"You wouldn't be interested. It's for my personal use."

Briar clapped her hands. "Oh, but I would. To see what a queen does!"

But her majesty turned away and waved them on. Appearing somewhat embarrassed, she declined their seeing the treasury. Instead, she signaled a servant to bring a dozen rings for Briar to examine. All were small and forgettable, but Briar selected one and praised its beauty enough to leave a self-satisfied smile on the queen's face.

On the ground floor they came to a gymnasium, where the clash of swords stopped them. A man was taking instruction from a fencing master. His back was to Briar, but from what she could see, his form was perfect, his motions fluid and precise. With three quick lunges, he drove his instructor back and touched the tip of his foil to the man's heart. They resumed starting positions, and the more Briar watched him and the cocky cant of his head, the more she was certain she'd seen him before.

The instructor made a few inaudible comments. Then came the ring of metal and this time the master acquitted himself better. But she saw no flaw in the pupil's defense, and his blade leaped like a striking cobra to the liver, spleen, and then the heart of his opponent. The victor bowed, turned, and his one eye fastened brazenly on Briar, the other one being covered with a black patch.

She should have recognized Diglan Crosse's arrogant

bearing immediately, but she dissembled. "That man frightens me. Who is he, and why is he here?"

The queen shrugged. "A promised payment for services rendered."

"He's accosting me with that eye of his. Thank the gods I can't see the other one."

"Back off, Diglan," said the queen. "This one's spoken for."

He returned to his lesson, but not before pressing his sword to his heart and bowing with that same rakish insolence he'd displayed at the Comb and Tap.

The queen was already stepping away. Vance glanced at Briar, his brow furrowed.

"That's all that's worth seeing," the queen said, when they reached the main level.

Briar pointed to a dim and narrow hall. "Where does that go?"

"The servants' quarters below."

"And … isn't there a dungeon?"

Impatience crept into the queen's tone. "Yes. Why shouldn't there be? Malcontents need encouragement to loosen their tongues." Her face darkened, but then she seemed to catch herself, and the cordial smile returned. "Nothing you need to worry over. Come along dear, you look piqued. A little fresh air will do you good."

Briar could well believe it. She'd explored the lower levels before and seen enough to break her heart. Screams and moans, echoing through the corridors. Desperate faces peering from cramped cells, reeking of human waste and despair. The memory steeled her determination.

The queen escorted them outside, where they meandered through gardens, fragrant with blossoms and alive with tinkling fountains. But once again, the chilly fog intruded so that the flowers and walkways faded to ghosts.

Briar had seen enough and wanted nothing more than to

get as far from the castle as she could. She tried to catch Vance's attention, but he was staring into the fog. An imp seemed to play in his eyes.

"Is your kennel nearby?" he asked. "I've never seen a sniffer up close."

The queen brightened. "So you shall. Come along, friends, it's a quick stroll to the back of the castle."

A few minutes later they walked down a stone path that bisected two rows of cages, the bars of which were as thick as those on a prison cell. A dreadful stench assaulted Briar's nose. Livestock droppings on Juniper's farm smelled sweet compared to this, and Briar guessed he would never let these foul beasts near his soil.

"They're my pride and joy." The queen's eyes sparkled as she gazed on the creatures.

Briar had never seen anything so ugly, so unnatural. They were the size of a half-grown calf. Their heads were overly large in proportion to their bodies. A flat nose with flaring nostrils seemed to fill their faces, and tusks like knives protruded from powerful jaws.

Briar hugged herself. "Whatever do you need them for?"

"Tracking, my dear. They make bloodhounds look like helpless puppies."

Vance raised a fist in the air. "That's the way to catch the rebels."

"Precisely, Quale. I bred them with the speed of a panther, the endurance of a camel."

"But like a bloodhound," Vance pursued, "you need a sample of someone's scent, no?"

The queen nodded. "Someday I'll overcome that detail."

"Is it true, one bite from a sniffer and you'll go blind?"

"Blind as a bat."

The thought turned Briar cold. If ever there was a creature she wanted rapport with, as she had with foxes and weasels since childhood, it was this brutish thing created to find the queen's enemies. She stared at one, attempting to probe its mind. She got nothing. She took a small step forward and tried again. A wall of granite seemed to block her. If push came to shove, she would not master a sniffer as she had the she-wolf on Einor.

They returned through the gardens. As they stepped toward a veranda, pigeons roosting beneath an eave suddenly took flight like one monstrous body. Their wings, like sharp blades, cut the air with a whistle.

***

One by one, Naryfel lit the candles beneath the beakers, the silly trio of Skyla, Quale, and Glodwell long faded from her mind. The tower windows were closed. Outside, a mizzling rain blurred the world.

She began to pace. "Am I to be trounced by a mob of fools? Defeated? No, the word is an outlaw, banished from my mind. The syllables mean nothing. Sounds a baby might babble."

The beakers began to steam, the liquid inside gradually changing colors. Up and down the length of the floor she went, her slippers hissing across the stone tiles.

"A ragtag rabble vanquish me? Do they think Purpura will find greatness under a Makken or a D'Arté? What greatness will they find in a serf reaping wheat? What brilliance in a miller grinding his wheel? What perception of mind in a soldier, born to spill his blood for the glory of others? Only I have a vision for Purpura. Generations hence will understand, vindicate, and venerate me."

The beakers bubbled now, and still she walked back and forth, running her fingers absently across the leather-clad volumes on her bookshelf.

"This is no time for diplomacy but for a strong hand. They are here for my glory, to serve me. They will know me. They will feel my wrath, but not a hot wrath, no! A cold wrath that bends them to my will."

With tongs, she began to pour liquid from the beakers, measuring it carefully while she muttered spells, gleaned from years of study, and added powders from several packets. Then from the casket Crosse had brought she removed the Nyctarix. The candles found no surface to reflect off. Rather, there was an endless shimmering and shifting like the waters of a lake at night. She placed the gem in a bowl formed from a moon rock fallen from the sky, and then poured the mixture from her beaker over it. Immediately a cloud rose and took the vague shape of a man. It hovered before her like a flag, stirring in the breeze, as though it awaited her command.

"What is fire, a kind of magic, no? It shifts, destroys, consumes, licks like a tongue, carries the scent of frankincense or devours trees with dragon's teeth, leaving nothing but ashes. It illuminates, penetrating the darkest night, even the vault of the dead, revealing the souls damned to eternity beneath its flames. Ah, but it nourishes, and by its art, milk is warmed for children. Lamb, deer, and oxen are seared into morsels that water the mouth and sustain the body. Fire is life, and a cold body is a dead body."

She filled her lungs with air and blew toward the thing stirring above her. It seemed to inhale, to expand slightly, and the watery properties of the gem now shone within the creature's depths.

She raised her hands, beckoning. The thing glided into her arms. They turned about the tower in a slow waltz, and though a sensation akin to frostbite struck her, for the first time she felt complete.

But there was work to be done. Stepping away, she pointed to the window.

"Know my enemies. Search them out. Punish them. Bend them to my will."

Though the thing departed out the window, her loneliness had vanished. She felt fulfilled, as if she had spent the night with a lover.

CHAPTER TWENTY-FOUR

The days shortened; the nights grew darker. Cold snaps struck. Winds heralded coming storms. Rain gave way to sleet, sleet to snow—driving sheets of it. The land was wrapped in ice, and even the trees huddled for warmth.

One morning, between gales, a proclamation went out across the land—nailed to sign posts, to the sides of buildings, on tavern doors. Preceded by trumpet fanfare, it was read in the marketplaces. Riders raced across the country and took it to villages, manors, and towns. Where official heralds missed, the message spread anyway with surprising accuracy, for the announcement seemed strange, mad, and impossible.

However the message arrived, it was the same. Lighting of torches outside of buildings was prohibited. Leaving torches on hillsides and roadsides was prohibited. The depiction of torches on walls, rooftops, bridges, and other places was prohibited. Those who defied the queen's order would be punished severely.

Falcon caught word of it near Desperation, the slave

shantytown, and bore it back to Briar and Vance at the forest hideout.

"Won't stop me," Falcon said, for she loved leaving torches where the queen would see them from her tower. "What can she do about it?"

"Every evil imaginable," Briar replied. "Lay off till we know her intentions."

Vance agreed and sent out his own emissaries to spread the word: no more torch lighting. Perhaps too few heard the message; perhaps they chose to defy the queen anyway. For a good week, more brands were lighted than ever before, even when lightning and thunder cracked open the heavens.

Then reports came in. A shadow stalked the land; it blocked out the stars on cloudless nights; it passed like the wind. Dead leaves scattered. Horses reared. Travelers hugged close their cloaks. Some said it had the vague outlines of a man, others that it was a demon unleashed by the queen. No two descriptions were alike, but it passed down chimneys, seeped through seams at windows or door-ways, and one by one, hearth fires went out and torches sputtered and died.

People took up flint and steel, but no amount of friction generated a spark. Soon citizens from lowest to highest huddled with loved ones beneath blankets or bedded down beside dogs or livestock for warmth.

There were exceptions. The queen's staunch supporters were spared, and people wondered in terror how she knew her enemies.

Cold wasn't the only problem. Without fire, no water could be boiled, no venison or boar turned over a spit, and the ovens went cold.

Where the thing originated, none could say, but the general consensus was that it had come from graves, tombs and crypts, and ancient barrows like a frosty exhalation.

Then it collected and coalesced from the barest whiff to a force, felt as it passed, like the chill cloak of Death.

Briar could well believe it as she streaked across the countryside on Dondle, warning people about the proclamation. Her journey took her by Juniper Donyman and his family. Though the farmer had maintained he stood apart from the politics roiling around him, it seemed prudent to alert him anyway.

As she approached the farm, a bitter blast whipped the trees and lashed her face. Frozen puddles crunched and cracked beneath Dondle's hooves. Lowering clouds threw a pall across the sky.

She found Reena and Juniper piling bales of hay before the chicken coop as a windbreak. Briar dismounted and lent a hand. When they were done, they spread more straw on the stall floors to form a warm blanket for the barn animals. As they returned to the house, she pulled Juniper aside and told him the news.

He studied her long and hard before replying. "That's bad. I was counting on melting ice inside the house so the animals can drink."

Briar gripped his arm. "What have you done?"

He looked toward Toivara. "Toted up a pile of brush. Burned half the night."

"You weren't going to get involved."

"It doesn't take a scholar to tell the queen's the problem. Besides, that tax collector got under my skin. Well, it's done now. We better get inside before the storm hits."

The air in the kitchen was as cold as outside. Joia, her belly swollen now, squatted at the hearth. Her face was as pale as snow, her hair gray. A haunted look had come into her eyes.

"It came right down the chimney," she said. "And the flames went out like someone doused 'em. I can't relight it."

She held out the flint and steel to her husband. "You better try."

The farmer knelt, but try as he might, he couldn't strike a spark. The candles were out too, and as the storm came on, blotting out the sun, the room dimmed, so that it seemed to Briar that she saw the outlines of the family through clouds of smoke.

"Pa, the animals won't survive out there," Reena said.

His gaze fell on his wife. She was shivering. A sheen of perspiration glistened on her brow, and now it was clear she wasn't just spooked. She was ill.

"Bring as many of them here as you can. Briar, you'll help?" Juniper asked.

Outside, the first flakes darted and spun in the wind like gnats, hurrying Briar's and Reena's steps.

As they herded goats and pigs, Briar said, "The baby's coming soon."

"Any day." One of the pigs sat and started breathing hard. Reena prodded him. "Don't you get scared on me now." The pig wriggled between his sisters and brothers, trying to make himself scarce. He liked it inside the kitchen though, and sat at Juniper's feet like a puppy.

Back in the barn, Briar and Reena gathered the cows and the two horses.

"What about Dondle?" Reena asked.

"There isn't room."

"He'll freeze!"

"He'll be all right."

Fifteen minutes later, the rooms were filled with the cows and the two horses, and chickens were pecking on the floor. Briar stepped outside and led Dondle from the barn. She whisked away snow collecting on his mane and then taking his face between her hands, leaned against his nose. Briar didn't have to say anything. He understood as he'd always understood. But she spoke her desire now, to reassure herself.

"Find Mirage. He'll take you somewhere safe. Come back when the storm passes."

Dondle stamped and nodded and then dashed away through a cloud of icy fireflies.

Reena still stood on the porch. "I don't like it," she said, when Briar joined her. "We'll find a place for him inside."

Mist came into Briar's eyes. "I wish more people had your heart."

Juniper had put most of the animals into the back rooms. Now he was working his hammer, boarding up the windows. "Close the flue, Reena. No chance of a fire now."

When he was done, he opened the inner doors. The animals roamed back in, and he began working on the back rooms. Then there was nothing else to do but huddle together beneath blankets and listen to the wind wail outside. Beside her, Briar could feel Joia shiver, and from time to time, Reena wiped perspiration from her mother's brow. Joia slept and sometimes muttered, the way people will when a fever strikes.

They sat in silence, the wind howling and whipping about the house. Briar guessed they were all thinking the same thing: would baby and mother survive?

Juniper's eyes were glued to his wife. "This queen," he said at last, "is a hateful, wicked thing. May her heart freeze."

The storm passed during the night, and Briar slipped from the house. Dondle stood waiting in the snow. She leaped upon his back and started up the road, her heart heavy for the family behind her. Lost in a cloud of gloom, she almost didn't see one of Donyman's neighbors prying loose two torch holders that had been nailed to a fence, one of the many places where brands had been placed in support of the Fellowship.

The man, who knew her in passing and always gave her a wave and a smile, gazed at her with suspicion. This troubled Briar, and she could think of no good reason for this change in him. As she topped a hill, she saw another farmer whitewashing the door of an abandoned barn where someone had painted blazing torches. Noticing that she had stopped to watch, he stared at her darkly, completed his work, and painted a crude version of the queen's insignia, as though it were a talisman that could ward off evil.

Most of the journey, she encountered people who were frightened and bewildered and asked her, when she stopped to speak with them, how they were to eat and stay warm.

The fear in their voices still ringing in her ears, she returned to the rebel camp by midafternoon and found Vance pacing in his tent. She told him what she'd seen, of the Donymans' plight, of others like them she'd seen on the road.

He sank into a chair. "Without bread, people will starve. How does it serve her to let them perish?"

"She's mad, Vance," Briar replied, flopping into a seat beside him. "It leaked out in the drawing room, raving to herself. Now she's throwing the country into chaos and taking everyone down with her."

He sprang up and began crossing back and forth like a caged beast. Periodically he stopped, looked like he was about to say something, but clenched his fist in frustration and began traversing the length of the tent again. "It's hopeless," he said at last. "Give me a sword, put me in front of an army; I'll fight until I'm no more. But this—how do I fight this?"

"We'll find a way."

"What way?" He gave a broad wave of his hand. "I've stirred them up. I've organized them. For what? To have them squashed beneath her heel? Their peril is in my hands, and I failed them."

"Not yet. Listen, I've been thinking—"

He shook his head. "It's over. We'll have to smuggle food in from Turlia, if they'll help us. And pray we can get it to as many as we can before it's too late."

"We'll do that. We'll go elsewhere if they refuse. But Vance, we'll stop her. Her weapon has to be in the tower. She took us pretty much everywhere else. Look, if we don't do something, people will lose faith in the Fellowship. I already saw signs of that on the road. They'll isolate rather than pull together behind us."

He paused in his striding and studied her. Understanding dawned in his eyes. "At first they defied her. But after weeks of this, they won't want to be associated with the resistance. They'll withdraw support. "

"People need to know we're strong, that we have something the queen can't extinguish." She held her hand aloft as though holding a torch. "Hope's Flame."

He sighed. "It's only a legend."

"What if it isn't? The queen may be a lot of things, but she's no fool. Purpura can't be a great kingdom without her people. Someone needs to grow the food, mine the ore, weave the wool. If the queen's magic can stop fire, it must be able to start it. She can't leave us like this forever. She needs a way to reverse it."

He gazed off, his eyes burning with their old fervor. "A flame—leaping from Mount Toivara. Is it possible?"

"I'm going back to the castle. Her secret is in that tower."

"Not alone. I'm going with you."

CHAPTER TWENTY-FIVE

*T*he roads were swollen with misery. What else could people do when their homes were no longer hospitable? They carried what they could in carts and on their backs. Glassy-eyed, they tramped along, hardly knowing where they were going, for what direction lent respite from the evil that had befallen them? Everywhere was destruction. Houses demolished. Trees blown over. Dead sheep, goats, and cattle littered the fields. Birds frozen, fallen from the sky. In dull shock, Briar watched a father dig graves for his wife and son, a little boy of five, by the look of him.

As Dondle threaded past them, people reached up to Briar for food. She'd given out the last of a meager supply of jerked meat an hour ago. The crying babies and wailing mothers filled Briar with steely determination to return on the queen ten-fold the ruin she'd wreaked on her people.

Briar's thoughts spun in an agony of worry over the fate of Reena and her family. Were they on the road too? It seemed unlikely, with Joia so near to delivering. Unless she had succumbed, the baby fallen gray and lifeless from her belly, and like the father digging graves, Juniper was now piercing the gelid earth with his spade.

Briar gripped the reins as she came to the turnoff to the farm. But she knew where her duty lay, and she fixed her face straight ahead.

"Say a prayer for them, Dondle. Say a prayer."

And Dondle tossed his head up to the sky bearing down on them, grey and oppressive, and trumpeted an appeal.

Her thoughts turned to Mount Toivara. A bonfire on the summit would defy the queen. People would look to it and know the Fellowship was there, fighting for them. But the fire would die out, and so would people's spirits. Briar wanted more: a flame that could not be quenched, that pierced the gloom of the darkest times. Old stories had a grain of truth to them. There had to be something to the legend surrounding the mountain. Farmers looked to its rugged peak and asked for abundant crops. Families invoked Hope's Flame when a loved one was stricken. And Juniper told her that a cluster of rocks surrounded a pit at the top, stones blasted black, as no ordinary fire could.

Even if the legend were true, a problem remained. How would she light it? All she could do was hope that once in possession of the queen's secret, Briar could turn it to good, for if magic could smother flames perhaps it could ignite them.

"It better," she muttered. The alternative was unthinkable. Starvation led to chaos. Riots. Normally good people tearing at each other like rats. The land would fall into anarchy that even the queen couldn't contain, and the Fellowship would be powerless to quell the tumult and turmoil.

Mile after mile passed, their progress slow and labored as they wove through people in flight, clogging the roads, though at times she pulled off the beaten track and cut through fields and woods, relieved at Dondle's speed.

She reviewed the plan in her mind. Don her disguise. Meet Vance at the queen's drawing room, where he would greet her as Haywood Quale. Then excuse herself. Get to the tower door. Pick the lock with a set of skeleton keys the Fellowship used when raiding warehouses. The castle was old, as were its locks. She had to hope these old keys would work. If not, she would scale the walls of the tower, if she had to, to gain access.

The morning wore on. Time had stopped. All that existed in the world was the endless stream of humanity on an endless and muddy track. Every face turned up to her, shattered with loss, was that of Reena, Joia, or Juniper.

With a moan of despair, Briar pulled off the road, and Dondle rushed her through a series of low-lying hills crusted with snow. But these ended in a ravine, forcing her back to the main highway, where an old woman stumped along, tapping a walking stick and making a good deal of progress among the wagons and carts, for people parted before her.

Briar rode up beside her and dismounted, leading Dondle along as she walked. "Do you need help, good woman? My horse can carry you."

The woman kept up her pace, the stick striking left and right, but she turned blind eyes to Briar. "Do I look like I need help?"

"Racca!"

Racca stopped and tangled a gnarled hand through Briar's hair. "Ha! The little fly escaped."

"Where are you going? I'll take you there."

"I'm already there." Racca leaned on her staff and pointed. "Is there a tree?"

An ancient oak offered shelter a short distance away. Briar laughed, and some of the darkness of the day lifted. "You know there is!"

"Well, what are you waiting for?" Racca offered her arm so she could be led.

It hardly seemed Briar's assistance was needed, but she took Racca's arm, and when they reached the tree, they sat beneath its boughs. Racca looked no older, no grayer, no more stooped, and a sharp light still burned in her eyes. She gazed toward the road, as though she were watching the stream of refugees.

"Much pain, much suffering," she muttered to herself. "Time to end it." Then to Briar, "So, you would steal the queen's magic and relight Hope's Flame."

Briar looked anxiously toward the road. They were out of earshot, and no one paid them any notice. Still, she felt as exposed as she had when she stood in Racca's hut, smelling of eldara and grass and the waters of Abunary Pond. Racca's prescience brought questions to Briar's mind, questions she did and didn't want answered. But something inside told her to ask. "I'll succeed in stealing the queen's magic?"

"How would I know? Even if you do, it's not enough." Racca reached for the jewel that Briar always kept on the necklace, close to her heart. Drawing it out from beneath Briar's tunic, the old woman removed it from Vance's hand-kerchief and turned it in her hand. "Tear of Tybaleth," she murmured.

A thrill went through Briar. She had long thought this was a Tear, for hadn't she heard crying from far above—as in Racca's tale. Hadn't this very gem drifted down from the black and sparkling heavens and kept her warm that day she almost died in the snow?

Racca was still feeling it with her fingers, her eyes shifting back and forth as they would of old, when she seemed to read the future. But she said nothing more and hummed to herself.

Briar was torn between respect and annoyance, but the

latter won out. "People will die. Help me, Racca. What do I need to do?"

And Racca told her in a whisper like wind in the trees. The jewel Briar wore was a tear of the gods. But the queen kept a Nyctarix in her tower, a jewel that swallowed warmth and light.

"Put them together, and—" Racca mimed an explosion with her fingers. "You'll see the flame from miles away."

A surge of hope flowed into Briar. "What does the queen's gem look like?"

Racca tapped Briar's jewel. "The opposite of this. Careful little fly, else you or those you love will get caught in her web."

Briar could get no more from Racca, nor would the old woman accept any help, but stumped back into the stream of victims and was soon lost like a cork borne off by the sea.

CHAPTER TWENTY-SIX

Tea went as usual, except the queen was absent—unexpectedly called into conference they were told—but would be down shortly.

Briar felt a funny vibration stirring within. Something was wrong, though she couldn't put her finger on it. She found herself scanning the drawing room, checking which windows were locked or open, how long it would take to dash to the far door. But she kept up a constant prattle and indulged the twins, complimenting them on their new dresses, while inwardly she was horrified to see them gorging on crumpets and teacakes, while people flooding the roads were starving.

One of the servants threw another log on the fire. Wilona observed that it was just delicious to be snug, while Lynette noted that if the population outside hadn't behaved like naughty children, they would be happy and cozy too.

It was all Briar could do to keep from thrashing both of them on the spot, but she smiled and nodded and added a dozen frivolous declarations on the subject. As for Vance, his faux chin wart noticeably twitched from clenched teeth, but he stated the usual inanities and kept his eyes from Briar. She knew the effort he was expending to not set the pampered kittens straight. At times, even Foofy glared at them.

Day was waning when the queen entered at last. "Apologies, friends. Duties of state never cease."

"Nothing untoward, I hope," Vance said, adjusting the ruffled sleeves Haywood Quale was famous for.

Of late, the queen had appeared older and tired. Now there was a spring to her step as she crossed to her chair, and rather than sinking distracted into it, she sat poised, flushed with confidence. And well she might. Her control of fire had more than given her the upper hand. "That's a matter of perspective, Quale."

Which didn't answer Vance's question at all, and Briar's disquiet increased. Vance's masquerade as Haywood Quale seemed unassailable. The real Lord Quale—a neighbor and close friend of Vance's—had gone in childhood to a sunny country far to the south, for the benefit of his mother's health. Should anyone track him down, he was prepared to protect Vance at all costs. Briar was not so sanguine about Skyla's cover. A messenger dispatched to Marendel would find no nobles named Silsken.

"What could be more untoward than the roads, Your Majesty?" she asked. "All those filthy people. Fleas hopping everywhere. One made its way onto my white kid glove. Where are they all going, anyway? Do clean the roads quickly. Last night I had to soak in a bath of rose petals to get rid of the smell."

The queen reached for the triumph deck and began shuffling the cards. "You will find that things are coming to a definite conclusion."

Vance sniffed indifferently at a crumpet. "What sort of conclusion?"

"I'm about to receive interesting intelligence. Nothing so

very great, really. Nothing that determines the outcome of the war. But small victories add up and bolster one's morale."

"I never saw you wanting morale." Vance sniffled and then sneezed into a silk handkerchief. "You must excuse me, Your Majesty. I'm a bit under the weather."

"Perhaps a bit of amusement will cheer you up." The queen proffered the cards.

Vance shook his head. "My head's a dizzy mess. I don't think I would be much sport."

"You're more diverting than you know."

A servant entered and handed the queen a note. She read it quickly and rose. "The emissary I mentioned. Now the game begins."

She left, and Vance shot Briar a worried glance.

A few minutes later he sneezed. "It's no good. I'm off to bed and a hot brandy."

He departed, rubbing his head. A short time after, Briar excused herself, pleading fatigue. She hastened down a corridor and turned up a flight of stairs. Guards and servants paid her no mind. Over the past months they were used to seeing Skyla Silsken carrying her little terrier from one end of the castle to the other.

At the top of the stairs, Vance emerged from behind a tall statue and pulled her into a shadowed alcove.

"I don't like it," he said.

"She's seen through us?"

"Unlikely. She wouldn't have allowed us out of the drawing room. But something's off. I can smell it."

Briar clutched his sleeve. "Don't call it off."

"I won't. We need to hurry."

"Vance, if something goes wrong—leave me. Get the jewel and go."

A pained expression came into his face. She put down Foofy and Vance crushed her to him. Then they were off, taking the stairs three at a time. When they encountered castle personnel they slowed and pretended casual conversation. When they were alone they rushed on.

They quickly found the passage leading to the tower. It made Briar wonder if maybe they were being jittery because so many lives rode on their success, and the cost of failure was unthinkable. Tension increased in her shoulders, and she realized how wound up she'd been.

She put Foofy down. "Keep watch," she told him, and he trotted to the end of the corridor, where he sat licking a forepaw.

The tower door was locked, but she took out the set of skeleton keys and tried one, jangling it in the opening. The lock failed to yield. She tried another key and another with the same result.

"You're rushing." He took the keys from her and began systematically going through the set, giving a patient jiggle with each one.

"What if none of them works?" she asked.

"Mirage breaks the door down."

"That'll bring guards."

"I know."

Briar studied him. "Then we need a signal. So we fight together."

He smiled darkly. "An element of surprise. Einor means attack right, eldara go left."

"Hurry." She nodded to the door.

The last key failed, but she'd watched and listened as he'd tried each one, noting the order. "Try the third one again."

He stared at her a moment, but he slowly inserted the pin, the key wards, the throat, the collar, and on down the shank, working gently left and right as it entered the lock. When he reached the bow, the lock gave, and the door opened. They slipped inside, shutting it behind them.

The tower was a small room with four windows, each facing one of the directions of the compass. The waning sun fell on the interior, so that the walls, floor, ceiling, and furnishings seemed to be burning. But the room was cold, despite logs smoldering on the hearth. A musty odor pervaded the chamber—probably from the scores of old parchments and books lining the bookshelves—and it seemed airless.

Briar scanned the room, uncertain where to begin. Bottles, beakers, and vessels with strange twisted glass tubing dominated a long worktable.

"Alchemy?" Briar asked.

"Or something darker," Vance replied.

They crossed to a specimen cabinet and began opening the tiny drawers as quickly as they could.

After half of them had been inspected, Briar dashed the foul-smelling contents of one of them on the floor, in frustration. "It's not here. It's locked up or hidden."

Vance scanned the tower. "Check those books. I'll keep looking here."

Briar crossed to the bookcase and began tossing the leather-clad volumes to the flags at her feet. She found no hidden spaces behind the books, nothing in the rolled up parchments. The press of time bore down on her, a weight as heavy as the closeness of the air in the room. If the queen's conference was about unmasking her and Vance, how long would that take? The alarm would sound at any moment, unless her intention was to trap them up here. Mirage would alert them from his side of the passage leading to the tower, but not the other. Briar cursed to herself. They should have brought a confederate to stand watch on the far end of the corridor.

She took up another book, large and old, and was about to toss it aside when something about the volume stopped her. She held it in her hands, staring down at the ancient runes, stamped onto the front leather. Then it dawned on her: the book was too light for its size. Her fingers leaped to the pages. They were glued together. The book opened at the middle, revealing a hollowed out space holding a pouch.

Her heart leaped. She snatched up the pouch, pulled it open, and dumped the contents in her palm.

A jewel! Roughly the same size as the one she'd received that stormy day on the mountain. But light didn't reflect off the facets of this gem. Rather, it shifted and shimmered like a lake at night. She found herself being drawn into its depths, as though she might discover secrets there—who she was, what destiny awaited her.

"Briar!"

It was Vance, calling, it seemed, from a distance. His hand closed over the jewel, and the spell was broken.

She drew a pouch of her own from a pocket sewn into a fold of her dress, and removed a plain rock with a flaming torch painted on it. This she put into the queen's pouch, pulled it tight, and returned it to the hidden space within the book. Then she closed the book and slipped the Nyctarix into an inner pocket of her dress.

As they crossed to the door, horns shrilled an alarm.

CHAPTER TWENTY-SEVEN

*B*riar and Vance raced down the tower stairs. The whole castle seemed to have erupted with the crashing of bells, blaring of trumpets, and the shouts and stampede of feet echoing below. Mirage bounded toward them in the corridor at the bottom.

"Lead them away!" Briar cried.

He streaked by her. His bulk melted away. In its place, a second Briar rounded the corner. Cries and the stamp of boots grew louder from that direction.

She didn't wait for the result. As she hurried down the stairs on the other end of the hall, Vance beside her, she heard a roar like thunder, and then shrill cries of fright. She smiled grimly. Mirage would lead them on a merry chase through the castle, appearing sometimes as Vance, sometimes as Briar. But who knew the mind of the big cat? Aside from returning to his preferred striped form, he might just present them with the queen in full fury, pointing in the wrong direction.

They reached the bottom of the stairs. A tramp of boots came from around a bend. Briar reached for her sword, then cursed when her fingers found silk and lace. She suddenly felt naked without her weapon, and ungainly in Skyla's dress. But she and Vance had talked about this. There was no way to bring her blade into the castle and maintain her disguise. As Lord Quale, he bore a sword. But who wore two? And he'd never carried a dagger in that disguise.

One thing was clear. Someone had stirred up a bee's hive. Odds were that Briar and Vance were the bears caught with their paws in the honey.

Briar grabbed a vase of flowers, slipped behind a statue, and watched while Vance pretended to tie a shoelace. Two guards rounded the corner and came charging toward them, swords out.

Vance stood, his hand on his sword hilt, and regarded them nonchalantly. "What's all the hubbub, gentlemen?"

"Are you Lord Quale?" one of the guards asked.

"Quale? Heavens no. That coward?"

The guards appeared confused and looked at each other uncertainly.

"You," Vance said to one of the guards. "Come here and help me with this cravat."

The guard hesitated.

"Come, man, it's just a cravat," Vance observed. "Surely, you've assisted a gentleman before." Then, to the guard's mate, "*You*. Better help him, in case he botches it."

Vance positioned them both with their backs to the statue. When the two guards were absorbed with the cravat, Briar came from behind and brought the vase down on one guard's head. The man crumpled to the ground. Vance shoved the other fellow back. His sword flashed out, tip to the guard's heart. The next instant, Briar disarmed him. With Vance's sword prodding him, the guard dragged his unconscious companion into one of the rooms off the hall, where they were both gagged and tied with a bell cord. Briar took one of their swords and wrapped it in a cloak she found in a closet. A surge of confidence ran through her at the weight of the weapon in her hands.

Mirage's ploy must have been effective. Briar and Vance glided down the next levels, unchallenged. The castle was a small city unto itself. Word hadn't spread to everyone, and there weren't enough guards to cover the whole palace. Nonetheless, they slipped into one of the many chambers along the way when they heard people coming, and didn't emerge until the stamp of feet faded.

Once, a guard saw them before they could hide. Briar gambled, hoping the months of Skyla wandering the castle with her little dog would pay off, and that the man was uninformed about who was being pursued.

She rushed up to him. "Have you seen Foofy? He ran off when those terrible bells and trumpets started."

He shrugged, bowed servilely, and strode on.

Near the main level, while hiding in an unoccupied bedroom, they heard the queen stop outside the door. With one hand clutching Vance's arm and the other gripping her sword, Briar held her breath. The queen bellowed orders to place a cordon around the perimeter of the castle. In the distance, Briar heard the crash of something falling—a suit of display armor perhaps—the tattoo of many boots on the flag floor, and knew the decoy was still working.

The queen moved on. So did Briar and Vance, taking the servants' stairs to the nether reaches of the castle, the floors below the entry level. Here they encountered washer-women, scullions, chambermaids, a seamstress, and a candle maker. The wardrobe mistress raised an eyebrow at the sight of nobles striding among them, but Vance scowled at her for presuming to look at them, and she quickly averted her eyes. After that, Briar kept up her act of searching for her puppy, and they descended without incident, nearing where Briar had long ago stashed a change of clothes.

Even while she peered at the doorways and intersecting corridors with the vigilance of a hawk, she allowed hope to brighten a corner of her mind. It really seemed that they would make it, and victory was in their grasp. No more fire-less hearths, no more cold meals, no more starving people. No more would the citizens of Purpura flee from their homes. And as soon as Hope's Flame was lit, the Fellowship would be strengthened. People would rally to their banner. They would rise up, storm the castle, and overthrow the tyrant.

She could almost feel what their lives would be like then. Juniper and his family would be free of weighty taxation. A fair treaty would be reached with Turlia and land belonging to them returned. Briar didn't care now what happened to her father's property. He'd never taken care of the people working on the manor. He didn't deserve to keep it. And Briar didn't want it. It held no meaning for her except as a loveless place of pain and suffering.

This was the revenge she sought—she knew it now—to see all evidence of the queen blotted from the land, replaced by joy.

Most of all, she saw a life with Vance. No cause would separate them. They could return to the forest with the music-box stream and the birds that serenaded them from the boughs of the trees. They would tread those paths again with no burden weighing on them. Each morning she would waken to his face, and she would see it serene and happy when sleep took her. But before it did, she would still taste on her lips the sweetness of his.

And on a warm summer day when they were old, they would hike to the top of Mount Toivara and watch the sun fall below the distant horizon and the moon rise and Hope's

Flame vying with the sparkling jewels above. And they would nod and say, "Remember when this pit was dark and only cold stars looked down? Bless the gods, those days are gone, and children only tease each other about Bad Queen Naryfel catching them and gobbling them up—not knowing where the name comes from." Then they would laugh and hold hands and watch the lights snuff out one by one in the snug and secure homes far below.

While these thoughts brightened a corner of her mind, never for a moment did Briar stop squinting down the arched hallways. Now some sixth sense alerted her that something was wrong. Bells and trumpets still sounded from above, insistent, frantic. But no drum of boots echoed through the dungeon. That could be deceptive. There were twists and turns in the passages that could mask pursuit until it was almost on you.

She glanced at Vance. Tension lined his jaw, but no more than at any point since they'd entered the lower levels.

Then she heard it. A faint vibration coming toward them. Vance glanced up, his brow wrinkled.

She tugged on his arm, urging him on. "They're coming!"

The tramp of many feet echoed off the stone walls, getting closer.

"Down here!" Briar pointed to an adjoining corridor.

They turned and ran. A cook with a pair of newly slaughtered chickens in each hand stopped to stare. The corridor seemed to narrow, to close in on Briar. Cries and the drumming of boots came from behind. She flung the cloak away. Her sword glowed dimly in the torchlight.

More shouts and footfalls pounding on the flags reverberated all around her. No! Yelling came from dead ahead. More behind.

The corridor ended at the terminus of an L. A dozen guards brandishing weapons and torches stormed toward her. She whirled to retreat the other way. More guards barreled down from that direction. Their backs to the wall, swords out, Briar and Vance prepared to meet them. In a heartbeat, they were surrounded.

Briar judged the enemy, looking for the weak link in the cordon, a sword held with an amateur's grip, a youth quivering at his first fight. To a man, the faces challenging her were grim and seasoned. They knew their business; they knew their fate if they disappointed the queen, making them a dangerous lot.

Pursued and pursuer alike, they stood eyeing each other, breathing hard, waiting. But for what?

The answer came shortly. The queen marched up. For a moment, Briar wondered whether she could reprise Skyla one last time and feign innocence.

But Diglan Crosse came striding along, escorting a tall older woman whose gaze probed Briar's face. She was grayer, thinner, and bent, but there was no doubt. It was her childhood tormentor—Budge!

The guards parted to let the queen into the circle. The best thing, Briar decided, was to act as Skyla would act, if she were a real person. It might cloud Budge's perception.

"Your Majesty, you must think it odd to find us down here," Briar said, smiling to conceal the terror running through her. "I'm simply frantic for Foofy. The bells and horns frightened the naughty thing, and he ran off. Lord Quale is helping me find him. He thought Turlians must have attacked the castle, and he gave me this sword he found, in case he couldn't protect my honor."

The queen ignored her comment. She studied Vance and Briar for a long while before calling Budge into the circle. "Well," the queen said. "Do you know them?"

Budge leaned forward, her gaze sweeping up and down

Briar, scrutinizing her face, her ringlets, her hands, even her posture in the way Briar's old tutor used to evaluate her deportment. Briar shrank inwardly, as though she was a girl again and Budge was about to reprimand and drill her for unladylike behavior. But Briar had absorbed her lessons well, had practiced them in court for months. Though in every other situation they were crippling yokes, in her role as Skyla, they felt natural.

A smile began to curl Budge's lips. "It's her."

"You're sure?"

"Oh, it's well done. The ringlets, the powdered skin. But the fire and impudence of those eyes—she can't mask that."

During Budge's examination of Briar, Vance remained inscrutable. But with Budge's pronouncement, his body tensed, ready to spring.

"And him?" The queen nodded toward Vance.

"I saw the young viscount only a few times—"

"Yes, but is it him?"

Budge surveyed Vance from head to toe. "I don't know."

"But it is, don't you think?" the queen said. "They loved each other as children. You couldn't tear them apart. Where you find one, you find the other. Quite a catch! Number two in the Fellowship and his sweetheart." To Briar she said, "You would have done better marrying the moron duke. It would've saved your neck. Seize them!"

"Einor!" Vance cried.

On the code word, Vance and Briar charged right. Six guards were amassed there. Surprised, four took a step back to avoid the blades bearing down on them. The other two were better trained and the next instant the clash of steel rang out. It had to be quick work. Those from behind would recover and attack. Neither guard proved a match for Briar or Vance. With a flurry of strokes, Briar sent her opponent's sword flying. Vance stabbed his man's sword arm. Then the lovers were flying down the corridor. Pursuit sounded from behind.

They turned down a narrow hall. It dead-ended at an air duct. Guards streamed toward them.

Vance stopped. "Go, I'll hold them off."

"We leave together." Briar engaged the first guard, and he retreated at her onslaught.

"We agreed. Go!" Vance attacked two at once, driving them back.

"I won't leave you."

"It's our only chance."

More guards came down the hall.

"You can't fight them all."

"Light the flame, Briar. Go!" He attacked three of them with the ferocity of a lion. One of their blades sliced his arm.

Briar went berserk at the sight of blood drenching his arm. She stormed into the knot of guards, sending them scrambling back down the hall. They clustered at the far end, and she could see more swelling their ranks behind, and then the queen.

There was but a moment. Briar flung herself into Vance arms and found his lips. Then she was racing up the air duct.

CHAPTER TWENTY-EIGHT

*I*n the growing dusk, the castle and the walls of the courtyard were silhouettes. The gown whispered as Briar crossed the flagstones. Every step increased the pull to return through the air duct and stand side-by-side with Vance until they fell. Every step tore at her heart.

But she set her teeth and pressed on. He'd made his wishes clear. To betray them now was to betray all he believed in, all he'd fought for. She knew her duty. It went beyond the two of them. The faces of the poor souls swelling the roads, the faces of Juniper and his family—and those like them—called out to her. Their fate lay in Briar's hands. If she betrayed Vance, she betrayed them.

At the far end of the courtyard a guard with powerful shoulders emerged from a door in the wall. He looked at her a moment, stunned, then barked for her to stop. She came right at him. In a few quick strokes she disarmed him, threw his sword over the wall, and then took his keys.

"Call out, and I'll skewer you," she said. "Maybe not now, but I'll come back and find you. Understand?"

He nodded. Perspiration beaded his brow. Keys in hand,

she went through the same door, and then locked it behind her. As she made her way along a path to the rear of the castle, she smiled with satisfaction that he didn't call out. Perhaps surprise at being so handily disarmed impressed him. She doubted he would report his failure to anyone. It was far too embarrassing to admit he'd been bested by a woman in skirts.

Blaring horns, the knelling alarm, and shouting came from the castle. But as Briar followed a track toward the perimeter of the grounds, the sounds gradually faded. She reached a bridge spanning a stream swollen from rain, crossed over it, and then made her way down an embankment on the other side. Beneath the bridge, unseen from above, Dondle waited.

She stripped off the gown and flung it into the icy water rushing by. After changing quickly into trousers, tunic, and a heavy cloak she took from a saddlebag, she leaped on Dondle, and off they flew.

She knew the roads surrounding Freyclif like the back of her hand. She avoided main highways. More often she cut across fields, the great stallion devouring the leagues beneath his hooves.

She wondered where Mirage was, whether he'd been surrounded and brought down. She couldn't imagine anyone daring such a feat, but her fear conjured a fisherman's net, and what could he do then? He might shift into another form, but she'd never seen him become anything smaller than Foofy, and she wondered if he could. Of one thing she was certain. If they took him, Briar would exact a heavy price on the queen. She could only hope that he had escaped, that at this moment he was helping Vance. If not, Vance would fall, for what could he do with the whole castle against him?

How had it come to this? She knew the danger going in. They both did. But now that she'd found Vance, now that she'd felt his arms around her and knew that he was hers, losing him was unthinkable. She couldn't imagine one day without seeing his face, without the tenderness in his eyes when he looked upon her. Yet here she was, riding farther and farther away, knowing his fate at the hands of the queen. Even now, he was probably stretched on a rack for torture. And then? Hanging in a public square, for all to see the fate of traitors raising a hand against the queen.

A crushing weight bent her in the saddle, so that for a moment, Dondle glanced back, eyes round with alarm, as though Briar had been spirited away, and now he carried a stranger. She threw her arms around his neck and wept into his mane. "No, it's me. But if they hurt one hair on his head, I won't be me much longer. And if they kill him …" Her sword smote at the bleak and soulless dark, and if a hundred had faced her at that moment, they would have fled in fright as her wail pierced the night.

Clouds marched across the sky like an invading army. A storm was coming. Briar could feel it in the air, in the snap of the wind. She needed to make it up the mountain before the gale hit, or she wouldn't make it at all.

Dondle suddenly picked up speed, as though he were racing the clouds, racing the wind.

A hundred times the urge seized her to return for Vance. A hundred times she resisted, throwing back her head and keening with despair.

When she reached the knees of Toivara, the storm struck. Wind whipped and howled, driving snow in sheets. At times she wasn't sure if she was going in the right direction, that perhaps she'd turned and was heading away from the mountain. But a lull in the storm allowed a brief view of craggy cliffs and a dark landscape below, so that she knew she'd been gradually climbing.

Her fingers went numb. Snow lashed. Ice crystals crusted

her eyebrows. They battled on, and it seemed that time stopped, as though they were trapped in a single moment, perpetually making the same steps, making no progress.

Dondle staggered and slipped in the heavy drifts. Her heart went out to him. He would struggle to his last breath for her, as she would for him. But even a will of iron breaks, as she'd learned the day her father drove her from the manse. She wondered if this was the queen's vengeance, that realizing her precious jewel was gone, she'd sent this storm to punish and stop Briar.

With a sick feeling, Briar felt darkness closing in on her, not from without but from within, pulling her into its fathomless depths. The storm was taking her. And with the blackness the last rays of hope faded.

She dismounted, pulling Dondle into the small shelter of a niche in a rock wall. His coat was slick with sweat. Foam hung from his lips. She rubbed him down with cloth from the saddlebag and let him drink from her water skin. Then she drank before the water froze.

The storm raged, daring them to venture out. All she could do was sit and wait and hope that it would abate. But her mind was no longer on the mission above. It was far below, filled with the horrors of what was happening to Vance in the queen's torture chamber, and Briar's heart ripped in two.

The gale bawled and shrieked its fury. Darkness spiraled and swirled like one of the queen's fiends. Briar bade Dondle to lie down. Pulling the cloak close, she pressed her body to his for warmth. The demon of sleep beckoned, promising peace. She fought him, eating snow, rubbing her fingers. It seemed he was winning. Her eyes closed. She forced them open, only to have them sag again.

From the depths of the storm she heard roaring. At first she thought it was a devilish quality of the wind as it strengthened and whipped past the rocks. But then she recognized the deep prolonged bellow of Mirage. He sprang into the shelter, and with him came hope.

Rising, she told Dondle to stay. He'd had enough, though his great spirit yearned to join her. But he'd done his part. The rest was up to her and Mirage, for the tiger was a creature of snow, born and reared on Einor, a mountain far colder and more savage than this.

She stepped back onto the road, expecting to ride him, but he forged ahead, and she realized he was acting as a windbreak, for the storm was sweeping down the mountain now, as though to force her back.

She leaned against it, and with Mirage's huge form before her, she waded up through the drifts, losing all sense of time, forgetting fatigue, forgetting all else but that here was a chance to forever end the darkness.

They climbed, battling the gale for every foot. The wind subsided for a moment, and she realized that the road was winding up the final loops before the peak. She came to stone stairs, cloven from the sheer rock of the mountain. Her muscles quivered. Energy drained from her with every step. And then she reached the summit, where she collapsed face first into the snow.

With one last effort she rolled over, exhaustion melting into numbness. In the swirling spindrift, a single face hung like a ghost ... a bold nose, a speculative brow, eyes that burned like two lamps. They admonished her, they scolded her, they forbade her to give up. They urged her on. Then like everything else, the face faded, the light in those lamps dying away, as though drop by drop the last of its oil had burned.

She was fading too, disappearing into a formless colorless dream ...

Mirage's thoughts intruded. *The Tear. Take up the Tear of Tybaleth!*

Her fingers inched to her breast until they closed over the jewel. Warmth flowed into her. With his nose, Mirage rolled her over. He latched onto the back of her cloak and pulled her up, and though the gale was fiercest up here where there was no shelter, no break from the wind, she staggered to a cluster of rocks at the center and began to climb.

At the top she found a pit lined with snowdrift. After taking out both gems, she placed them in the center of the pit. Then, eyes closed, she slammed down on them with the butt of her sword.

Light, white and dazzling, streamed through her eyelids. She reared back from the heat. When her feet found the edge of the pit, she opened her eyes and beheld a column of fire, shooting into the sky.

CHAPTER TWENTY-NINE

The storm passed, suddenly expending with a whimper. By morning, only a few defiant thunderheads shadowed an otherwise bright sky. Snow hadn't fallen on Freyclif, and though the air was cold, grosbeaks and warblers scoured the mud for worms and insects.

With heavy feet, Naryfel plodded up the tower steps. She had found her private chamber ransacked the previous evening. However, the pleasure of capturing Vance D'Arté more than compensated for overturned drawers and spilled powders. But when she had discovered the Nyctarix missing, her first impulse was to tickle the prisoner with a hot branding iron. In truth, she had not altogether discarded this delicious thought, except she wanted him in reasonable condition for his execution that afternoon. If the foolish citizens of Purpura saw that he'd been tortured, it might illicit sympathy, make a martyr of him. That would not suit her purposes.

Oh, he'd been beaten as soon as he'd been taken down. The hiding places of the Fellowship, their leaders, their current location, their plans, these were too valuable not to pursue. But she knew that as soon as word went out that he'd been taken, they would slip away from the nooks and crannies they occupied and, like lizards, find new cracks to slither into.

D'Arté knew this as well. He would hold out a few hours, and whatever information he spilled would be worthless.

Oh, he had suffered, she'd made sure of that. But when he was led to the block, little outward sign of this would show, other than an unsteady step and a haggard mien. And when his head was separated from his shoulders, she would stick it on a stake for all to see, a reminder of the fate of traitors.

Mollified, she trod to the tower to pass the time bathed in pleasant thoughts of revenge. Almost as soon as she stepped into the chamber, she sensed something was wrong. With a sinking feeling in her belly, she lowered herself into her chair, a chill upon her. An unaccountable loneliness took up residence within her, as though a long lost lover had vanished forever.

Seized with panic, she rushed to a window and looked out. All was normal. All except the emptiness inside.

For the first time, Naryfel fled the tower.

***

Rupert Alamond Glodwell sat at breakfast, absently pushing a sausage link back and forth on his plate. He had no appetite for food, no appetite for drink, and no appetite for his mother and her overstuffed face.

"Are you feeling unwell, dear?" she asked. "Your eggs are getting cold."

"No, I'm not feeling good," he replied. "I'm not feeling good at all."

"Are you hot? Let me feel your head."

He glared at her. "That's sure to make me worse."

"Nonsense. You must eat, Rupie, to keep up your strength."

He pushed the plate away. "I don't lack strength; I lack purpose. Everything I do is silly and hollow."

"How strangely you talk, Rupie."

"I feel strange."

"It's news of that traitorous viscount that's upset you. The blood drained from your face a moment ago when I told you."

"Did it?"

"You mustn't let it upset you. Don't give him another thought. He made his coffin. Now he'll lie in it."

He stared at her, wishing he were anywhere but here. "You mean bed, don't you?"

"Coffin. Grave. What does it matter? He's out of our lives, and you can breathe easy. He'll never interfere with your affairs again."

"My affairs? And what are those, Mother?"

"Whatever you choose, dearest. You're rich. You can buy whatever you want. Either of the Orendale twins, if you wish." She winked. "Or both!"

He looked down in disgust, preferring the crisscrossing trail of fat on his plate to the world from his mother's point of view.

It was a blessed relief when a servant entered, ending the frivolous exchange. The man stopped and stood at a deferential distance.

"What is it, Quimby?" the duchess asked.

Quimby spoke to the duke. "A little girl, Your Lordship. Insists on seeing you. A ragamuffin, if I may say. Most disagreeable. I tried to turn her away, but she refused to leave. Said she would glue herself to one of the giant vases if we turned her out. Says it's most urgent."

The duchess scowled. "You know better than that,

Quimby. Take a dog whip to her. That will send her flying fast enough."

"Yes, my lady, I would, but—" He held out a fuchsia-colored fan. "She gave me this."

Excitement fluttered inside the duke like a hummingbird. "Send her in."

The duchess held up a finger and looked sharply at the servant. "Have her thrown off the property."

"No, Mother, I will see her."

"Silly dear. Don't get yourself worked up. You know it makes you dizzy."

"Enough, Mother. I'll see whom I please, when I please." He turned to Quimby. "Send her in."

"She insists on seeing you privately."

The duke rose and tossed his napkin on his plate. "Good. I need air, anyway. Bring her to the fountain."

He stepped from the dining room onto the veranda and out along the meandering pathways of the garden. One could get lost here, a fact he took frequent advantage of. The worst of last night's storm had passed him by, leaving the many blossoms along the walkway intact. He reached the fountain, and a moment later Quimby arrived with the girl. Her pants and shirt were nothing more than a patchwork of rags, the colors faded. But she wore a beat up yellow hat that brightened her face, and he decided on the spot he liked her.

"That will be all, Quimby."

When the man disappeared around a bend, the duke said, "Walk with me. The shrubs have long ears."

"They do in my neck of the woods too."

"Where is that?"

"Desperation." She watched for his reaction.

He winced, well aware of the shantytown where the queen's slaves eked out an existence.

When they were deep inside the garden's maze, he drew

her to a bench surrounded by a tall thick horseshoe of hedge, and asked her name.

"Kids like me don't have names," she replied. "You can call me Falcon. Listen, you've heard that Tich—Vance D'Arté—was captured."

The duke sagged against the bench. "It's terrible. Poor lad, I always liked him."

Falcon smiled and nodded toward the fuchsia fan he held in one hand. "She needs you. You'll come?"

He jumped to his feet. Ten minutes later he was galloping up the road on his snow-white stallion, following Falcon's pony.

They met no one—she led him on little used trails and byways—and when they arrived at the Shady Bone, she took him around the back to the kitchen.

Briar was there, talking to a plump man who promptly took off his apron and left through an inner door.

Rupert looked anxiously after him.

"You can trust Geoffer with your life." Briar's eyes were bloodshot. Her hair, usually glossy and bewitching, was tangled and wind blown. "You heard about Vance?"

A fire seemed to pulse through every fiber of her being, sending a thrill through him. He guessed it always would. "It pains me."

"You saw him as your rival."

"Miss Briar, I want to be loved for me. I'll find some girl as silly as me, and we shall be happy."

She took his hand and holding it between both of hers gave it an encouraging shake. "I hope you find her soon."

"You didn't bring me here to discuss my marriage prospects."

"You once said if there were anything you could do—"

"In a heartbeat."

"Even if it's dangerous."

"My soul would sing to do something for once, really do something. You don't know how much I long for it."

"Good." She gave his hand an affectionate squeeze before letting it go, and the sensation lingered as though she'd touched him with hot spices.

***

Naryfel could never stomach introspection. She was who she was. Let others deal with it. It was better to gloat, and she had much to gloat upon. The capture of Vance D'Arté was a delectable prize indeed, and she played out his execution in her mind to the finest detail—not the blood so much but the resounding chop of the sword, the expressions on the spectators' faces, a head balanced on a pike, its expression frozen in horror. These were worthy of deep contemplation.

With these happy thoughts, her early morning flirtation with loneliness soon passed but not the feeling that something was amiss. That was not to be ignored and worth inquiring into. Her whole career was based on attention to detail, on missing nothing. Sitting in her audience chamber, she considered the mountain of scrambled eggs, sausages browned to perfection, biscuits, scones, muffins, and marmalade, arranged artfully before her—hers precisely because she listened to those little alarm bells sounding within, guiding her this way and that.

This warning system rang loudly when a servant stepped in to announce that the Duke of Glodwell asked for an audience.

"I said I was not to be disturbed." She stared at the man, trying to quiet the bells. Her mouth went dry.

"I thought I should check, being he's a favorite of yours. I didn't think it fitting to call the guards."

She gave a dismissive wave and then busied herself

spreading whipped cream on a strawberry scone. "Tell him I'm occupied with affairs of state."

The servant bowed and left, but came back a few minutes later.

"Well?" she asked.

The man twisted his hands nervously. "He won't leave."

"He's that insistent?"

"Adamant, vociferous, persistent."

She regarded the half-eaten scone in her hand. She had half a mind to see the duke. Perhaps he could shed light on her trepidations. But the man was a clown. What could he possibly have to say that concerned her? "Tell him I'm meeting with a foreign dignitary. He can call tomorrow."

The man left, his brow knitted.

Almost as soon as the door closed, the duke burst in and stumbled across the floor like a donkey on ice.

***

Rupert caught the edge of the table with his hand and righted his balance. With a deep breath, he straightened and faced the queen.

She stared at him, fingers raised to hide the amusement quirking her lips. "My dear duke, I have state affairs to attend to. You understand."

He clasped his hands passionately. "That's what I've come about. You captured my enemy at last!"

"D'Arté? I didn't know you were so keenly against him."

"He took from me the only girl I'll ever love. Of course I'm against him. It will be my happiest moment when your headsman severs his limbs from his body."

She spread cream cheese on a strawberry turnover, the juice inside spilling out. "You'll have a front-row seat."

"I have to look my enemy in the eye first. He may have won the game of love, but by Jyd, I'll have the last laugh."

The turnover stopped halfway to her mouth, and her eyes narrowed with suspicion. "That will not be possible. No one is allowed near the prisoner. You understand. It wouldn't be safe. In case there's an attempt to rescue him."

"A chance I'm willing to take. I have to stare him down, to smite his face." With a powerful slapping motion, the duke spun all the way around and almost fell. "Don't worry about me. I can handle myself." He brandished his sword and winced painfully, rubbing his shoulder. "An old injury. It won't stop me from showing him who's the better man."

The queen shook her head while trying to stifle a laugh. "I appreciate your feelings, but—"

"Nay, hear me out! See how much it would mean to me? Accept this token of my gratitude." He took off one of his enormous rings and let it glitter in the morning light streaming through a window.

She licked her lips like a lizard. "It would be amusing ... Yes, I believe we can make it safe for you."

"Safe? Do I care about safe? I must have satisfaction, Your Highness. Because of him, my heart is broken forever. *He* led her astray. Now she's an outlaw too. All because of him. You can imagine how it will crush me when you hang her from a gibbet. I don't think I'll recover. He's the author of my sadness and grief, the destroyer of my happiness."

That did the trick. Under the escort of a dozen guards, she led Rupert down the levels of the castle to the dungeon. He'd heard of the atrocities there and steeled against what he might encounter. It was damp and cold. An odd smell permeated the corridors, beyond what might be expected from centuries old stone, as though the walls had absorbed the suffering of the victims.

They stopped before a cell. The light was too dim to penetrate the shadows beyond the bars.

The queen asked Rupert to give up his sword before entering. "For your own safety. The traitor is capable of anything."

"I don't need a sword to show I'm his master," Rupert replied.

She watched him as a guard let him into the cell, then leaned against the bars to observe all that passed within.

The slender form of Vance lay crumpled on straw in one corner, his clothes torn and bloodstained.

Rupert winced inwardly at the sight. When he was within toe reach, he stopped, hands akimbo. "Get up, dog. Meet a better man."

When the form before him gave no response, the duke prodded him with his boot. "Stand before me, coward."

A cracked voice drifted up. "You've come to gloat, Rupert? Haven't I always shown you kindness?"

"Kindness? To steal love, rightfully mine? Stand up, man. If we met anywhere else, I should demand satisfaction."

Vance rose unsteadily to his feet. His lips were cracked. Crows' feet cut the corners of his eyes, which searched the duke's. "I'm truly sorry I've caused you pain."

Rupert glanced at the queen. "You see how he stands humbled before me, all contrite now that he is going to die?" He removed a glove. "If we were on the field, this is what I should do." He slapped the leather fingers across Vance's cheek, though not as hard as perhaps it looked. "In a few short hours, when you face your fate, remember *that,* and take it to the grave."

"We should go," the queen said. "He's got plenty to meditate on."

But the duke, pretending to be overwrought, took out a crimson handkerchief and patted away perspiration. Then he wadded it up in such a way that only Vance could see the silver eldara leaves, embroidered on the silk. "You're not worth the sweat on my brow." He threw the handkerchief into Vance's face.

"There, I've done it," Rupert said. "I told my mother this morning, *'I'm coming for him.'* That's what I said, *'I'm coming for him.'* Do you understand? There's nothing I wouldn't do for her. Nothing. Do you understand? And now I have done it."

A light shone in Vance's eyes. "I understand."

CHAPTER THIRTY

Falcon wove through the crowd, clutching a long object wrapped in rags. There must have been at least two hundred assembled—merchants, fishmongers, butchers, nobles, farmers, drapers, seamstresses—milling in the square. The earth, usually packed hard from many feet, was muddy from the storm, for it had rained here. No one minded. They elbowed and shoved for position, the better to see the stage where the afternoon's drama would unfold. The platform, a good six feet high, was constructed of wood. Today, no rope hung from the high crossbeam of the gallows. The victim was doomed to bleed out his life as first his arms, then his legs, and finally his head were severed from his body. A table hewn from the thick trunk of a tree served as the block.

The stage was built before a wall made of stone, except for a single door of stout oak through which the prisoner would be led. On the other side of the door was a holding cell. A cordon of guards, triple the usual, made the cell impenetrable. Guards were also positioned in a ring before the stage. Soldiers were scattered through the crowd, and two companies of the queen's finest fighters surrounded the area, more than enough to quell a rescue attempt, should one be mounted.

Falcon sighed, eyeing the block with trepidation, and gripped her package fiercely. Tich was friend, brother, and father rolled in one, and though he worked tirelessly for the cause, he'd always found time to hold her and rock her to sleep.

Her heart wrapped in sadness, she turned away, making for one of the three low-lying hills that overlooked the square, and took up her position. She no longer wished to see the ugly faces, lifted with hunger to watch a man die.

She gazed across the flat valley to the hill opposite her and tightened her grip on the package.

No birds wheeled in the sky.

***

At a quarter to three, the door to the stage opened. Guards, armed to the teeth, streamed out and took up positions along the back and sides of the stage. The executioner emerged next. He strode with a heavy step—denoting the mass of muscles in his arms and legs—his sword resting casually on one shoulder, his face hidden beneath a black mask. When he reached the block, he propped the sword against it. Hands free, he rotated his head several times, then rolled his shoulders and swung his arms. Sufficiently loose, he took up the sword and began the series of whirling motions he was famous for, his blade whistling like the wind.

Meanwhile, servants brought out three cushioned chairs, one larger than the rest. After these were placed to one side of the block, a magistrate entered, wearing a long crimson robe trimmed with ermine, followed by the steward and then the queen.

She sat in the largest of the chairs, folded her hands, and gazed impassively at the crowd. Despite the coolness of her expression, those closest to the stage might have seen that she probed the mass of spectators and eyed the hills just beyond them.

A full minute ticked by, in which one could hear nothing but the rustle of clothing and the breathing of a neighbor. Then the door opened and two guards led out Prisoner 946, Vance D'Arté, Viscount of Pendley, beloved leader of the Fellowship of the Flame. He staggered, and guards needed to support him as he crossed the stage. His lips and cheeks were swollen and bruised, his eyes puffy, one almost shut. He was made to stand on the block, his hands bound behind him. He took a deep breath, his chin thrust forward, defiant.

The magistrate stepped forward. "Vance D'Arté, you have been found guilty of crimes against the state: arson, stealing from national granaries, killing her majesty's soldiers, incitement to insurrection, and high treason. The sentence upon you, by most merciful pronouncement of our sovereign queen, is death. Are you prepared to confess, to cleanse your soul from eternal damnation?"

The prisoner found strength from some hidden source: he stood tall, squared his shoulders, and his voice rang out clear and strong to the far corners of the square. "The only crimes that have been committed are against the people of Purpura, trampled under the foot of a tyrant. Fear not, sisters and brothers, the day will come when our suffering will cease. Let the blood spilled today nourish our cause. Long live the Fellowship!"

A few people hooted and hissed, and several citizens pelted him with rotten vegetables. No doubt the queen had paid the hecklers. Vance remained poised and unruffled.

The magistrate shook his head sadly. "I knew your father. He would gnash his teeth and tear his hair out if he knew what you had become."

Vance smiled. "He would gnash and tear if he knew what the country had become, and would be standing beside me today, facing the same fate." He turned to the executioner. "Get on with this circus."

"Let it be noted," the magistrate said, "that Prisoner 946 refused to confess. He is stripped of title and lands. These revert to the crown." To the executioner, he said, "Quarter and behead."

With a guard holding each of Vance's arms, his bonds were cut. Though he struggled, four guards took him down. First his legs, then his arms were fastened to the block.

On the hilltop, Falcon removed the cloth scraps from the object she'd been carrying, revealing a stave with rags soaked in animal fat wrapped on one end. She tipped a hot coal from a lead-lined wooden box onto the wrapping and blew.

It leaped into flames.

***

On the opposite hill, the queen's soldiers patrolled a nearby road. Lying facedown, hidden in foliage not twenty feet from them, Briar couldn't see what was unfolding on the stage. Her gaze was riveted on the small figure of Falcon across the valley from her. Flames shot from a torch, held aloft in the little girl's hand.

Briar jumped to her feet. She threw back her head and sent a shriek to the sky. The call was answered in the hundreds, the thousands. A shadow passed overhead and descended on the valley. She paid it no mind, nor did she give a glance to the squad of soldiers that turned and gaped at her. Mirage sprang from a tree and landed beside her.

Dondle thundered from a copse of box elders. The rumble of a stampede came from behind him.

Briar leaped on Mirage. The three of them tore down the hillside. A moment later hundreds of wolves poured from the trees and followed in her wake.

More swept down Falcon's hill like a wave. Above, eagles, hawks, crows, jays, and—smaller but no less fierce—thrushes, wrens, and sparrows swooped down on anyone wearing the purple and gray insignia of the queen's army and guards. A tornado of them descended on the executioner.

Men and women of the resistance, scattered throughout the crowd, flung aside their cloaks, revealing weapons. More streamed down the hillsides behind the wolves. By the time Briar reached the foot of the stage, the valley was ringing with swords. Anyone fleeing the scene—from spectator to soldier—was spared. Anyone who stayed to fight for the queen was flailing to protect his eyes.

Mirage bounded onto the stage. Briar leaped from his back. Sword out, hair flying, she fell like a fury on the four guards between her and Vance. From the corner of her eye, she saw Mirage streak toward the queen. A dozen guards formed a cordon around her and rushed her from the stage and into the holding cell. With a roar, Mirage charged at those guarding the door.

Briar's sword pierced the arm of a guard. A moment later she disarmed another. She drove the remaining two across the stage. Then she was at the block, cutting Vance free.

"Can you stand?" she cried.

He scrambled to his feet. "Give me a sword."

She handed him one a guard had dropped. His eyes flashed as he gripped it, but he staggered under its weight.

A squad of soldiers rushed from the holding cell. One held a net.

Horns sounded, signaling the arrival of a troop. Most of

the birds and wolves had left, chasing stragglers from the square.

"We have to leave," Briar shouted.

She drove their opponents back in a dizzying blur of blades, Vance following behind. She turned to rush down the stairs. Diglan Crosse was coming up, two of his cronies behind him.

Briar met his sword, sending out sparks. "Thought you'd run with your tail between your legs."

Grinning, Crosse parried. "And miss the chance to finish what I started."

Briar laughed. "Almost *your* finish, as I recall."

"Nay, you were lying on the floor, bleeding."

"Then it's blood for blood. Time to spill yours." Briar delivered a wicked thrust that he dodged by a hair but which sliced his arm. Crimson bloomed on his sleeve, shoulder to cuff.

The cut did nothing to erase the smug impudence from his face. He redoubled his attack, forcing Briar up the stairs. The improvement she'd seen of his technique in the gymnasium was no fluke. His stance was correct. He delivered sharp, crisp strokes, and kept her off balance. Everything was working for him. She found no opening in his defense, no flaw to exploit.

"I won't kill you." He smiled with satisfaction, turning on her a look that made her flesh crawl. "I'd rather tame you in bed."

With a series of quick thrusts, he drove her onto the stage. On level ground, he gained the advantage of height, and her confidence waned. A quick glance to her right showed Vance being forced toward the block by Crosse's men. It appeared either of them would be a formidable opponent, and all Vance could do was fall back. From the corner of her eye, she saw Mirage pacing back and forth, keeping a dozen soldiers from reaching Briar and Vance. They were about to cast a net over him.

The wolves were gone, the birds departed, the sky empty and lifeless. Beyond the stage, knots of rebels, too far away to be of any help, struggled against soldiers. The square was littered with the fallen. The injured on both sides lay writhing and screaming from their wounds, and the air was redolent with mud and the stench of blood.

Briar heard the shift and slide of her feet, that of her opponent's, and the rasp of their breath. Unlike their last fight, when his arrogance faded, now Crosse's face was flushed with excitement, a man about to taste triumph.

Trumpets sounded from the central hill. A unit of the queen's cavalry appeared at the crest and thundered down the slope.

The net dropped on Mirage. He struggled but could do nothing more than flop like a fish and roar in outrage. Soldiers began reeling him in.

Then she saw it—the slight dropping of Crosse's guard that Briar had spotted in their first fight. She let the first opportunity pass, in case it was a trick. She waited patiently, watching, gauging the timing of the next opportunity in relation to his attacks and counterattacks.

She sensed the instance coming. A grim smile came to her lips.

His guard dropped.

"Tame this!" She struck, sinking her blade into his belly. He stood a moment, eyes flared in surprise. She yanked her sword free. He tilted off the stage and pitched face first into the mud.

Mirage swelled in size, stretching the mesh until it burst. The soldiers dropped the remnants and ran.

Briar whirled on Vance's opponents. She took the crony on the left, leaving Mirage the one on the right. A quick flurry and her opponent was disarmed. The other man fled. Then Briar was off the stage and on Dondle. Vance swung up behind her. Together they raced away, Mirage following like a shadow.

PART FOUR

CHAPTER THIRTY-ONE

*T*he perfume of pines, music from the brook, and streams of sunlight filled the air. Arm in arm, Briar and Vance wandered the clover- and fern-lined paths, while wood thrushes serenaded from the boughs of the trees. Her heart sang with them, and for the first time, she was at peace.

At last they came to the bridge. Where the rebel camp had been, no tents occupied the glade; no crackling fires warmed the cooking pots. The place was deserted but for Falcon, who sat cross-legged on a rock, turning her yellow hat anxiously in her hands.

Briar hurried to her. "Did you find my friend, Juniper Donyman?" she asked, when they were beside her.

"I did. Joia's fine." Falcon remained tense.

"And the baby?"

The girl mustered a smile. "Named after you."

Briar exhaled in relief. "That one will grow up loved."

"They're good folks. Offered to take me in." Falcon shrugged. "The Fellowship's my family."

Vance gazed around the empty encampment, perplexed. "Where is everyone? We were to rendezvous here."

Falcon looked inside the hat, put it on her head, removed it, and began wheeling it in her hands. "They're at Jolby's Mill."

Vance's face went blank. "Why?"

She nodded toward Briar and Vance. "Packs of sniffers looking for you. Things are hot right now. Too dangerous for the rest of us."

"I won't be intimidated," Vance replied. "I won't stop until she's off the throne."

Falcon paled. "You can't, Tich, you can't. The sniffers know your smell. *She* got it when you were in prison. You gotta go. Makken and Irem ordered it. For awhile, until things cool down."

He looked at Briar, lost. She understood. From childhood, the Fellowship had burned like a flame within him. Now it had suddenly been extinguished, and he was a child in the dark, searching for a way home.

"What do we do?" He took Briar's hands, as though she could lead him back to daylight.

She stroked his fingers, usually supple and strong, now hanging limp.

She gazed west, as though she could see beyond the trees, beyond the hills and farms, and out past the minarets and towers of Freyclif. "There's a place where the sniffers will never find us."

He searched her face, questioning.

"Like we always dreamed." Her heart fluttered with excitement. "Where the wind and spray dance with the waves. Let's pepper the queen's ships with cannon fire."

His eyes lit, and he followed her gaze, seeing it too. "A new front. Pirates!"

While Briar packed a few supplies, Vance took a blanket

they'd slept under, one with the crossed-torch crest of the D'Artés woven into the wool, and cut it into small pieces with a knife. When all was ready, they stood near the footbridge, Mirage and Dondle beside them.

Mirage's tail switched disconsolately. Dondle nosed Briar, pushing her back a pace.

She reached up and stroked Dondle's neck. "I can't fool either of you. You know what I'm going to say." Her throat swelled as she fought back tears. "Go back to our mountain, to the hawks and the wolves. Remember me when the poppies and bluebells paint the meadows."

Mirage shifted form until he stood before her, ethereal with light, as he'd been when he healed her in the tent. They embraced, trembling with emotion. When they parted at last, his head tipped to one side, and his lips formed silent words: goodbye, Mother. Then he melted back into tiger form, and soon, he and Dondle disappeared over the bridge and into the woods.

Falcon stepped up to Vance, turning her hat, and kicked up a plume of dust with her sandal. "Better go, better just get out of here."

"Not so fast, my brave little friend," Vance replied. He handed her a bundle he'd made of the blanket pieces, now wrapped in canvas. "Divide this among your troop. Let them divide it, and divide it again among the Fellowship."

Falcon looked at the bundle in wonder. "What is it?"

"A part of me. And something more. Have them take the pieces to the four corners of Purpura—everywhere except the way between here and Misty Cove—attached to a pair of crossed torches."

Falcon blinked back tears. "Will I see you again?"

"Count on it."

She rushed in and hugged him. "Who will rock me to sleep?"

He lifted her in his arms and clasped her to him. "I'll return. Soon. All the queen's armies couldn't keep me from you. Now ride. Draw those sniffers away!"

Face hardened with determination, she climbed on her pony and raced toward the hills.

The rest of the day, Briar and Vance lurked in the densest part of the forest. Once, so far away they could not be sure if they heard it, the cries of a tracking party came to them, and the low roar of sniffers.

Later, they slipped through the night, shadows within shadows, until they came to gold and emerald sands sparkling in the moonlight, and heard the waves calling. Beyond rose the swaying silhouette of the Golden Gull, anchored in the cove.

Next morning they stood on the prow, the sun rising behind them, the salt air crisp and bracing. They'd been there for some time, senseless of all around them, lost in a kiss that left Briar breathless.

When at last they drew apart, she looked to the coast, certain that from Purpura's snowy heights to her glittering sea, scraps of a blanket fluttered like pennants, while high on the summit of Mount Toivara, a beacon of hope shot skyward, never to be dimmed.

Briar and Vance are back for another magical adventure!

Dark Enchantment Hides a Secret ...

A sorcerer's spell throws the kingdom of Purpura into bloody chaos. Briar's one hope to protect her friends and stop him is to find a mythical treasure.

She's mastered swordplay. But how can she fight the sorcerer's mesmerizing allure?

How can she keep her heart true to the pirate, the man she really loves?

How, in the vast, unchartered waters of the Teeth, can she find the greatest treasure ever known?

The one thing that will stop Purpura from plunging into madness ...

AUTHOR'S NOTE

Dear Reader,

This story was a labor of love, and I'm thrilled you shared part of the journey with me by reading it. Writing can often be a lonely process! Your heartfelt response to my writing can be just the thing to keep me going. One of the best ways to do that is to take a moment to post a review. It can do a lot to help the book gain notice. I promise that I read each and every one of them, and they touch me deeply.

This link will take you right to your favorite seller's page, where you can post a review:

Universal Book Link

In gratitude,

A. R. Silverberry

WYNDANO'S CLOAK GIFT EDITION

Evil looms over the kingdom of Aerdem ...

Three girls, swept into a battle they're not prepared for. And don't know how to fight ...

Jen, frightened of the very thing she once loved, and maybe needs.

Bit, longing to spread her wings, but chained by a past shrouded in mystery.

Pet, sharp as a whip, but forced to pursue her father's dreams. At the cost of her own.

With their world about to shatter,

A sorcerer's cloak holds the answer ...

Limited edition hardcovers of *Wyndano's Cloak*! Only available through the author at www.arsilverberry.com. Get your signed collectible today!

ACKNOWLEDGMENTS

Creating a novel requires a seemingly endless number of artistic decisions. Without the valuable input of my wife, Sherry, I don't know that I could have completed this. The toughest part always comes at the end, when it seems that any metaphorical brushstroke on the canvas, no matter how small, will ruin the whole. I'm sure it's an illusion. Nonetheless, I need that extra input when it comes down to a few words, lines, and phrases, and she graciously put up with the myriad variations I handed her.

Deep gratitude goes to my editor, Betsy Beard, who believed in the story from day one and whose thoughtful comments and suggestions pushed me to make this story shine. I felt her cheerful and positive attitude in all our interactions on the book.

ABOUT THE AUTHOR

Adler wouldn't do—I needed the right handle to go where I was going. Silverberry unlocked the magic door. Now I quest through the limitless realms of the imagination, here, official scribe to bold knights and treacherous kings, there, intrepid recorder of the future and the far reaches of outer space. Wherever I land, I promise to hold nothing back.

This portal takes you there ... www.arsilverberry.com.

ABOUT TREE TUNNEL PRESS

Tree Tunnel Press is an award-winning publisher of fiction and nonfiction, including *I Love Birds, An Enchanting Coloring Book*, featuring twelve beautiful hand-drawn illustrations of birds. We create products that entertain, encourage, and inspire. Requests for rights or permissions should be directed to: Tree Tunnel Press P.O. Box 733 Capitola, CA 95010

Visit our website, www.treetunnelpress.com, to purchase books and for more information.